*A
Harlequin
Romance*

OTHER
Harlequin Romances
by ESSIE SUMMERS

Many of these titles are available at your local bookseller,
or through the Harlequin Reader Service.

For a free catalogue listing all available Harlequin Romances,
send your name and address to:

HARLEQUIN READER SERVICE,
M.P.O. Box 707, Niagara Falls, N.Y. 14302
Canadian address: Stratford, Ontario, Canada.

or use order coupon at back of book.

A TOUCH OF MAGIC

by

ESSIE SUMMERS

HARLEQUIN BOOKS   TORONTO
WINNIPEG

Original hard cover edition published in 1973
by Mills & Boon Limited, 17 - 19 Foley Street,
London, W1A 1DR, England

© Essie Summers 1973

SBN 373-01702-2

Harlequin edition published July 1973

*All the characters in this book have no existence outside the
imagination of the Author, and have no relation whatsoever to
anyone bearing the same name or names. They are not even
distantly inspired by any individual known or unknown to the
Author, and all the incidents are pure invention.*

Printed in Canada

1702

To

Naire and Ron Gordon, who took Bill and myself rambling among their hills in the time of autumn gold and in winter snows

and to

Jessie and Cap Jardine who, in a spring twilight, showed us the Remarkables through the circle of their moongate.

This book is also dedicated to all our other dear parishioners of St. Andrew's, Queenstown.

The author records her thanks to the
Australian *Woman's Mirror* for the
use of the poem *The Bell* by Norma
L. Davis

CHAPTER ONE

How odd it seemed that the strongest feeling of which she was conscious was peace. A deep and inner peace possessed her as if, having plumbed the depths, nothing could perturb again, except on the surface. Yet everything that had been hers hitherto had been swept away. It didn't even seem the same world any more, yet Lucinda knew a freedom of the spirit that was paradoxical.

Most of all she was aware of being very close in heart to her father—or more correctly, her stepfather. Because this serenity was a legacy from Kenneth Darling. Every word of wisdom and love he had spoken to her was hers for always, some hidden in her subconscious, probably, to be brought to light at those times in her life when she would most need them. As now.

She realized so well that some of the things he had preached and practised had been underlined by him, especially for her, if ever in the years ahead she might find out, or be told, the truth about her real parentage.

It would have been more in Kenneth Darling's nature to have told her, when she was old enough, and relied on her not to let it bite too deeply, so he must have kept silent for her mother's sake, who in turn must have felt it was better for Lucinda not to know. Lucinda couldn't agree with that, but she could understand that it had been done for her sake. Of course, if her mother and stepfather had not died so suddenly —and so heroically—they might have told her on their next New Zealand furlough.

The twins, of course, belonged to both Kenneth and Anne. Lucinda was glad they were in England just now, because it would have been hard to hide it from them. Trudy was too gloriously happy in her newly-married state to read between the lines, and Ivan was deep in study at Oxford. How lovely for them to be so near each other still.

It was just as well the knowledge had come to her after she had broken it off with Harvey, otherwise, no doubt, she would have told him, would have felt it was his right to know. What a blessing she hadn't consented to marry him when first he had asked her. If she'd said yes right away, instead of saying she needed time to consider it, she could have blurted it all out in the first shock of receiving that letter from her real father, posted from Brisbane in Australia, by the neighbour to whom he had entrusted it when dying.

Even before that letter came, it seemed as if fate had already linked her with Queenstown. She had been sitting in the travel agency where Harvey worked, waiting for him, when she first knew this strong desire to see Lake Wakatipu. Now she was actually in the Lake County, choosing this place in which to forget him. It was ideally far from Wanganui ... not only vast land distances rolled between but also the waters of Cook Strait, dividing the North Island from the South Island. Though neither sea nor land made much difference in a jet age!

Lucinda, sitting on a ledge of shingle in the Arrow river-bed, laughed at her thoughts. Jets had nothing to do with that miniature airport at Frankton, at the foot of this lake, even if tourists from all over the world came there in tiny planes; even if the Queen, the Duke, and Prince Charles and Princess Anne had landed there one perfect gold and sapphire day not long ago.

She watched one of the artists daub more colour on a palette and splash it on to the bright canvas in front of him. Only the most vivid colours could do justice to the flaming torches of the poplars and willows here, thrown into relief by the sombre shadows of the narrowing gorge as the river snaked out from the steep mountains to spread itself across the shingle of the river-bed in several streams.

Lucinda had never seen such living colour on any trees. It was as if the essence of all the gold that had been won here in the rip-roaring days of last century had been caught up in the sap of the trees and by some strange alchemy, flung against the precipitous sides every autumn, year after golden year.

Yet, when in Christchurch that letter had caught up with her, she had almost changed her mind about coming; hadn't wanted to be linked in any way with the scene of a past that belonged to the man who had so cruelly deceived her mother, all those years ago. A man who had proved to be a bigamist.

Yet something had driven her on to Queenstown, after the

first shock. No, not *something*, nothing as vague as that. It had been because of that will her father had enclosed for her. Lucinda thought it would be valid. It was just written on a printed will-form, but was duly witnessed.

She'd taken it out of the envelope before she'd read the letter, so had stared at it uncomprehendingly, positive it was not meant for her. Because what had the will of a Brisbane man, one Sylvester Mordred, to do with Lucinda Darling? She'd never heard of him. Then she had picked the letter up. . . .

It was almost a death-bed repentance. Lucinda had to school herself not to feel cynical about that. The way he had asked her to forgive him—though he knew he might be gone before she received the letter—had sounded sincere. He'd made no bones about it. He had known she bore the name of Darling, but had assumed she had known the circumstances of her birth. Lucinda had to piece some of it together, guess at other things.

He had been a merchant seaman, had deserted in Singapore just after the war, meeting and marrying her mother there. Lucinda was born just a year later. He had been married before, to a girl in Queenstown, and had one son, also Sylvester. He had deserted her there. There had been no divorce. When his bigamy had been found out, his first wife had divorced him and he had been given a stiff sentence. When Lucinda's mother's parents had retired from Army life, she had gone with her little girl to live with them in England, but later he heard she had married and lived in Hongkong. Seemingly he had never done well in life, but in the last year he had fallen heir to an aunt's estate. He had not made a will till now. Naturally, if he died intestate, his money would go to his son, but his conscience would not let him rest till he had made some sort of restitution to the child he had deprived of a name. He had seen the report of her mother and stepfather's deaths, trying to rescue a family in a flood in East Bengal. He thought she might now be alone in the world, and though it was not a huge legacy, he thought it ought to be divided between his son and his daughter. Hence the will, enclosed, leaving them equal shares. Some months before, toying with the idea of contacting her, he had had her traced, and now had asked this neighbour to post it on.

9

It had taken Lucinda a week to recover from the shock and to decide what to do, which was precisely nothing, because this whole thing could bring nothing but grief to her half-brother, this Sylvester Mordred junior, and to his mother, reviving old sorrows, best left interred.

It would be bad enough when the legalities caught up with them, as they would. The will simply gave the son's name and said, 'of Queenstown'. Some strange compulsion had driven Lucinda to come here. She thought she would like to see her half-brother, might be able to find out, unobtrusively, whether or not he had recently come into money. If she did not bring this will to the notice of the authorities, the legitimate son would naturally receive it all. It was an unusual name, and no doubt there would be something in his father's papers, to enable the Brisbane lawyers to get in touch with him. It was a name with unpleasant associations ... that had been the name of King Arthur's nephew, who had brought ruin to his kingdom.

She daren't make open inquiries, to arouse curiosity, because for all she knew she might resemble her father, but in a place like Queenstown, with a small resident population, even if it was fantastically multiplied with tourists, it ought to have been easy to find her half-brother's name in the telephone or street directory. Now, after fruitless searchings, she felt she was not meant to find it and ought to give up her search.

Besides, this place had lulled her into an acceptance of what had happened, and Dad's philosophy, seeped into her through all the vicissitudes of their adventurous years, had given her an outlook on life that would not allow her to dwell on shadows of the past.

She shook herself out of her reveries, and made her way back to Arrowtown where she had parked the car before walking down to the river-bank.

After a delightful smorgasbord luncheon at The Stone Cottage she decided she'd fill in the afternoon with a jet-boat trip down the rapids in the Kawarau Gorge when she went back to Queenstown, but first she must buy some postcards of Arrowtown to send to Trudy and Ivan. All the shops here had a tourist and pioneer flavour, with a heavy accent on the romance of the goldmining days. No wonder, in this village of lilliput houses nestled under the immense English trees that a hundred years ago had been tiny saplings planted to give shelter from the savagery of the elements. Quite ordinary run-of-the-mill grocery shops had family antiques displayed and pictures that had belonged to that fabulous period.

This one must have been connected with provisioning the district right from the digging and sluicing days, because there were pictures of the shop in all stages of development, right back to the lean-to corrugated iron shack. She wandered round looking at the photos, some brown with age. Some had names beneath. There was one here, taken when the store still had a form outside, for patrons to sit on while they waited the arrival of the papers. By the fashions of the three women in it, it must have been taken in the thirties. Her eye ran idly along the typed names on the gummed paper.

Then it hit her. In the second row ... Sylvester Mordred. She closed her eyes against the impact of it. When she opened them again she felt as if a long time had passed. But no ... that woman was still trying to decide whether to take baked beans or spaghetti, and the girl with the Jane Austen hairdo was still flicking a feather duster over tins of green peas.

Lucinda swallowed and took a closer look. Yes, she hadn't just imagined it. Her eye ran along, checking his position in the group. He looked quite young and had a decidedly rakish air. Dark like herself, though photographs often made people look darker, even redheads. He was tall and slimly built, had one foot up on the form, and his hand resting on a woman's shoulder. But the woman wasn't Mrs. Mordred. She was somebody Smith.

The woman decided on spaghetti, the cash register clicked and the shopkeeper came across to Lucinda. 'I'll just have these postcards, please.' Then she had an inspiration. She indicated the man at the other side of her father. 'I have a feeling I've seen this man. He's much older, of course—must be in his sixties. He lives in Wanganui and I believe he came from here years ago. It says M. Jones. Could it be Morgan Jones? Or wouldn't you know?'

'I know the lot. I've always lived here. That chap worked at the shop. It was Meredith Jones. Rather an unusual name.'

Lucinda nodded. 'Yes ... in fact there are a lot of quite unusual names here ... Uriah Falkington, for instance, and this one, Sylvester Mordred.'

He nodded. 'We sure had a collection of characters ... Old Uriah was the son of one of the first goldminers. But that one, Sylvester Mordred, was a fly-by-night regular scoundrel. Charming fellow, but I wouldn't have trusted him far as I could see him. Weak as water. And lazy! Married a wonderful girl, then, when she had a baby, deserted her. They were tough days, you know, the nineteen-thirties. She was a brick. They lived in a little stone cottage up one of the valleys, and she had it a fair picture. He disappeared and later there was no end of a scandal. He'd contracted a bigamous marriage with someone else overseas and was gaoled—a nasty business. But of course he wasn't a local.'

Lucinda's voice was very casual. 'Must have been tough on the wife.'

She felt she shouldn't ask if she still lived here. He'd take that for sheer nasty curiosity and would close up like a clam. But it was a lead. The son, of course, might have moved away, even if his mother was still here.

She allowed herself one more question. No doubt tourists often asked seemingly irrelevant questions about places they would see once in a lifetime. 'Where was the cottage? Has it been preserved as so many are?'

He shook his head. 'No, not this one, but perhaps some day the Historical Places Trust will take it up. But it's off the beaten track for tourists. It's along an access road leading to a terrific track made right into the hills by the miners to a gorge way back in, that yielded a lot of gold in the early days. My great-uncle was a keen photographer and snapped it because he was fond of the two old characters who ended their days there, long before the Mordreds took it over and did it up. Look at them ... the one on the left is old Once-upon-a-time, so called because he was always yarning, and that's Blue Duck Jake. He was a terrific shot and always had a blue duck feather in his hatband.'

It was certainly faded and dull, and only one stunted tree grew against it, but no doubt when her father and his first wife ... his *only* wife ... had lived there, her garden would have softened the grim outlines. Underneath the caption read: Red Spur Gully.

The shopkeeper added, 'There's just grazing land round

there now. It's one of those valleys leading back into the foot-hills past the Ben Lomond Station. No, past Drumlogie Station, on the way back to Queenstown. Do you want envelopes with these?'

'No, thanks. I'll just send them as they are. I'll go along to the Post Office now. How much? Oh, thanks very much.' She handed over the correct change and got away.

She scribbled a line or two on each and posted them. Trudy had no idea the break with Harvey had been so hurtful. Lucinda had merely written and told her that she'd decided, after careful consideration, not to marry him. Trudy had written back, 'I had hopes, of course, that you'd met the right man at last, but you were very wise, Lucinda, if you felt he wasn't quite that. I'd like you to meet someone you could be really sure about as I was, with Gordon. After all, we're such world citizens as a family, you're not tied to New Zealand. It was simply the place where we spent most of our furloughs. You could come over here now.'

It had been more than that to Lucinda. It had been the place where her dearest friend had lived—Janice. The place where her parents had planned to settle after their busy, dedicated lives in refugee centres.

Lucinda drove up the hill out of Arrowtown, past A-shaped chalets and quaint pioneer cottages, modernized and used as holiday homes or residences, and turned right. On her left was Speargrass Flat, rich and fertile, bounded by huge grape-blue hills that hid the lake. In front and above her was Moonlight, where you could hire horses for long treks, and further up still, the aptly-named Coronet Peak of the ski-slopes and the chairlifts, a tussock-tawny mountain until the time of the snows.

Before long the road, winding round the foothills, would cross the Shotover River at Arthur's Point, where a man in rags and tatters had struck a fabulous lot of gold, and a few bends further on, the sapphire of Lake Wakatipu and the tree-sweet hills of Queenstown would come into view.

There was one thing, leaving her beloved Wanganui had dulled the sense of loss she had known when she first realized that Harvey belonged to Janice. And even now she was beginning to suspect that the biggest blow had been not so much that she had lost Harvey, but that she had lost a planned and settled future. She had drifted into that, she knew that now.

On top of leaving the place where she had hoped they might live, the impact of the knowledge that she was not, after all these years, Kenneth Darling's daughter had taken her mind off it still more.

When Janice and Harvey got the letter she had recently written them, they would feel less guilty, and free to get on with their own lives. And now she was away from Wanganui, friends would stop saying how badly she had been treated, and laying sympathy on with a trowel. There had been times when Lucinda could have screamed her head off.

Shortly she would take a position here. Even though the ranks of the tourists were thinning a little, so was the seasonal help now so many students had gone back to the universities at the start of the academic year in March. She could become a waitress or receptionist without much trouble, she thought. There would be only a brief lull between the autumn tourist traffic and the snowsports season.

Janice would have that letter by now. Lucinda had written so many drafts of it, she knew it by heart. She had worded it so they would think she had already obtained a position. She'd kept it light.

'I'm writing to tell you I've lost my heart to Queenstown. Never in my wildest dreams would I have imagined I'd love any place more than Wanganui, but after the desolate and crowded places we've lived in all our lives, this is sheer heaven. I feel this is the place I want to strike roots into.

'Positions are easily come by here, and what office routine could compare with working at a guest-house with people from all over the world booking in? Not only tourists, either, but conventions and conferences galore. I love it. Nothing had gone as deeply with me as you two chumps—and a few other people—thought, so you can say poof to your guilt complexes and get married. And I do hope you'll ask me to be your bridesmaid if I can get time off. That ought to make people stop muttering: "Poor Lucinda ... hiding a breaking heart." I've a pretty good idea I wasn't half as much in love with Harvey as with the idea of settling down in Wanganui for the rest of my life. If I had been, no doubt I'd have really agonized over losing a boy-friend to my best friend, but honestly, Janice, that's all he ever was. Just someone to go to the theatre with, to dances, picnics. Believe me, if it had been anything more I'd have snapped him up when he proposed, instead of asking for a few weeks to consider it. Cold-blooded, wasn't it? And when your people moved to Wellington, and you came to share the house with me, Harvey also realized that we had just drifted into our relationship.

'It was a darned good idea to take a holiday like this ... it gave me time to see things in their correct perspective. I've written Mr. Ames and told him to set about selling the house, now you've got board. And Janice, I just couldn't bear this situation to spoil our lovely, almost lifelong friendship. And I know you and Harvey are just right for each other.

'Now, an end to all this. I must tell you something hilarious that happened the other day, Jan. How you would have enjoyed it....'

Yes, Lucinda had been rightly proud of that letter. Even knowing the anguish it had caused her, the time it had taken, it had sounded authentic; yet when it had gone she had been conscious of a great emptiness and had walked for hours on Queenstown Hill to tire herself so she might sleep, lest in writing it, she had revived the disillusionment and loss of two months ago.

Now she shook her head impatiently as if to clear it of these thoughts and told herself to concentrate on finding Red Spur Gully. It was very foolish, but she'd like to explore that old miner's hut, even if it should prove entirely unproductive. It wasn't likely she would find any clue in it to the whereabouts of her half-brother. It might be best, anyway, if he and his mother were away from Queenstown, because she had this inexplicable urge to stay. It was stupid, because she had no feeling for her father, other than that of revulsion, and it wasn't even the place where he grew up.

She saw a sign pointing to Drumlogie Guest House, though apart from the gateway and a long drive snaking away into the hills, not a habitation could be seen. She slackened speed and looked for the Red Spur Gully sign. It hung crookedly from a sycamore trunk at the corner and the road was hardly more than a wagon track, rutted, with very little metal on it, and grass quite high between the ruts.

There were two stone cottages not far from the corner, but from the photograph, neither was the one she sought. They

15

were little more than heaps of stones, tucked into hollows, relics of the days when the only way to get shelter from the icy winter gales and the hot blasts of summer, was to build in a depression. That was why Queenstown was an instance of man enhancing nature not spoiling it—at least not so far—it was a pictured example of man adding to the handiwork of God, clothing once bleak hills with all the glory of English trees, setting the flags of autumn flying in an evergreen Pacific land.

The road was worsening and the pile of shingle her wheels were straddling was getting ominously higher. The road turned a bend and ended, and there on the left was the cottage. No mistaking it. A gate gave access to the old track beyond the cottage. Lucinda turned her car into the gateway. She could reverse there later, but right now she was going to explore this cottage and garden.

The roof was rusty but still intact, the windows had unbroken panes and everywhere about it was an unrestrained garden, evidence of the green fingers of a girl who had lived here long ago, had loved, and lost, and had a small boy to bring up solo.

Daisies and geraniums were prolific, and roses rampaged over rotting rustic arches. Cornflowers that must have seeded year after year, starred the long grass with blue as deep as Lake Wakatipu itself.

The gate was so overgrown with clematis vines it was impossible to open, so she climbed over the low tumbledown wall of loosestone, and found that under the mat of weeds was a path of smooth stones set in the turf. No doubt they were glacier-planed rocks borne down these mountainsides aeons ago in a river of ice. She doubted if the miners had set them there. A girl-wife would have done it, to keep her feet dry, unable to afford a concrete path.

It was skirted by bushes that caught at her trews as she brushed by and the scent of crushed balsam came up to greet her, and lavender. There was a large square of the stones at the front door, and a huge rock, flat and almost a rectangle, served as a step. The door was ajar, but it sagged and wouldn't open fully. She squeezed in.

It was just like a dolls' house, with a tiny hall, bare and thick with dust and festooned horribly with cobwebs. The door to the left led into a small sitting-room, with a huge fireplace

16

of hand-set boulders, and the grate a mass of straw and feathers from old nests. On the left was a bedroom, with faded patches on the plain wallpaper, showing where pictures had hung, and a door led off this. She pushed it open, then had to blink back tears.

It was so tiny, evidently built on later, and on the walls were tacked the remains of a home-made nursery frieze. She could imagine that girl-wife cutting them out of books and pasting them on the cardboard, pinning them up at a low height so that the little boy could see them properly. He had lain there in his cot, drowsily content, with Bo-Peep and her sheep, Jack and Jill running up the hill, and that absurdly chubby-faced cow jumping clean over a grinning crescent moon. The girl would be sitting beside him in the twilight, saying the rhymes over and over again. The wee boy, because *she* was his safe and secure world, would never know that she was listening for a step she would never hear again. Had she ever sung to him,

'Clap hands for Daddy coming down the wagon way,
With a pocketful of money and a wagon-load of hay!'?

No, that would have been one song she couldn't sing.

Suddenly Lucinda was angered at herself for coming here. This little cottage was best left to itself and its lonely memories. *She* had no part in it. She almost ran down the uneven path, scrambled over the wall, got into the car.

She began to back. There was an ancient stile by this gate, but though the folds of these hills looked so tempting, she still felt a usurper and resisted the temptation to explore.

On the opposite side to the stile was a clump of willows, their trunks swathed with evidences of past flooding where the stream came through and under, in the shape of great solid lumps of uprooted tussock caught there. She backed, felt a bump, heard a heart-lurching squeal and a scrambling.

Lucinda braked, leapt out, stared in absolute dismay as an injured hare, dragging a leg, gazed up at her with great liquid amber eyes, petrified by terror. Then, turning in utter desperation, it scuttled somehow through the long grass at the foot of the fence, and began a painful progress towards the hillside.

Lucinda clutched her head at each side ... what on earth could she do? She couldn't allow an injured hare to drag itself away to die slowly or to be set upon by farm dogs. It would haunt her.

She rushed at the stile, was over it and running after the wounded animal in a trice. The hare kept to the lower slopes, obviously aiming at the bend of the hill that might take it out of sight to a gully where there would be more cover. It must be badly injured or she wouldn't have kept up with it. But she wasn't gaining. She had no idea what she would do with it if by sheer and persistent effort she did catch it. She might even have to put it out of its misery. Her mind flinched from the thought.

It would be no use going for help once she caught it, because no farmer would keep a hare. They did far too much damage to pastures. Hare drives were held quite often. She kept running madly, gaining a little now.

Lucinda put on an extra spurt. She slipped, fell into something that made her shudder, rushed on after she picked herself up, right round the shoulder of the hill where the hare had dragged itself and went pell-mell through a crowd of young steers advancing towards her. They threw up their heels in panic, bellowed, rushed in all directions, scattering through a shallow stream and most of them tore into a patch of native bush.

But the hare had stopped, crouched close to the earth, petrified at this new menace, so she gave no thought to the stampeding cattle and tried to pounce. The hare came to life, ran on, but was tiring now. It dived down towards a tarn fringed with willows where Herefords were drinking. They scattered too, bellowing wildly, and the hare dived into a broom bush and tumbled exhausted into the roots.

From nowhere a man sprang up into Lucinda's headlong flight and cannoned into her. He grabbed her. 'What the hell do you think you're doing, stampeding my stock?'

He was slightly below the track, and when she wrenched away he almost went sprawling down the hillside. She dived into the broom bush and picked up the hare. Then she turned round to face a look of comical, but furious astonishment.

Well, at least it checked his speech. They stood glaring at each other, Lucinda automatically stroking the hare with soothing movements. Then the sounds of cattle still crashing through scrub jerked him back to speech.

'You've not answered. What in flaming hell are you doing stampeding my cattle?'

Lucinda glared back. 'I didn't do it on purpose! I had to catch this hare—I'd wounded it. *You* mightn't care about that ... farmers don't, mostly, but *I* do. I wouldn't let any wounded animal crawl away to die a lingering death, a horrible death, no matter how many cattle I stampeded—and anyway, I thought this was sheep country!' She made it sound a crime to pasture cattle.

He made a resentful noise.'We aren't in farming for fun! We have to make a living. And at the present time there's more money in cattle!'

'And that's all that matters to you! A wounded animal doesn't matter, of course, you can't make money out of hares!'

He gave another muffled bellow. '*I* didn't wound it! *You* did. I suppose you're a rotten shot, and in any case you have no blasted right to be shooting over my property without asking permission. You——'

'*Shooting*? Who said anything about shooting? I've never handled a gun in my life. I don't go round killing things. I was backing my car and ran over it. It bolted out of a clump of tussock right under my wheels! What do you mean, shooting?'

'Ach! You said wounded. Naturally I thought you'd been shooting. You should have said injured.'

Lucinda actually gritted her teeth at him. 'I wasn't thinking about being pedantic. I hate purists.' Then she looked down at the hare and her face changed. 'What on earth can I do for it? It's badly hurt, isn't it?'

He stopped glaring and put a hand out to the hare, not struggling at all now. He gently extended the leg, which was bleeding freely, and examined it closely. 'It's not broken, it's scraped to the bone, but——'

Lucinda made a protective movement.

He said irritably, 'I'm not going to hurt it. I'm just wondering what can be done with it. The best thing——'

She broke in hotly, 'Oh, I know! The best thing will be to put it out of its misery. Kill it! But I won't let you. I know it's all one can expect of you Farmer Giles types, but I just w——' She broke off, her mood changed. She looked up at him. 'Sorry, I'm not being practical. I do know that's all that can be done. We can't let them overrun the country and ruin its economy. Only——'

To her surprise he grinned, said, 'That's better. But——'
Was he looking embarrassed? 'It's the same with our deer.
They have to be kept down, or we'd have no forests left. I help
a chap at that on the other side of the lake sometimes. But at
times I've seen them playing. They do, you know. They paw
the ground and prance round it like kittens, for the sheer delight of being alive. Makes it very hard to level a gun on them.
So sometimes I've lowered my gun and come away. It's
seemed so wrong to put an end to that spontaneous happiness.
I was going to say the best thing to do would be to pen it up in
one of the fowl-houses till it's healed. Oh, I daresay it'll get
caught in one of the hare-drives, but I don't think I can kill it
this very moment. I've got a sack on my saddle. My horse is
tied up over there. Good job he was, or he'd be over Ben
Lomond heading for Glenorchy right now.'

Lucinda had the grace to look ashamed. 'I—I can't do anything about the cattle, I suppose? Will they have done themselves any damage?'

He shook his head. 'But I'll have to come back tomorrow to
shift them. No use trying now, they'll be as skittish as they
come. And there would have to be two of us.'

Lucinda looked appalled. 'A morning's work gone!'

He looked rueful. 'Yes, and I'm trying to run a guest-house
too—time is precious. Never mind, hang on to that hare for
grim life while I get that sugar-bag.'

Lucinda put the hare gently and reluctantly into the sack.
His mouth tightened. 'You think I'm not being honest about
this, don't you ... that the moment you're out of sight I'll take
it out and give it a rabbit punch on the back of its neck? Well,
this Farmer Giles isn't like the rest of the Farmer Giles types
you seem to have met. I'll do exactly what I said I would, and
if you don't believe me, you'd better come to see for yourself
tomorrow—at Drumlogie, about a mile back towards the
Arrow from the track you must have taken up here.'

Lucinda nodded slowly. 'I might just do that.' (Because if
he thought she would he would spare the hare.) 'What name
shall I ask for?'

His grin annoyed her for some reason. Why *should* he grin,
anyway? 'You know it already,' he said.

'Know it? How could I?'

His face was solemn. 'Search me ... feminine intuition, I suppose. It's Giles!' He added, 'Farmer Giles ... Giles Logie.'

Lucinda gave a short offended nod and turned away. His voice halted her, full of hateful amusement. 'I see you haven't got a sense of humour.'

She swung round, looked him straight between the eyes and said, 'That's a most offensive and smug thing to say. It's hard to laugh when you've made a fool of yourself. And it's just a question of not seeing humour in sarcasm. I'll be out in two days to see that hare, Mr. Logie,' and she stamped off.

As she turned the shoulder of the hill again, she stopped, furious with herself for being so petty, and started to giggle. Farmer Giles! It reminded her of the time at that reception in Hongkong when a young boy who was helping them had unknowingly collided with Lady Cingleby from the back, clutched her to steady them and said, 'Whoa, Emma!' and wondered why they had all, including Emma Cingleby, laughed.

She looked down at her once elegant scarlet trouser-suit, plastered with cow platter, streaked with blood and ginger hairs, and decided she'd better go into the boarding-house by the back door if possible.

Mrs. Millister ran a bed-and-breakfast place and was washing up the family lunch dishes when her guest appeared. She stared in alarm, fearing Lucinda had had an accident, but on hearing the explanation said to the girl who was helping her, 'Marny, go and put some soapy water in the tub in the laundry. There's a brush out there. If you scrub it all off first, I reckon we could get the deeper stains out later.'

Lucinda accepted the help gratefully and Marny went running up to her bedroom for a wrap. They giggled as they scrubbed.

'And I called him Farmer Giles,' said Lucinda, 'then asked him what his name was, so I could call out to see the hare in a day or two, and he said I already knew his name, that he was Giles Logie of Drumlogie. A big shot here, I presume. Do you know him?'

'Not to say know, and wouldn't want to. I've been here only a few months. But I believe he's a very poor type, a real womanizer.'

Lucinda blinked. He hadn't struck her that way. Or was it just that she associated womanizers with city-slicker types? A very ill-formed way of judging men, she supposed.

Something made her push it a little further, put up a slight defence of him. 'Is he really? Or do you mean he's just a flirt ... fond of the girls?'

'Oh, he's a bad one all right. Likes the experienced ones, the married women. Bit off more than he could chew last year. Woman he knew somewhere else followed him down here and there was a real good shindy when the husband arrived.'

Lucinda pulled a face. 'Well, the fact he thinks I'm coming out to see will make him look after the hare. I don't think I'll go if he's that sort of chap.'

Marny nodded. 'Very wise. He probably only offered to do it because he wanted to get you to Drumlogie. In that scarlet trouser-suit you're really something.'

Lucinda said slowly, 'Oh, I don't think so. He told me that if he sees deer playing he can't always bring himself to shoot them.'

Marny looked staggered, as well she might. 'Well, that for a tale! Not a high-country farmer. They've *got* to keep the deer down. No, he was all out to impress you, get you out there.'

Lucinda considered it, then picked up her trews and looked ruefully at them. She laughed. 'That just couldn't have been the reason. It wasn't exactly one of my more glamorous moments. I smelled to high heaven, I was covered with gore ... and worse! And my hair was all over my eyes and my temper very short. Well, thanks, Marny, you've been a sport. Just leave them to soak. Good job they're Crimplene and not wool. I'll put some salt in to get the bloodstains out. Even on red they'll show. I have a feeling this suit will never be the same again.'

The letter that was awaiting her in her room drove all thoughts of the encounter out of her mind.

It was in Harvey's writing. How odd ... her letter to Janice would not have reached them yet. She slit it open, her hands trembling a little. The conventional opening that didn't mean a thing now....

'Dear Lucinda,

'Jan and I have been talking things over and we feel it's only fair to you if we get away from Wanganui. It's not too difficult in a job like mine. Your home is here, and I know how

22

you've loved having a garden. Although you said you'd think things out on holiday and might take a job in Christchurch or Dunedin, we feel we should be the ones to move, not you. You'll be coming back soon, of course, but I thought I should let you know right away that an opening has cropped up for me, so there's no need for you to look for a job in either of those towns now.

'I'm sorry it had to be like this. I feel no end of a heel, but I feel you understand, though not many girls would. I'm taking charge of the Queenstown branch. I'm looking forward to being in one of the main tourist resorts, and of course it's not only a good advancement, but it's an ideal solution to our problem. Jan will be writing to you separately. We'll get married quite soon and move south. I can hardly realize I'm writing all this. *You* were the one who wanted to be sure, yet *I'm* the one responsible for the break. Not that I would have broken it up, once I'd asked you, if you hadn't found out, Lucinda.'

The rest of the letter didn't matter. Poor Harvey. He'd tried to chat on as if it were an ordinary friendly letter. What mattered so horribly was that by now they would have her letter and would be positively appalled to think she had fallen in love with Queenstown and had taken a position there. Now they would feel worse than ever. If only, if only Harvey had written a week ago!

Now one of those ridiculous situations would arise with both sides trying to back out. Well, she could not jeopardize Harvey's standing with his firm. *She* could not stay. But they would feel it very deeply.

Oh, how ghastly! She'd better ring Mr. Ames and tell him to take the house off the market. Yes, she'd do just that. But before she got to the door she stopped. No ... she just couldn't face going back to Wanganui where people were too nice to her, where they sympathized, scanned her face for signs of strain, urged her not to fret, that men weren't worth it.

Meanwhile, she would not go jetting among the rapids; she needed to walk, somewhere where she would not meet people. She picked the road to Glenorchy, past the One-Mile Creek.

She looked on every tree, every curve of the road, completely deserted today, every viewpoint of the lake with eyes that felt they were taking a lasting farewell. How could a place take hold of you in so short a time? It was absurd.

She hoped the physical exercise would have tired her to the point of exhaustion, but the longer she walked, the more alert her mind became. And the hours between sunset and sleep were going to be hard to pass. As she went up the steps of the boarding-house she looked up at Bob's Peak to the Skyline Chalet on top, saw the coloured bubble-cars of the gondola-lift ascending and descending their cables in the bare swathe cut between the fir trees of the massive hillside.

Up there tonight would be bright lights and people intent on pleasure, delicious food prepared by experts, above the beauty of this lake whose Maori name meant The-Trough-of-the-Goblin. Better to be there, Lucinda, feasting your eyes on loveliness, than down here in your room, staring at a wall.

She'd been to the Chalet before, in a party they'd made up at the boarding-house. She supposed you didn't often see a solitary woman diner, but what odds? One could please oneself. She even managed a smile. The mystery figure ... that would be her ... the one who waited and dined alone, sad, remote. The woman in black lace! Only it wouldn't be black lace. She would wear that cerise georgette blouse with the full bishop sleeves and the high stand-up neckline with the sequins. The cerise and lime-green pinafore dress would go over it and she would bind her hair back with that twist of pearls.

Strange how clothes could make one feel glamorous, not just look it.

Not even the fact that she sat opposite a hand-holding young couple in the gondola quenched that confidence. The girl was nervous as it first ascended and still more when it swung in close to the bluffs, but her escort enjoyed that and put his arm about her. Lucinda smiled at them indulgently and felt sophisticated.

She didn't go into the dining-room at first. Her table was booked. She'd rung an hour ago. No need to hurry. She went out on to the huge lookout platform and watched the sunset fading above Walter Peak and Cecil Peak, saw the very last rays touch the jagged edge of the Remarkables above Frankton, with the windows of the houses below reflecting back the light blindingly, looked down on the boat-harbour that lost the sun so much earlier and therefore was already folded in the purple wings of dusk, and thought how she would have loved

24

to have seen this lake rimmed with the purity of virgin snow, to have seen these needle-toothed summits beneath the paler skies of winter. She shivered suddenly despite the mildness of the night and turned to go in before the next gondola should disgorge its passengers.

A waiter seated her by a window at the smallest of the tables. She thought he looked at her a little curiously. She said, looking round, 'You have a big crowd tonight?'

He nodded, a Continental accent in his voice. 'Yes, mad-ame, a tour. All middle-aged. And how they are enjoying themselves! These are the ones perhaps who came through the Depression and were denied these things in their youth. It makes me happy to serve them.' Lucinda warmed to him.

'You'll be very busy indeed for a few moments. I'm in no hurry. I'd like to watch the twilight coming down on the whole lake before I eat. I'm just filling in time tonight.'

He twinkled urbanely. 'There is probably someone, some-where, wishing he could fill it in for you,' and he went away after telling her he could really recommend the *paua* fritters.

The chatter and excitement and obvious enjoyment of those older people alleviated the loneliness somewhat. Lucinda was glad the floors were not filled with courting couples or honey-mooners. She sat in a dream, her profile against the window, looking out on an angle, her chin in her cupped hand.

Up against the window like this, one was in a world of one's own, suspended in space above an immense lake, with only the lights of the gondolas above the town below.

Suddenly someone came to the table with a most purposeful tread, pulled out the opposite chair, dropped into it, leaned across and said, 'It's me, Giles Logie ... for Pete's sake look as if you've been expecting me. Look joyous ... quick, oh, catch on, will you? This is an emergency!'

Lucinda had looked up, blinking, to find it was indeed Farmer Giles, and despite the desperation of his words, he was smiling as if he had just joined the one person in the world who mattered to him.

Her response was instinctive after that first startled moment. She put out both hands across the table to him and said loudly, 'Why, Giles, I'd gone into a daydream over this magnificent scenery. So you made it reasonably early after all!'

She hoped that met the situation.

His eyes, sparkling and daring, met hers in a look that was almost as much of a tribute as a toast would have been. He said in a voice below a whisper, 'You beaut! Oh, you beaut! You wizard of a girl. Keep it up, ask no questions. Just keep it up.'

Lucinda felt mesmerized. She waved a hand to the window. 'I didn't think it could possibly be more beautiful by twilight than by sunset, but it is, isn't it, Giles?'

He nodded. She thought he was a little breathless. 'Didn't I tell you it was? But you've yet to see it at its most beautiful of all, of course ... in winter, when Walter Peak is mirrored ice-sharp in waters that are almost Prussian blue.'

Lucinda swallowed and whispered smilingly, so it would look as if they were murmuring sweet nothings, 'How long do we have to keep this up ... can you brief me?'

He whispered back, looking pseudo-lovingly into her eyes, 'All night, probably, but tell me quickly in case they come across, what's your name?'

'Lucinda.'

'Lucinda *what*? They *are* coming. I'll have to introduce you ... Lucinda *what*?'

Her eyes danced wickedly. 'Just make it darling.'

His voice hissed urgently, 'Of course I'll make it darling, but the surname, quick!'

She collapsed into laughter. '*That's* the surname. I'm Lucinda Darling. There are hundreds of people surnamed Darling in the world.'

Laughter took him too, and they were still chuckling when a man and a woman arrived at the table. Lucinda had a vague idea that this woman too had been sitting alone. So the man must have come in with Farmer Giles. Then what——-?

This man was suave, with an undercurrent of something else. What could it be? A sort of suppressed fury? Why? And the woman seemed to be in the grip of some emotion too. Her neck was slightly mottled with diffused colour. In fact Lucinda had the impression that she was struggling with several emotions. And very possibly chagrin.

Giles rose, said to the woman, 'Oh, hullo, Arlene. Back in Queenstown? I didn't know till Mark joined me in the gondola. I don't think you've met Lucinda. Arlene and Mark, this

26

is Miss Lucinda Darling ... Darling by name, and darling by nature, as you can see. Lucinda, this is Arlene Oliver and Mark Oliver. What a pity there appear to be no bigger tables left. We could have all dined together. But we'll see you later, perhaps have coffee with you in the alcove with the potplants.'

Lucinda felt weak with relief when they went back to their table, and still more when she realized they were out of earshot.

Giles Logie picked up the glass of sherry Lucinda had not started, drained it and said, 'Phew! I needed that!' then, 'Of course I'll pay for your dinner. Unless ... oh, of course, you must be waiting for someone, surely? Oh lord ... if so, how can I——'

She surveyed him coolly. 'Calm yourself, Farmer Giles, I'm not. I'm having dinner on my own. Aren't you the lucky one!'

'I certainly am,' he said fervently, 'I couldn't believe my incredible luck. I thought if only I could see one woman sitting alone, or someone in a party with a spare chair, I'd make straight for them and throw myself on their mercy. I left Mark at the entrance, I dared not hesitate, saw your profile at the window, recognized you immediately and made a beeline for you. I feel a good diplomat or a spy was lost in me.'

Lucinda said softly but with meaning, 'You had help.'

'I sure did. You were magnificent!'

She opened her mouth to ask what on earth it all meant, but at that moment the waiter arrived, quite evidently, by the greeting, a friend of Giles. Well, in a tourist town, and both of them catering, they were bound to know each other.

He beamed, 'I said to Madame I was sure someone would be wishing to be here to share a table with her ... and here *you* are, Giles, just like that.' He beamed as if he had personally conjured up her escort. Then he looked puzzled. Giles interpreted it, said quickly, in case a hush should fall on the buzz of conversation, 'Marcel, I was in a spot, and Lucinda came to my rescue. Mark Oliver was on the gondola. I'd no idea either he or his wife were in town, or that she was up here. She's run out on him again. He said, most unpleasantly: "Well, which of us is going to give my wife dinner tonight?" All I could think of was: "Well, it can hardly be me. I have a rendezvous with somebody else, believe me." I hadn't dared hope for luck like this. I was just going to drop into the first vacant seat I saw. And if there wasn't one, I was praying for an empty table, and would have had to pretend to wait for someone.'

Marcel put his head back and chuckled. 'My wife is helping in the kitchen tonight. I would have got her to come to you. But instead you extricated yourself ... and found a most charming dinner-partner. I shall personally see you have the best of everything as if it were a very special celebration. This has made my day. I feel as if I am taking place in a television series. High intrigue indeed!' And he went off, still chuckling.

Lucinda looked across the candles. Her voice was low, but a tart tone crisped it. 'Yes, it's very much in the best James Bond style, isn't it? Never without a woman in it.'

He grinned unrepentantly. 'It is. You're a good sport, Lucinda darling.'

She said shortly, 'Lucinda will do ... when we're alone.'

His eyes gleamed. 'Did you think I was making it an endearment? Using "darling" with a small "d"? I wasn't. I called you Lucinda Darling, just as you might call me Giles Logie. But let's not waste time on things that don't matter. We've only got the time it takes for dinner to investigate each other's backgrounds and cook up a really good tale to satisfy Mark Oliver.'

'Why should I? I got sort of pitchforked into this. I must have been mad. But I was taken off balance. I've no intention of embarking on a wholesale deception. Why should I?'

He looked at her soberly. 'Because Mark Oliver is a very decent chap, one who deserved a wife better than that ... she likes to play the field. The only way I can convince him that a recent affair I had with his wife was never meant to be serious is for me to appear really serious about somebody else. And, since you responded so nobly a few minutes ago, it has to be you! You're hooked!'

Lucinda thought, with a curl to her lip, it was the old tale ... the woman tempted me. She drew in a deep breath and was about to let him have a broadside when the wine waiter appeared and a waitress with a menu.

Giles Logie took one look and burst out laughing. 'I can tell you this, Jill, my companion won't be wanting hare soup. You don't, do you, Lucinda darling?'

She shuddered. 'No, I'll settle for crayfish chowder, thank you.'

When they were alone Giles said, 'We haven't time for any explanations re my little peccadillo with the wife of Mark. Let's fill in the gaps and decide on our line of campaign. Be a sport, Lucinda. Do it for Mark's sake—and,' that audacious eye gleamed again, 'it *could* be fun.'

Lucinda said faintly, 'All right, but with one proviso. No hanky-panky. The minute I feel it's too unsavoury, I'm getting out from under.'

'That's understood. Just get your mind fixed on the fact that you're saving a marriage, plus saving me embarrassment, and you'll enter right into it.'

Lucinda said, 'I'm afraid the latter cuts no ice with me at all. The former does.'

His mouth twisted. 'Don't let's argue. Let's get on with it.'

It was punctuated with the most delicious courses. Over the chowder he found out where she was staying and how long she had been in Queenstown. With the *paua* fritters pan-fried in lemon butter, he asked her if she could prolong her stay a little, and she found herself confessing, to her own amazement, that she was a free agent at the moment and actually thinking of seeking a position in Queenstown.

'Oh, splendid,' he said, heaping the lemon butter over his fritters with a knife, 'you can come out to Drumlogie. I'll give you a job.'

Lucinda felt as if she were being swept along and hadn't the power or the wisdom to say no.

Over the venison, cubed and marinated, and served with mushrooms, glazed cherries and ground almonds, he told her that he had met her first some time ago when he had visited Wanganui. They had taken a jet-boat up river to Jerusalem and Pipiriki, then had had a fabulous time at the Chateau Tongariro. 'Your mother and father were with us, of course. All very right and proper.'

'That would be difficult,' said Lucinda squashingly, 'seeing all my parents are dead.'

He waved his fork as one to whom diversions of plans mean less than nothing. 'Oh, I'm sorry about that, but your aunt could have accompanied us. I do trust you have an aunt. It would be very remiss of you not to have one.'

He saw the dark brown eyes narrow to slits of laughter and one lop-sided dimple appear in her smooth cheek. 'I haven't, but I'm sure you wouldn't let that matter ... haven't you got an imagination? Let's invent one. Let me see ... Aunt Thomasina. I've always wanted an Aunt Thomasina. The only thing is that the sort of aunt I have in mind ... ultra-respectable ... wouldn't have approved of you!'

The grey eyes in the sun-tanned face went solemn. 'You're so wrong. Your Aunt Thomasina belonged to the generation who believed that the best husbands were the ones who'd sowed their wild oats in their youth. And she recognized my basic sterling qualities. In fact, she made the match. She's bound to be a matchmaker—all aunts are.'

Lucinda relaxed and began to enjoy herself. It was all so gloriously mad. 'Yes, she did, really, but her innate cautiousness made her insist that we got to know each other better before we became engaged. So I came down to stay at Mrs. Millister's. Taking it all round, it's just as well Aunt Thomasina doesn't know as much about you as I do!'

'Lucinda darling, I'm beginning to suspect you have a very sharp tongue. You ought to watch it.'

She grinned at him. 'Careful, I might walk out on you.'

He grinned back. 'So you might, though I feel you're too good a sport to do that thing.'

'Well, don't push your luck too far. I'm sporting, yes, but I'm not——' She paused, picked up her glass, surveyed him over the rim.

He held her gaze. 'You aren't what?'

The brown eyes went sober. 'I'm not cheap. I was sort of—well, bulldozed into this, or mesmerized or something. But it's just for as long as it takes us to get away from here.'

The grey eyes under the thatch of sun-bleached hair were very serious. 'You're reneging on me. I could have sworn a few moments ago you were prepared to come out to Drumlogie, take a temporary job, see this thing through. Why the change of heart?'

'Must have been the mention of Aunt Thomasina. So respectability settled upon me again and I knew suddenly that this is the sort of thing one should not become involved in. I'll see it through tonight. It should convince Mr. Oliver you were not coming here to meet his wife and——'

She was very firmly interrupted.

'I *wasn't* coming here to meet her, if that's what you think!'

Lucinda put her glass down, picked up her knife and fork. 'I find that hard to believe.' She didn't try to keep the derision out of her voice.

His voice was rueful, not offended. 'Anyone would find it hard to believe. But it happens to be true. I didn't even know she was back in Queenstown. I have to see the manager here about a group who are coming to my guest-house. Nearly all tours come up here for a dinner, but they book well ahead. This group just rang from Nelson today, and it's short notice, so I thought I'd have a personal chat with the manager. We all work in together. I was staggered, when I realized coming up on the gondola-lift that Arlene was here. Mark had been told so at the motel she's staying at. I'm just wondering if she rang Drumlogie and they told her I was having dinner up here. It was sheer coincidence otherwise.'

Lucinda looked at him appraisingly. To her amazement a flush ran up from his throat, an angry flush. 'You'd just *better* believe me,' he said.

She dropped her eyes. She wanted to believe him, but all sorts of warning bells rang in her ears. Then she looked up, smiling, 'We'd better not appear to be quarrelling, Farmer Giles, or that would really spoil things.'

He relaxed. 'You'll stay, for a few days at least, till they go away?'

'Is it necessary? Will you have to see anything of them?'

He grimaced. 'Oliver told me he'd booked at Drumlogie from Dunedin, when he found out Arlene had come up here. He must have got the only girl who wasn't with us last year when it happened. My aunt, or the other girls, would have said full up. He's booked for them both. *Will* you stay?'

Lucinda said, 'Your aunt keeps house for you?'

'Yes, with her husband. They, like your aunt, are ultra-respectable.'

'All right.' Lucinda's voice was reluctant, and she had the shaky feeling she was committing herself to something more than a lighthearted deception. 'How will you explain the fact that I'm not staying at Drumlogie already?'

He considered it for a moment, spearing the last cube of

venison on his fork, then, 'Till now, you've just come out as a visitor. Your aunt felt much happier if you stayed with Mrs. Millister at first, someone she'd met once on a visit here. She wanted you to get to know my background, but she's relenting now, and you've decided to stay on here for a few weeks, helping Aunt Stella. But of course I may not let you go back to Wanganui at all!'

'I trust Aunt Stella will concur in all this.'

'She will. In a little while, before we leave the table, I'll ring her, from behind the scenes here. You can sit quietly alone. I don't want to leave you on your own with them. We've got to know exactly what the other has said. Ah, here's our pavlova coming.'

The confection was all that a pavlova should be, faintly creamy, crisp and sugary outside, soft meringue inside. It was filled and decorated with fruit and whipped cream by the hand of an artist.

Giles Logie said, 'I'd better know a bit more about you.'

Lucinda said, 'I spent most of my life going from one country to another. Dad was a missionary and finally took on refugee work. He had a year back here in an administrative capacity but missed the field work horribly. I stayed on in the house they bought and to which they were going to retire in about five years' time. Then——' She faltered a little.

He said, 'Didn't you want to go back with them?'

Her words came slowly. 'There was someone I met. Mother was so thrilled—she felt that the life they lived kept us from meeting people of our own age. My sister and brother are in England. Trudy is married, Ivan at Oxford. They're twins. Mother thought it was lovely that it looked as if at least one of her children would settle in New Zealand, which was Dad's country.'

She seemed reluctant to go on. He prompted her.

'And—things didn't work out that way? You felt at a loose end?'

She decided to be honest. 'I had a great friend. I always left my other childhood friends when we moved on ... Korea, Singapore, Pakistan, Indonesia ... but all our furloughs were spent here, in Wanganui, with Mother's best friend. She had a daughter my age, Janice, a kindred spirit.

'Her people got transferred to Wellington, and she went

32

with them, but when my mother and father lost their lives in a flood in East Bengal, she came up to Wanganui to live with me. Harvey Renfrew, this man, had wanted us to get married before Mother and Dad went away, but, foolishly, I asked for time to think it over. I said Mum and Dad could fly home any time, for a wedding, that there was no need to rush things, marriage was a big step.'

She paused, went on unemotionally, 'I think I knew from the start how it was with Janice and Harvey, even though I pretended to myself I didn't.'

Giles Logie's eyes held hers, 'And——?'

'They fell in love. Oh, they were very decent about it. They weren't going to say anything to me. Janice was going to say she was missing her parents, and was going back to Wellington. I happened to overhear that, so it was all over. I told them these things happen. I decided to take my holidays, but my boss knew I wasn't coming back. Then I wrote Harvey and Jan saying I'd fallen in love with the South Island, and would probably take a job in Christchurch or Dunedin. Then I reached Queenstown, and wanted to stay.'

'Then why not? You can have a permanent job at Drumlogie if you like——or till you find an office job. I'd like to think there was something I could do for you in return for what you've done for me.'

Her eyes went out to the dark lake below them, rimmed now with tiny lights in the remote bays. 'But now I can't stay. For long, anyway. I wrote to tell them I was staying here. I—my letter crossed with one from Harvey. He's in a travel agency. He and Janice felt I was more tied to Wanganui than they were—because of the house. So he applied and got a transfer to ... Queenstown! One of those horrible coincidences you can't quite believe. So I've to pack and go before they get here. But I can spare you a few days. It won't be too long, will it?'

But he didn't answer that. He leaned forward, his elbows on the table. 'Lucinda, isn't this the answer? Couldn't it be a two-way benefit? Harvey will probably feel worse than ever now—I think he must be mad, mind you, letting a girl like you slip through his fingers—but if he came here to find you interested —seemingly—in someone else, wouldn't that solve your problem? And it would suit me to have you stay on. I don't want

Mark Oliver ever to guess this was a put-up job. How about it, Lucinda darling ... with a capital "D"?'

She turned back from her contemplation of the lake, found her eyes very close to his, knew an overwhelming tide of relief ... it could be the solution to all her problems, and said, 'Right, it's a bargain!'

He pushed back his chair, but first patted her hand as it lay on the table, said, 'Won't be long, my sweet,' and disappeared into the kitchen regions.

CHAPTER TWO

THEY lingered a long time over the cheese-board and no one would have guessed they were other than a couple deeply in love.

'We'll have a second cup of coffee with the Olivers,' said Giles.

It was suddenly fun. Giles had a thought. 'Fill me in with your likes and dislikes, save me tripping up. I'll think up mine.'

Lucinda admitted to preferring films and plays to musicals and vaudeville, didn't care much for ballet, but loved Gilbert and Sullivan if not grand opera. Was fond of skating, had never had the chance to try skiing, but best of all liked long, long tramps. Had never liked living inland, though she had had to, very often; much preferred to be somewhere where she could climb a hill and see the ocean.

Giles said, smiling, 'Till you came here and found great waters over a thousand feet deep, land-locked in the Trough-of-the-Goblin. This lake gets a hold of one just as the sea does. Carry on, Lucinda ... no wonder I fell for you in Wanganui, this is adding up to kinship of spirit.'

She thought of something, looked a little alarmed. 'Do you know Wanganui? If you didn't, and Mr. Oliver did, you might make a bluey.'

'I do. I've been through that huge tunnel in the centre of Durie Hill and up the lift. Weren't they going to have used that tunnel as an air-raid shelter in World War Two if the Japanese had got here?' He looked at her face and grinned. 'I

34

don't believe you knew that yourself,' he accused.

She laughed. 'That's something I hadn't caught up on. But I *have* taken that trip you mentioned—to Jerusalem and Pipiriki. I've done it by road as well as jet-boat, going from Pipiriki to Raetihi over the tops of the ranges.'

Giles said dreamily, narrowing his eyes, as if remembering, 'I'll never forget that hunter's moon over Virginia Water ... there were cinerarias under the trees, remember, faintly purple in the moonlight. There were sleeping water-fowl at the edge, and that little bridge; and the curves of the phoenix palms against the starlit sky was something never to forget. And you wore that blue dress.'

Lucinda said quickly, anxiously, 'It's Virginia Lake, not Virginia Water.'

His lips twitched again. 'Wrong. Most people call it Lake now, but it was named after Virginia Water just off the Bath road on the way to Windsor Castle. I visited there—I had three years in United Kingdom, by the way. You could be supposed to have known that. You see, my Aunt Caroline lives in Wanganui, on St. John's Hill. I spend holidays there. That's how we met, of course. Our aunts play bridge together.

'Lucinda, do you know my favourite place? Long-Acre Valley—a no-exit road winding back about fifteen miles or so, I think. A deep narrow valley, with hundreds of poplars, aspens and lombardies. Magnificent *totaras*, too, with tall, branchless trunks for a great height, and the stream winds under the road so often there are umpteen humpy-backed bridges. When I was a schoolboy, there used to be a peacock farm there. I wonder if there still is. It gave a touch of magic to our wanderings—we used to go up there as a family—to suddenly see one spreading its tail and adding to the green and the blue and the gold.'

Lucinda answered with an equal nostalgia, 'Yes, I remember Long-Acre last autumn. We went there on a still, dreamy day. All of a sudden a little wind sprang up, a wind as small as a sigh, really. It loosened the leaves so gently, but kept them fluttering in the air like golden snowflakes, till they finally drifted to the carpet of leaves on the ground. It made it a fairy-tale place.' Suddenly her face shadowed, remembering.

Giles Logie said quickly, 'Sorry ... am I recalling something you'd rather forget?' He touched his hand to hers,

35

swiftly.

She shrugged. 'Forget it. I'm not going to keep looking back, or if I do, not with a sense of loss. I very much doubt if any man is worth wearing the willow for. Do you think we could join the Olivers now? They appear to have finished. I'm a little apprehensive, so let's get it over and done with.'

He was very attentive. He picked up the vivid green stole she had draped on the back of her chair, put it round her shoulders lingeringly. Lucinda was aware that Mark and Arlene Oliver were watching them closely. She smiled up at Giles, holding his gaze; were his eyes really grey, or blue?

There was a great contrast between this Giles and the Farmer Giles of this afternoon. This was a suave man, mocking, very sure of himself, something his experience with women had given him, she supposed. But what did it matter? Being cautious and sensible hadn't served her very well. It had lost her Harvey.

Giles seemed very at ease with the Olivers. What an actor he must be. He said to them, 'Come on over here, I'll get Marcel to bring us some more coffee. It's thinning out now that tour is going back to its hotel.'

Arlene was very beautiful in a brittle, hard sort of way. Her hair was a glorious natural chestnut, and it showed burnished gleams in the glow of the lamp next to her. Giles had man-oeuvred the Olivers into two deep chairs and he sat very close to Lucinda on a low couch.

Arlene had to pretend too, though Lucinda didn't know if it was to placate Mark, or just face-saving as far as Giles was concerned. 'I hadn't realized Mark was going to be able to get away as soon as this. A nice surprise. I was pining for these mountains—they get into one's blood. And I love this chalet. Mark was very clever to find me here.'

Mark grunted. 'Oh, not so clever, since you'd told them at the motel you were coming up here.'

Arlene smiled, 'Well, I'm thankful I did, darling.'

Lucinda could not decide whether Arlene was covering up an assigned meeting, or simply so furious that Giles had another girl in tow, she was trying to make him jealous by pretending all was well between herself and her husband, be-cause if they hadn't arranged to meet, Giles and Arlene, she would have no idea what her husband had said to Giles on the

36

way up.

Arlene turned to Lucinda, and only the nervous screwing-out of her cigarette betrayed the fact that she wasn't perfectly at ease.

'Have you been in Queenstown long? I don't remember you when I was here last year. Are you a resident?'

Lucinda felt confidence flow into her. 'Well, I wasn't then. But Giles spent some time in what could be called my home-town, Wanganui, in the winter. Our aunts play bridge to-gether. Later, Aunt Thomasina suggested I came down here on a working holiday to see how I liked it.' Her eyes went to the window. 'As if anyone could help loving a fairyland like this!'

She saw Arlene's lips tighten. Mark Oliver, visibly relaxing, though his eyes remained watchful, said, 'But I don't think you're a New Zealander, are you? Your voice suggests you're from England.'

Lucinda laughed. 'I was born in Singapore—my mother was English—and we had some holidays there, with our grandparents. But by upbringing I'm what could be termed a world citizen. We're a motley lot. My twin brother and sister were born in Madras, but my father was a Kiwi, so we spent many furloughs here, especially after my grandparents died.'

Mark said with interest, 'Was your father in oil?'

'No, refugee work. So Wanganui became for me the place where I could put roots down.'

'Till you came here,' said Giles, with a satisfied inflection they could not miss. Mark Oliver leaned back and crossed his legs. Perhaps he didn't know a small, relieved sigh escaped him.

Nothing could have been more natural than Giles's small talk. He was certainly some actor. Perhaps he was; no doubt there'd be some local drama group. Lucinda felt unreal. Giles built it up, so carefully, phrase by phrase, teasing comment and light-hearted flirting, that she found herself almost believing in their fabricated past. Mark Oliver became so free with them he even grew confiding. 'In the past, I've stuck rather too closely to my business, I think. I've been finding out lately that no one is indispensable. I've a jolly good staff, and I think they rather enjoy taking more responsibility. Arlene seems to have developed itchy feet, and you can't see much in one holiday a year. I've a good mind to run my business on a more relaxed schedule and take time off for a long cruise, say. How about that, Arlene? And right now, I'm in no hurry to return. I think we ought to go to Milford Sound from here. I've never seen it.'

Arlene said swiftly, 'A cruise sounds marvellous, but don't let's go to Milford Sound yet. Queenstown is my favourite place.'

Mark smiled, 'But how do you know you won't like Milford still more? By the way, Logie, I just booked for three nights at Drumlogie ... if we decide to stay on, perhaps it would be awkward for you?'

Giles said nonchalantly, 'Depends on how much booking the staff have done between your ringing them, and getting home tonight. And Lucinda is coming out tomorrow.'

Lucinda said quickly, 'Oh, I could stay on with Mrs. Mill-ister if that would ease things.' She laughed. 'I'm out at Drumlogie for all except night-time as it is.'

'No fear. You've been there too long now, to my way of thinking. And Aunt Stella knew no one was to be given the room I'd set aside for you.'

(He must have told his aunt to reserve one when he rang her.)

Mark said, and you could sense the iron behind the light tone, 'Oh well, if you can't have us longer, we'll go on to Milford. I cancelled the motel when I arrived there and they were jolly glad. They were in no end of a flap because some double booking had just been discovered. I put your cases in the car, Arlene.' Then he added, 'I think we might get weaving now. I daresay you want to stay on, Logie.'

Giles shook his head. 'No, we're both going out to Drum-logie now. Lucinda wants to have a look at her precious hare before she goes to bed.'

The other two looked slightly startled. 'Hare?' exclaimed Mark.

Giles grinned. 'I was moving some cattle near the back road today. I'd got Lucinda to take her little Mini round to the far gate to meet me there. She backed into a hare she disturbed, right at the gate, and injured it. To please her I had to take it home, bandage it, and put it in an old fowl-house till it's able to fend for itself.'

Mark Oliver burst out laughing. 'Well, all I can say is she must really have bewitched you! Imagine any farmer playing doctor to a hare. It beats all!' He looked so delighted Lucinda suddenly felt deeply for him. He was like a man who has suddenly had his chance of happiness renewed. She felt a blinding surge of anger against these two people, Arlene and Giles, who had obviously caused this man great anguish. For Mark's sake, not Giles's, she would see this thing through.

They came out into a world of ineffable beauty. A moon was riding high above Walter Peak and making a golden path across the fathomless waters of the lake. Nature had carved this out with a loving hand and man had embellished its sculptured loveliness with the grace and symmetry of trees. She hoped achingly that they would not spoil this demi-Paradise by building too many high-rise hotels in the centre of the little dreaming town. Surely they could build them against the hills where they would spoil no views.

With one accord they all moved to the look-out, leaning on the rail above the fantastic drop of the gondola-lift. Isolated lights twinkled goldenly in the over-lake bays, whose only access was by water. The little town with its continental atmosphere lay below, still with the old-world air of houses huddling together, a legacy from lawless days when proximity meant protection.

Behind Bob's Peak was the long, higher line of Ben Lomond and limitless ranges reaching westward. Northward, behind and below the chalet, lay the Skipper's Gorge Road and Drumlogie. *And a very tricky situation!* There ought not to be intrigue and unfaithfulness in a setting like this, fouling one of the fairest places on earth.

The four of them, closely facing each other, swung out over the precipices in the steel-and-glass bubble of a yellow gondola and stepped out into the control-house. Lucinda had walked from the boarding-house. Now she got into Giles's car, finding it a relief to be away from the other pair for a brief time.

She said, anxiously, 'I hope no one gives us away at Drumlogie.'

He seemed to have no apprehension. 'No one will—relax. They're good employees. And they knew the former situation, except for one temporary hand, and Aunt Stella was going to brief them all.'

How cocksure could a man get ... the arrogant male, for sure. He was sublimely confident none would give him away.

Her tone bit. 'You're extremely sure of their loyalty.'

'Why shouldn't I be? Our employees have the habit of becoming friends. And they didn't like Arlene. They'll be well primed by Aunt Stella, believe me. They'll appear to recognize you. I'll call them by their names, so you can do the same. And by the way, I call Aunt Stella Star when I'm speaking to her. When I was a small boy I couldn't say my "L's", so it turned out "Star." You could do the same—a nice intimate touch.'

A small boy who couldn't say his "L's" seemed a far cry from an adult who got himself involved with married women.

It didn't take long till they were turning in at the Drumlogie entrance. Not long enough really, in view of that following car. Lucinda had thought once they turned the first bend in the poplar-lined avenue, they would see the lights of the guesthouse, but they drove on and on and up into the quietness of tall hills, their way outlined by great white quartz rocks at the foot of each tree.

She said, 'How ever far is it?'

A smile sounded in his voice. 'The old homestead is incorporated in the guest-house, and if we'd built nearer the gate, we'd have lost our view of the lake ... our greatest tourist asset.'

Lucinda's voice was squeaky with surprise. 'But you couldn't possibly see the lake from here! We've come several miles.'

He laughed. 'It's a case of wait and see. We wind among the hills and go steeply up the Footstool of Ben Logie, as it's called, to a ridge. There the first Giles Logie built his home. You know the view from the Chalet is called the Million Dollar View? Well, ours is known locally as the Half-million View. It's the same, but a slightly lower level.'

Lucinda's voice held enchantment, a sort of dreaming half-belief.

'You mean you look right down the lake over the Peninsula and the Frankton Arm to the Remarkables from away in here?'

'Yes, Lucinda darling. And also across the lake to Cecil and Walter Peaks through a cleft in the heights at the back of the house. It's framed, with these closer hills dividing for the

40

glimpse. You'll have seen it a dozen times on calendars and postcards. We always have artists painting it.'

If it hadn't been for the following lights reminding her of a man who, for the sake of his own happiness, must be deceived, Lucinda would have known sheer delight.

In the beam of the headlamps larches and pines were silhouetted in a cavalcade of serrated tops, then came the thicker foliaged trees of a big garden, and the unmistakable perfume of roses, prodigal in their second blooming. They turned a bend in the great avenue, took a rise up a steep cutting on to a huge terrace, where lights like golden poppies blossomed out in the moonshine. Lucinda had an impression of a house with old gables and modern patios and a welcoming warmth.

The door swung open and a slim figure appeared against the light.

'Aunt Stella,' said Giles's voice in Lucinda's ear as he helped her out. The Olivers' car drew in behind them. Giles put a hand under Lucinda's elbow, turned. 'I'll have your cases brought in in a few moments, Mark, come away in.'

The slim figure advanced, greeted the Olivers, then Stella Adair held out two hands to her nephew's companion, said, 'Lucinda dear,' and touched her lips to Lucinda's cheek. 'Now, don't you two go running off to see your hare. It's curled up in some straw fast asleep at last, and I'd like it to stay that way.'

Lucinda laughed. 'Thanks, Star. I've been imagining it trying to burrow its way out. But perhaps the leg is too sore to attempt that. Giles thinks it will soon heal, given a good start. He says it's even eating.'

They came into the hall. Giles said, without noticeable haste, but fairly clearly, 'Meg, would you ask John to bring the cases in and to take Mr. Oliver's car to the carports?'

Meg, busy with some papers, swung round, said, 'Oh, hullo, Lucinda—look, see me before you go, will you? There was something I meant to ask you this afternoon and forgot.'

'Right, Meg,' said Lucinda, 'I'll come out after you've rounded John up.'

Mark signed in and Stella whisked them into a small sitting-room. 'I lit a fire in here. Any excuse for a fire, that's me. Would you like to sit down till your cases go up? Lucinda, what time tomorrow do you intend to come out? Morning? Oh good, because I have Mrs. Haigie coming for morning tea and she'd like to meet you. Of course she's known Giles since he was a baby and is interested.'

It was very cleverly done. What a family!

The Olivers, to Lucinda's great relief, decided they'd rather have a tray brought to their room than stay down for a cup of tea, and before long Meg came in to take them up.

With one accord the three conspirators waited till footfalls faded, and there was no chance of being overheard. Then Giles and his aunt looked at each other and burst into uncontrollable, though quiet laughter. Stella was certainly a young-looking aunt.

Finally she sobered up, wiped her eyes and looked at Lucinda. 'Do forgive us. You must be feeling absolutely bewildered. Even I did, at first, when Giles rang me. Though why I should after all these years of pulling him out of scrapes, I don't know! But this certainly must have meant some quick thinking. Giles, what a blessing you'd already met Lucinda this afternoon. Otherwise you might have got entangled with a stranger who almost certainly would have smacked your face. Or she might have been waiting for an escort, who could have cut up rough. Really, Giles! But tell me, how long are they going to stay? I suppose we can't keep this up too long.'

Giles merely grinned. Really, he was maddening! He was taking it far too lightly. He ought to be worried. 'Only a few days, Star, then they'll be off to Milford Sound, never to return, I hope. Once Arlene is convinced the fun and games are over, I shouldn't think she'd come chasing up here every time she wants to spur Mark into making more fuss of her.'

'If that's all she's after,' said Star gloomily. Giles laughed again.

Fun and games ... that was how he regarded it, yet when he'd been persuading her to back him up he'd said she must get her mind fixed on the fact that she would help save a marriage. Just cunningly appealing to her better nature, she supposed. He'd said that just after she'd told him she'd get out the moment she felt it was too unsavoury. What a man! Yet his aunt looked the essence of integrity and was backing him up. But then when your dear ones were involved you helped them even if you didn't approve. Unless they went too far and you had to take the prop away.

Giles said, 'Look at Lucinda, she's gone into a daydream. I guess she's wondering what in the world she's got herself into.'

'No wonder.' Stella's voice was tart. 'I hope you realize and appreciate your incredible luck, Giles. Fate brought her into your path this afternoon, and arranged for her to be where you needed her most tonight! Added to which she's no end of a sport, entering into the spirit of it as she has ... in something which can't possibly benefit *her* in the slightest!'

Giles sobered immediately. 'But it can ... though she didn't know that to begin with, and I give her all credit for being so quick on the uptake.' He looked across at Lucinda. 'May we tell Star or——'

Lucinda said instantly, 'I think we'll have to tell her, though in any case, I somehow don't mind her knowing.'

A look passed swiftly between Lucinda and Stella and sealed a friendship. Stella's blue eyes flashed with pleasure. 'Thank you, Lucinda. You've been pitchforked into this crazy set-up, and have hardly got your bearings yet, so I appreciate this. I hope it doesn't mean an intrusion on your privacy.'

Lucinda said slowly, 'I might resent *some* strangers knowing, but—well, we've taken a few fences very suddenly to-night, and I have a feeling you'll understand. It's simply that it would help me very much to appear to have someone romantically interested in me just now.'

Giles said, 'Would you prefer me to tell it, Lucinda?'

She hesitated, then said yes. She'd an idea she could tell what sort of a man he was by the way he retailed this to his aunt. If he embroidered it too much, she'd know he could not be trusted.

Giles said, 'Lucinda came here to get away from Wanganui. She'd been keeping company with someone who'd asked her to marry him, but she wasn't quite sure of her feelings, so she asked for time to consider it.'

'That was a mistake,' said Lucinda.

Stella Adair's eyes darkened as if a shadow of feeling passed over them. 'It might seem so, just now, Lucinda, perhaps not later. Some of us rush into marriage without enough thought. Yes, Giles?'

'Meanwhile her best friend came to live with her. She and Harvey fell in love and Lucinda found out. They hadn't been

43

going to tell her. Lucinda decided to make a complete break and leave them to it. But they thought she was just taking a holiday. She came here, fell in love with the place, decided to stay. She put her house on the market, then wrote to Janice, to say she had a job here.'

He paused, as if considering how to put it. 'Then a foul coincidence took place. Before Janice could have received Lucinda's letter, but when it was on its way, she got a letter from Harvey herself. In fact, just today. Harvey and Janice had decided *they* ought to leave Wanganui. So Harvey asked for a transfer. He's with a tourist agency.'

Stella Adair drew in a sharp breath, sensing what was coming. She caught her lower lip between her teeth.

Giles continued, 'He's to run the branch here! Lucinda feels she wants to rid them of a certain guilt complex which is inevitable in the circumstances, I proposed that we keep this deception up—that when they arrive, they'll find Giles Logie very interested in Lucinda Darling, and Lucinda Darling very taken with Giles Logie!'

Stella's eyes had widened and she clapped her hands in delight, just like an entranced child, laughing. 'Oh, how too marvellous! What a fascinating situation—a sort of reciprocal agreement. So neither of you need feel under obligation to the other!' And suddenly they were all laughing in a perfectly relaxed sort of way.

Lucinda realized what a terrific tension she had been under ever since Harvey's letter had come and how relieved she was that she need not ... quite yet ... leave this cornflower blue lake in this immense and idyllic hollow of the mountains.

Meg came in and wheeled a tea-trolley near the fire. Stella said, 'Stay and have some with us, Meg, and get to know Lucinda.'

Meg shook her head. 'John and I are doing the most fascinating and tough crossword. We're determined to get it out if we have to stay up till midnight, and that's not far away. You can prime me in the morning if there's anything else Rena and I should know. John thinks it's hilarious.'

Giles said, 'Good job you three are as safe as houses ... and there's no danger of you just bursting to share the secret with other people.'

Meg looked serious, in so far as someone with such a merry,

round face, could. 'We won't, believe me. We're only too anxious to see that one get her come-uppance. Her husband's a decent chap and deserves better.' She added a moment later as she put a dish of hot buttered toast near the fire, 'And weren't we lucky the children were away in Alexandra? They'd have given the show away for sure.'

She went out, and Stella said, 'The children are my grand-children, Fergus and Mhairi, my eldest son's children.'

Lucinda said, 'Oh, how right to have such Scots names, to be tacked on to Adair.'

There was a little pause and she had the distinct impression that both Giles and Stella checked themselves from saying something and even glanced uncertainly at each other, antici-pating speech. Then Stella said, rather irrelevantly, Lucinda thought, 'Well, you see their mother is Scots—Kirsty. My son's name, by the way, is Christopher. You could be expected to know all this. The children are visiting their other grand-parents who emigrated here years ago. Their first holiday was in Queenstown. Rob and I ran motels there then. That was how Chris and Kirsty met. She's the most gorgeous daughter-in-law a girl could be.'

'Where do they live, Star?' Lucinda smiled because it was so strange to be on nickname terms with someone met less than an hour ago.

'Oh, they live here, in the other house, across the Six-Miler. Only they're in Australia just now. On—on a holiday.'

A slight hesitation. Why? It didn't matter to Lucinda whether it was a holiday or a business trip.

Lucinda nodded. 'Much better to leave the children here. Australia is so vast, the distances exhaust children who are not interested in scenery as such, just in staying at beaches or lakes.'

'She knows her onions, doesn't she, Star?' said Giles. 'A very understanding girl to have about the place. She'll do Drumlogie. Kirsty and Chris won't be back for a few days, but the kids come home the day after tomorrow. They've been away a fortnight, so they won't be able to give away the fact that you've just met us.'

(No, and they were probably so used to Giles having new girl-friends, they wouldn't take it seriously, either.)

Aloud she said, 'How old are they?'

'Fergus is eight and Mhairi six. You'll wonder why they're away from school. They had measles; fortunately both picked them up from a contact at school at the same time. As soon as we suspected it, their grandparents in Alex came and got them. We didn't let their parents know. Kirsty would have come back like a lintie if she'd suspected they had as much as a cold, and we thought Chris needed her with him.'

That was an odd thing to say. Naturally he'd want his wife with him on holiday.

Stella said, 'I must be right in the picture. Where were you two supposed to meet? In Queenstown? How long ago?'

Lucinda chuckled. 'No, in Wanganui. Giles was visiting his aunt there. Oh, what's her name ... did you say Caroline?'

Stella thought of something, a line between her brows. 'Lucinda, you said you had a house—that's unusual for a single girl, isn't it? Oh, am I putting my foot in it? Had you planned on living in it after you were married? And what about your parents? What do——?'

Giles said quickly, as if he wanted to spare Lucinda, 'Oh, all Lucinda's parents are dead.'

Stella looked slightly embarrassed and to cover up said quickly, 'What an odd way to put it, Giles—*all* her parents. I'm sorry, Lucinda, I'd no idea. You aren't very old, so I naturally expected you to still have your people. Does this mean you're all alone in the world or——'

Giles interrupted her, in a puzzled tone. 'That *was* an odd way for me to put it, but I've an idea it was because I was repeating just what Lucinda herself said. Or am I mistaken?'

Lucinda suddenly had a flake of carnation colour in each cheek. 'I *did* say it, and it *was* odd. Just a slip of the tongue. I mean *both* parents.' She looked across at Stella. 'Don't be embarrassed. I was taught to take death naturally. We saw a great deal of it, the way we were brought up. My parents were medical missionaries—at least Dad was, and Mother a trained nurse. We lived all our lives in dangerous places with not only the perils of flood and fire, but of major epidemics, typhoid, cholera, the lot. We had contacts with lepers and all the attendant diseases that go hand in hand with bodies weakened by malnutrition.' Suddenly she looked a little remote, as if she saw scenes they would never see. 'We knew all about "the arrow that flieth by day and the pestilence that walketh by

46

night," but we seemed to bear a charmed life for so long. Mother told us once she had always prayed she might be spared to see us launched in life, old enough to cope. And she did. I've a twin brother and sister. Ivan is at Oxford and Trudy is in England not far from him, married. Dad was a New Zealander and wanted to retire here, so they bought a house in Wanganui. I was to keep it warm for them, till they finished over there.

'They lost their lives rescuing villagers in one of the tragic floods in Bengal last year. Earlier, their flood-boat—one of those designed in New Zealand—was destroyed by fire. Another ought to have reached them before the time of the monsoon. But there was a strike on here. The only boat available was flimsy, hard to handle, and needed more depth of water. It overturned. But it was the last boat-load. They would have been glad of that.'

She looked up to meet very sympathetic expressions. She managed a smile. 'But Dad imbued us with a certain philosophy that has made it easier to bear our loss. Not that'—she looked away from them for a moment—'we don't have our moments wishing they were still at the end of a postal service, to share our jokes and our difficulties by letter ... but they taught us life was for getting on with.'

Stella said quietly, 'Yes, you have your memories of them, memories of two wonderful people—something you'll always treasure. No disillusionment.' Again it seemed as if a slight shadow passed over her face. Lucinda wondered if she were a widow, or separated from her husband. It could be.

She said, 'It's very late. I must go.' They rose with her.

Stella said, 'When would you like Giles to pick you up? Tomorrow morning or afternoon? Which would suit you best? Either will do us.'

Giles ruffled his aunt's hair. 'That's a polite lie if ever there's one! If I pick Lucinda up in the morning you won't be able to go out to the airport yourself to meet Uncle Rob. I believe you're so grateful to Lucinda for rescuing me, you'd even forgo that. Could you make it the afternoon, Lucinda? One of us should be at the helm here, especially with Chris and Kirsty away ... Star's husband has been away for a fortnight and it's been like a year to her. You never saw such a pair.'

That answered Lucinda's surmise about the shadow. About Stella Adair's thinking it wise to have second thoughts about marriage, about death being easier to bear than disillusionment. But maybe someone dear to her had known these things. A daughter, perhaps.

Lucinda wouldn't—quite—trust Giles Logie, but she knew beyond doubting that Stella Adair had an integrity that could not be questioned.

Just as well she did have these doubts of Giles. He was so—apparently—sincerely grateful on the way back to the little dreaming lakeside town, that she could have thought him a fine fellow. But she had been forewarned, even if she hadn't been embroiled tonight in evidence of his unsavoury affairs.

He took her on to the veranda of her guest-house. He paused for a moment, then said, a little awkwardly, 'I think if I were you I wouldn't mull over that letter Harvey sent you. Think rather of all the adventures that can lie ahead of you. There are times when we come to the parting of the ways. But a new road is sometimes a good road.'

She was startled into being natural. 'Oh, Giles, thank you ... For the moment you sounded exactly like my father.'

He said quietly, 'Then I take that as a great compliment.' Then he laughed. 'I've entered into the spirit of this masquerade so fully, I almost feel I ought to kiss you goodnight.'

His voice was only teasing, but he took a half-step towards her there on the moonlit verandah, with the lake-wind sighing in the pines and the perfume of the late roses heavy on the air. Lucinda took a quick step backwards, and put her hand on the door handle. She spoke softly because above all she didn't want Marny to know who had brought her home, but her tone was very damping.

'Oh no, Giles. We play our parts only when the Olivers are about. Goodnight. I'll be ready at three, and don't forget, as far as the folk here are concerned, I only heard tomorrow morning that you wanted someone to help at Drumlogie and applied for the position.'

He laughed and went away.

CHAPTER THREE

To Lucinda's great surprise she slept dreamlessly and woke with the eagerness to greet a new day she had known long ago before she had lost Mother and Dad, and before she had met—and lost—Harvey. The lake lay shimmering like a giant sapphire beneath the early morning sun and a dawn cloud, infused with rose, hung lovingly above the jagged peaks of the Remarkables, which, after a summer of perfect tourist weather, were innocent of as much as a gleam of snow.

Oh, it was good to feel this zest again, this expectation of adventure. She must be careful what she said to Mrs. Millister and Marny, so she went out, spending the morning prowling round the town and leaving her Mini to have two new tyres fitted.

She came back to tell them that at an agency, where she had inquired about a position, they had told her they could do with some help at Drumlogie, and right away, so as her car was in the garage they were coming in to pick her up after lunch.

Marny burst out laughing, 'Well, at least you'll be able to keep an eye on your hare. But just imagine having for your boss the man you bawled out yesterday!'

Lucinda grinned quite naturally. 'Well, he turned out reasonably kind—towards the hare—and with some of his casual staff back to Varsity now, I expect he thought he'd overlook my outburst. I just had to say when I spoke to him on the telephone, applying for the position.'

Oh dear, she did feel a liar.

Lucinda felt it had gone well, just the same. Nevertheless, she was glad when they were on the road to Drumlogie. It was a great relief to know Mark and Arlene were away up-lake on the steamer, an all-day trip. Giles grinned. 'It's not Arlene's cup of tea, but Mark was adamant. Said if you loved the lake, you ought to be on it, not just loafing round the edge. It'll give me time to show you round so you can orientate yourself. You could be expected to know where certain things and places are, having visited us so much!

'Fortunately we have practically a full batch of new guests, so no one can give away the fact that you're a newcomer.' He chuckled. 'I'm finding things out about myself ... I seem to have a taste for high intrigue.' When he got no answer, he looked at her sharply. 'I take it you haven't.'

Lucinda turned a very serious face towards him, caught the mock-rueful expression on his face and burst out laughing. 'I don't know what's come over me,' she confessed. 'I feel I ought *not* to be enjoying it, but I am! You aren't the only one finding things out about yourself.'

He slapped her knee. 'That's the style, girl! Might as well get all the fun we can out of it.'

She sobered up. 'Fun, yes. But let's keep it that way.'

He lifted an eyebrow. 'I get it. You're warning me off. I'm not to take too much advantage of the situation?'

'Exactly,' said Lucinda gratefully. He didn't answer. She glanced at him. His mouth had quirked up.

She said, 'I notice you're not promising.'

'I'm not in favour of too much promise-making. It would be an easy one to break. Look, let's take it as it comes. By the way, you have a pressing problem yourself. Let's talk about that.'

'About what?'

'The letter you'll have to write to Harvey, replying to the one he sent you. They'll have your letter by now. Imagine the flap they'll be in.'

'I know. I shall have to write him tonight, and just what to say I don't know.'

'I do. I have it all mapped out. It's just like writing a story. Perhaps I should have been an author, not a farmer. Write it in the light vein. Say you realize now you ought to have been completely honest with him in your last letter, but you thought it was a little early to say, but your real reason for not going back up north is very much a girl's reason ... the chap you're working for is rushing you off your feet! So, though no doubt Harvey has felt awful about his transfer to Queenstown, and the crossing of the letters, he's not to give it another thought, and you're sure they'll love Queenstown too.'

He cocked the comical eyebrow at her again and they both succumbed.

Lucinda stopped laughing and said ruefully, 'I feel like putty in your hands. You go too fast for me. I can't even think! Tell me, do I say you know why I left Wanganui?'

'You do, Lucinda darling. It makes me appear a very understanding sort of chap, just the sort he'd hoped you'd meet some day and fall for. Tell him we'll look round for accommodation for him if he likes, right in Queenstown. I expect he'll be down here on his own before they get married.'

There was a long pause, then he added, 'And if this feeling for Janice has been just a sudden infatuation, he might——'

'No,' said Lucinda vehemently. 'No, Giles.'

Their eyes met. Then he looked back to the road. He said gently, 'Is that pride? Or have you gone off him? Or is it because Janice is your best friend and——'

'I don't know.' Lucinda's voice was tight and hard. 'I just don't know.'

They drove a mile or so in silence. Then Lucinda laughed. 'You must have taken my breath away. Giles, I only hope the Olivers leave long before Harvey gets here. Wouldn't he wonder what was going on if he heard any talk of us having met in Wanganui, especially if my mythical aunt were mentioned! I'd never be able to get out of that one!'

By daylight Drumlogie was even more beautiful, built as it was on the ridge of the Footstool, a setting that looked as if it had been designed for just such a house as this, before the earth had cooled. It nestled in against the curve of the hill, with great gardens each side and below, lying in a blaze of sunlight, lit by the gold of birch and willow, oaks and poplars, with here and there a splash of red and russet. The house blended into the tawniness of the tussocks of the hill behind it. A kingfisher flashed down from a *kowhai* tree, into the creek below, with a dive that was a streak of vivid emerald and blue, and soared back to its perch again, to gobble some morsel.

Tuis were chuckling and twanging in the huge pussy-willow that overhung the table where Stella had shallow bowls of elderberry jelly mixed with water, for their honeyed delight. Two of them winged down, the white wattles at their throat justifying their nickname of parson birds, and dipped their brush-like tongues into the syrup, flying back to pay their dues in trills of joyous notes. Sparrows and wax-eyes feasted on crumbs on another table, and there was the soft coo-cooing of doves near the cotes.

Lucinda looked everywhere, drinking it in. Giles slowed, stopped, said, 'Well, what's the verdict?'

'It's a house with a history, isn't it? It's grown, and keeps growing. Has it been in your family always?'

'Yes, the first Giles was a goldminer. That bit in the middle, where the loggia with the clematis has been added on, was a little stone hut he built away up here to get away from the quarrels of the canvas-towns. He had another away up Red Spur Gully, but he was a wise man and didn't win a fortune one night and lose it the next. He decided, once he got a bit behind him, that there was more money to be made out of provisioning the miners. Prices were sky-high, of course, but he won for himself the name of being a just man, and a generous one. He never saw a man have to turn back from the chance of a lucky strike because he couldn't buy mutton and tea, and he married a Scots girl who came out with her aunt and uncle to work on William Gilbert Rees's station. Rees was a cousin of the great cricketer, W. G. Grace. She was a thrifty lass too, and had her head screwed on the right way. When the fabulous strikes of the Red Spur were worked out and the men began coming through here on the way to the Arrow, they built some stable-like accommodation—over there, see? They had half-doors and bunks with mattresses made out of sacks and tussock, for the men to sleep on. A certain amount of mining went on for years and years, of course, but when things slacked off, they bought more land and stocked it with sheep. It's sheep country, of course.'

The nostalgic note did not escape her. What a pity wool wasn't as profitable as of yore, that there were problems facing the frozen meat trade, with the altered situation overseas.

She said so, but her voice was crisply devoid of self-pity when he answered her. 'Oh, farming has always fluctuated, Lucinda. The Drumlogie homestead has survived the depression of the eighties and of the nineteen-thirties, and has always been versatile; one must adapt to changing times. We're running more beef cattle, and bringing in calves for fattening from the stock firms. They give us so much a pound for the weight they put on; and if there's one thing really booming, it's the tourist trade.'

She nodded. 'Only it must be a bit tough, having to share the home you love with strangers.'

'At first, yes, and would have been tougher on Mother and Father, but it so happened they retired to Roxburgh while wool and lamb prices were still high. Uncle Rob, Star's husband, has always been in the tourist trade. He managed motels in Queenstown, and when Chris married Kirsty, they took on the job as married couple at Drumlogie. When we saw the writing on the wall, Stella and Rob—who owned the motels by then—sold out, put the capital into this, and help me run it. It meant we didn't have to borrow too much for the extensions and year by year we plough the profits back in and extend it more. I've come to terms with it now and even enjoy it.

'I get a kick out of the way the tourists enjoy the sheep-station atmosphere. We feel we're giving them something unique ... farm and lake and mountains. It's by no means a luxury hotel, but it's not cheap either. We give good value and make a reasonable living. Look, we'll leave your cases here and take a look at the view first, then visit your hare.'

He took her hand, murmuring, 'Local colour only, of course, Lucinda darling, for all who might be watching!'

He led her across a green lawn where sprinklers were going, up some rough mountain-boulder steps, under an arch covered with briar roses, and came to an abrupt halt by some delphiniums that were no deeper blue than the waters far below them. Silence was the only possible tribute.

Lucinda thought she would never be done drinking in the beauty ... the living, breathing depths of the lake sent a myriad shafts of light upwards as from some gigantic gem, faceted by a master craftsman to mirror back the sun. The lake turned the corner southwards and lost itself in an infinity of mountains that were lavender and purple against the azure sky. The Remarkables looked as if someone filed them freshly every morning so their jagged outlines would never become blurred, and, straight across from Queenstown, a ruled-off line of fairy mist cut across Cecil and Walter Peaks, isolating the tips so that they looked disembodied, like mountains of a castle in the air. Lucinda looked down suddenly, but evidently Giles caught the shimmer of tears in her eyes.

He had forgotten to relinquish her hand, though they were out of sight of everybody now, so he squeezed it. 'Don't be embarrassed, girl, it's a compliment to our view.'

She swallowed, said, 'I suppose so. It was so perfect. Al-

53

most *too* perfect, as if it couldn't last. Oh, isn't that a foolish thing to say about anything as permanent as mountains?'

'Perhaps, but I know what you mean. So would Star. She said once that perfection like this is almost too much to bear, that such sheer beauty belongs only to Heaven. That it's just as if this was a remnant of Eden, left over to show us what an unstained world could be like.'

Lucinda stood quite still. If she moved, *when* she moved, she might shatter the beauty of this moment. How odd, how very odd that it should have been given to her by a man who was quite unworthy of a girl's trust. But wasn't life like that? Showing you a glimpse of heaven and shutting it out? Those were the things Harvey had never said. He was so prosaic. She had chided herself for feeling disappointed in him over it. Had told herself she was looking for a second Kenneth Darling, the old, tiresome father image. Yet this man, the lighthearted trifler, had it.

The visit to the hare over, they strolled over the stone bridge across the creek and up to a ranch-style, modern house on another rise. The restaurant that Chris and Kirsty ran joined it. It had a terraced garden too, and a patio with small tables, sun-drenched, and sweet with perfume from flowering creepers. Inside, the restaurant had windows on three sides and was panelled in pine, lightly varnished, and the pillars that divided off the sections to give an air of seclusion to groups of tables, were of rough-barked tree trunks, surrounded by vines wreathing up from rustic troughs. The hangings were in tawny shades, with vivid marigold here and there, and the tables were already set for dinner with sparkling silver and glass and coarse-weave table-mats, but the family atmosphere was still stressed, with no hint of pretentiousness. Only guests staying at Drumlogie were catered for.

Lucinda met the cook, a Northumbrian man in his thirties, his wife, and the waitress. They would be glad, they said, when Chris and his wife were back.

As she and Giles emerged into the sunshine again, Lucinda said, 'I expect it was still pretty busy when Chris and Kirsty took off, but sometimes, even when you're in the tourist trade, you must yearn for other than a winter holiday.'

Giles said, 'Well, it was hardly——' He hesitated, changed it to: 'Well, you're right. Chris and Kirsty deserved for once a

54

holiday in decent weather.'

It was queer ... they all seemed a bit cagey over this Australian trip. Perhaps they had had a family shindy over it. Maybe Kirsty had become fed up with all work and no play, and it was none of Lucinda's business.

They paid a visit to the old stables, though the horses and ponies were out in the paddocks. Then they crossed to the guest-house. Giles pointed upwards. 'That end dormer is to be yours. It's quite old. That storey was put up at the beginning of the century. It has a gable at the back too, so you can look right up Ben Logie as well as down the lake.'

Lucinda was delighted, 'How marvellous to have a room that's seen so much of life, so much change, people coming and going. Would you know its full history? Whose room it was first, and second and third? I've always lived so short a time in so many places. And in our furloughs in both New Zealand and England we just had rented houses. I expect you've lived here all your life?'

'Yes, my father was born in that dormer—just as dawn was breaking. His mother wondered what sort of world she was bringing him into. It was in the first month of World War One. And I was born there too. Evidently I beat the gong and she didn't have time to get to Queenstown. My father was fighting in one of the islands of the Pacific. But he came back and the other children were born—my young brother, who's at medical school in Dunedin, and my sisters, who both teach in Roxburgh. I suppose you *would* feel strongly about putting roots down, if you led such a nomad existence.' He looked at her sharply, the grey eyes keen under the heavy tawny brows. 'Was *this* why you wanted to settle down with Harvey?'

It jerked Lucinda back to the present, to the thought of that letter that must be written tonight. For some reason his inference stung. 'It could be, you know, that I simply fell in love with him.'

'M'm. I think if you had, you wouldn't have taken so long to make up your mind. I think, because of your early life, home was your lodestar, you wanted to fall in love and mistook that for the real thing. That was why you drew back.'

'Well ... Giles Logie! You *have* got it neatly parcelled up and tied. Even labelled! Who made you an authority on love?'

He didn't look set back, merely puzzled. 'Darned if I know!

55

I never talked to anyone in my life before, like this.'

'Do you expect me to believe that? I'd an idea you were well experienced in the ways of women!'

That got him. He stopped in his tracks and glowered down on her. Grey eyes were usually cool. These weren't. 'That's one below the belt. I can see you've been listening to gossip! I put up with enough of that sort of thing last year—having my name bandied about—I don't think I quite appreciate the fact that the moment you knew you were coming out here, you must have begun to ask questions about me. I think you could have taken me on trust, as you appeared to do last night! I thought you were a blamed good sport then. But——'

'I did *not* ask questions about you. I heard about you *before* you gatecrashed my table last night. And the gossip was thrust at me, not asked for. I'm not interested enough to ask questions about you. I wouldn't be likely to, either, if you had enough sense to realize it ... I'm supposed to be playing a part and pretending I'm madly attracted to you. I resent you labelling my feelings, and analyzing my motives in being drawn to Harvey. It just isn't any business of yours!'

To her surprise and chagrin he burst out laughing. 'Pax! Pax! We've got our lives well snarled up ... one can't do without the other just now, so it *is* my business.' He looked down into her stormy face, the brown eyes flashing, her breast heaving. 'Look, I rather like to think I'm helping you out too, I don't have to feel so infernally grateful and apologetic that way. And—you may not believe this, but in saying that, I thought I was sort of comforting you. You expressed some of your father's philosophy last night, on life and death, and getting on with things and not looking back. I seem to have bungled it, but I was trying to create a sort of father image for you, as you seem to be so alone. I was attempting to minimize the blow you must have endured when the man you thought you'd probably marry fell in love with your best friend.'

Vivid colour flamed into Lucinda's cheeks and she felt the unwelcome prick of tears behind her lids. She blinked rapidly, then said in a very small voice, 'I'm sorry. I don't know what made me like that, all prickly, like a hedgehog. And it *did* sound like Dad, but——'

She bit it off, rather appalled. She had so nearly said, 'But I don't particularly want *you* to sound like Dad.' Now why *should* that particular thought have popped into her mind?

He cocked that comical eyebrow at her. 'But——'

She gave him a frank look. 'Giles, I'm not sure what's come over me. I've always been regarded as fairly easy-going and I've been a bit vitriolic ever since I met you. I'll start having second thoughts about my words, I think. Don't press me.'

He said interestedly, 'Was it going to be another dirty slam? That you think of me, as per local gossip, as more of a gay Lothario than a hander-out of pearls of wisdom?'

She had to laugh. 'That's better,' he said, and swooped before she knew what he was doing, and kissed her cheek. 'Just making up,' he said audaciously.

She made a face at him. 'You're right in full view of the whole loggia.'

'Yes, I know. That's why I did it. It looks like the Olivers' car coming up the drive. After all, we are supposed to be playing a part, not spitting sparks at each other, though of course, even lovers have their tiffs.'

Lucinda glanced at the drive. The car stopped. The driver got out, a portly figure, hurried round to the other door and opened it. Out came a weird feminine figure in a violent-checked trouser-suit, dumpy and twice as old as Arlene. Lucinda and Giles were still giggling as they came into the reception hall.

Stella was just terminating a telephone conversation. She saw them, said, 'He's here now, just hold on.' Then, 'Giles, it's Nanna Ramsay. She wants to know if you're going down for the children in the morning or the afternoon.'

Giles excused himself and went to the phone. Stella said, 'Lucinda, come and meet Robert. He's in our sitting-room. I've primed him.'

Oh dear. Still someone else to enter the deception. Not all men would approve, though Stella apparently had no doubts.

However, it was evident quite soon that Robert Adair had such faith in his wife he'd go along with anything she did. You were instantly conscious of the bond, just as one had always been with Mother and Dad. How refreshing in this rather decadent and permissive world to meet up with lasting love and simple trust.

Robert was as dark as Stella was fair and chuckled over the whole thing, even adding a few suggestions of his own, for the

57

further underlying of the supposed attraction between Giles and Lucinda for the benefit of the Olivers, and for Harvey when he should come.

Meg called Stella and suddenly Rob Adair became serious. He said, putting out a hand and holding hers, in quite an affectionate gesture, 'Jokes aside, Lucinda, we're most grateful to you. We went through a bad time last year thinking Giles was going to be cited as a co-respondent in a divorce case. Then the Olivers patched up their differences, and we thought we were rid of them. Why on earth they have to turn up again, I don't know. Or why they didn't stay somewhere else. If only one of us had answered the phone when he booked, we'd have been full up. Giles and Stella think we'd better not make too much fuss about it, now they are here, or people will start to talk again. We'll just hope they fade out pretty damn quick.'

Lucinda didn't say anything. Robert probably thought she knew the whole story. She didn't dare ask anything, because Giles might come in and would think she was probing.

Robert looked at her shrewdly from under his dark brows and said, 'You're a little bewildered, aren't you? Perhaps you find this deceit distasteful. Don't. It's been in a very good cause. Try to keep it lighthearted. It's a mild deception that may help both you and Giles out of awkward situations.' He looked at her a little more closely. 'My word, you do remind me of someone. I wonder who? It's a strong resemblance, I'm sure . . . but blest if I know who. Let me see!' He released her hand and used both of his to push the hair back from her face. 'M'm . . . even more teasing. Who the deuce can it be? You're like someone I know—or knew.'

Knew. The past tense. Perhaps long ago. Lucinda held her breath. That stone cottage where her father and his first wife —only wife—had lived long ago, wasn't very far away. The Drumlogie property must join it. It was quite on the cards that Robert Adair might have known her father, his wife, the little son called Sylvester. She didn't want to have a likeness traced. No one would think the more of her for being Sylvester Mordred's daughter. It made her uneasy.

She said, seemingly idly, 'Mr Adair, have you always lived in Queenstown?'

'No, I'm a North Islander, of Scots extraction, of course. Came from Waipu where there's a small Scots settlement as

58

remarkable in its own way as Dunedin—though this one came via Nova Scotia. I ran a guest-house at Tauranga. That's where I met Stella. We were married up there and when we came down to Drumlogie for holidays, I fell in love with Queenstown, sold up and started off here in the same line. But I went into motels—they're much less demanding than full boarding, especially when the family is small. We've another son and daughter. The boy is taking engineering in Christ-church, and our daughter is at teachers' college there.'

At that moment Giles burst in. It was the only way in which to describe Giles's method of entering a room. He always seemed to be propelled in. Both their early meetings had been in the nature of catapulting into her presence. He seemed to have such energy it needed an outlet. 'I want to show you over the rest of the house before the Olivers get in.'

Well, that was wise, except that—'Giles, they won't trip me up much on things in the house, will they? They won't know it so very well themselves.'

'Arlene will, unfortunately. She was here as our receptionist last year. That was how we got involved.'

She loved her room. It had a very fine, if worn, colourful Persian carpet on the floor, and a couple of deep armchairs, possibly shabby rejects from the guest-rooms. The bed was an old-fashioned, but once again popular, spool-bed, and it actu-ally had a genuinely old patchwork quilt on it. Could she but have known the story of each patch, she was sure it would trace the cavalcade of the Drumlogie years. There was a roomy wardrobe under the eaves and a bookcase of books both old and new. It was certainly a half-million-dollar view down lake from the back gable, with the added charm of the close-ness of Ben Logie itself.

Giles looked at her cases. 'Do you want to hang up some of your things? Might get too crushed otherwise ... though there's a laundry downstairs with ironing boards. Oh, there are plenty of hangers here—hand over some of your frocks, Luc-inda.'

She wanted to laugh. He was irrepressible and his vitality made him dash at things. It even revealed itself in his crisp tussock-coloured hair, inclined to stand on end, and in the way he bounded up and downstairs as if anxious to cram as much action as possible into his lifetime.

He was entering so fully into this part he was playing that he *was* the devoted swain. She might as well go along with him. She snapped open one case and took out some frocks, handing them to him. He hung them up, extended an arm for her to lay some more on it. Suddenly he took one down again, surveyed it critically.

Lucinda wrinkled her brow. What now?

He answered her look. 'I'd like you to wear this tonight, for dinner.'

'I was thinking of wearing a trouser-suit. This purple one,' and she flicked it with a finger. 'Your uncle and aunt don't have a thing about trouser-suits, do they?'

'No. Not in a touristy sort of place, but I like this colour—russet, isn't it?' He caught a peculiar expression in her eye, said, 'What's up?'

'I didn't expect you to make that fine distinction. Most men, expecially horny-handed sons of the soil, would have said, "This reddish-brown thing."'

His mouth twitched. 'Oh, but I'd a special reason for recognizing this as russet.'

'Did you? What?'

He grinned, annoyingly. 'You'll find out, later tonight.' He looked at it critically. 'See this long sort of scarf thing, slotted through these tabs—haven't got a blue one, have you?'

She gazed at him. 'I have ... one that doesn't belong to that outfit, but why in the world? The green is much better with it.'

'Just a whim. Will you?' He added: 'Please?'

Had he demanded it, Lucinda wouldn't have consented, but he'd said please with just a hint of that little boy who couldn't say his 'L's' properly. It was somehow disarming. So she said, laughing, 'All right, I'll go along with that, you ridiculously mysterious creature. But now I'd like to unpack the rest myself. After all, you are virtually a stranger.'

He turned at the door, looked back over his shoulder, said, 'Am I? Think that one out, Lucinda.'

She shrugged her shoulders. He was quite, quite mad, provoking, tantalizing, fascinating ... and thereby a little dangerous to a girl's peace of mind. But whatever he was, or wasn't, or should be, he was definitely fun. And how marvellous it was not to feel any longer that weight upon her spirits concerning

Janice's feelings, and Harvey's or being constantly tormented with thoughts about her own unstable father. For days, since getting that letter, she had thought of nothing else and it had tired her brain and given her a nagging ache in her heart. It seemed to have hurt her memories of her mother. Mother had been so gay always, so loving, so clear-eyed and candid, happy with Dad, as if no shadow had ever lain across her heart, her earlier years.

But she must have known sheer agony. Must have known that in the eyes of the world, her little girl was deemed illegitimate. Her mother's father had been high up in the Army service. They would have been very well known in Singapore. It must have been hell. If only her grandparents were still alive, if only there had been someone to ask. How fond her grandparents had been of Kenneth Darling. Some of it might have been sheer gratitude for patching up their daughter's broken life, for giving their grandchild a name.

Lucinda suddenly wanted her mother, wanted her with a searing sort of desperation, with a stab of realization at the irrevocableness of death, the sheer impossibility of ever having the chance to discuss this with her. Oh, how she longed to reassure her mother that it did not matter ... that she would not regard herself as illegitimate; that all she grieved for was the sadness and disillusionment her mother must have known when she was even younger than Lucinda was now. She flung herself on that quilted patchwork in an agony of longing. She *would* not cry; she *must* not cry. Presently she had to go down and face dinner with a family of strangers. Later she must mingle with guests who were in happy, holiday mood, and play her part convincingly, to save Giles and his nice family from being embroiled again in Arlene Oliver's toils.

Lucinda had an arm upflung over her head and it shut out all sound. The other ear was buried in the quilt. She did not hear the little tap or the door opening. But suddenly someone sat down on the bed, put a hand on her shoulder and said with a wealth of tenderness: 'Lucinda dear.'

Lucinda turned a little, brought her face up out of the patches, looked embarrassed. Stella Adair said, a hand on the dark, ruffled hair, 'I expect you're overwhelmed with it all. We've been so selfish, so demanding, only you seemed the ideal answer. And you have problems of your own. Only I hope that this too will solve yours. But I expect you had all sorts of dreams woven about this young man. Words are clumsy, I know, but——' and her hand made a gesture that was purely maternal.

Lucinda's embarassment fled. She managed to smile a little. 'Star, it wasn't that. It was just that suddenly I so missed my mother and father. It's so hard to get used to the idea that I can't just sit down and write to them. Even the tough hard things always turned out to have a humorous side if I could write them out. And I've been haunted by the feeling that if only I'd gone back with them this might not have happened, that they'd have taken less risks if I'd been there. But they saw I was attracted to Harvey and didn't want to break it up.'

Stella slipped an arm about her. 'Lucinda, it's hard not to think about the might-have-been, but there would have been no reason for supposing your presence could have held your parents back from attempting that rescue in a less-than-safe boat. They'd spent all their lives, I gather, doing those things. Say your mother had been lost and your father rescued. You wouldn't have wanted him to grieve that he'd taken her into that way of life, to continually reproach himself that because she'd married him and become a fellow-missionary, she had died, would you?'

Lucinda felt as if a load borne too long had rolled off her shoulders. She sat up erectly. 'Oh, Star, how right you are! I'm so glad I'm here and that you said just that; suddenly Mother doesn't seem so cut off from me. Because now I remember once, ages ago, Dad saying rather ruefully to Mother that if she'd married someone in a different walk of life she wouldn't have known so many perils, not have known agonizing separations from her children—we often had to be in mission schools, or left with friends in safer areas. And Mother said, "Oh, Kenneth, how can you even begin to think such a thing, when all the happiness I've known in adult life was the happiness you gave me?" Oh, Star, you brought it all back to me.'

Lucinda thought Star had the most beautiful blue eyes she had ever seen, as if her spirit looked out through the azure of the sky. Stella said, 'Well, I'm glad I did. Sometimes it's so hard to say the things one ought to say. I wish I'd known your mother—she sounds a kindred spirit. The way she felt about your father is the way I feel about Robert. Now, dear, run along and have a shower. I brought your towels up. And whenever you feel like it, talk to us about your parents. You would if you were in England and could talk about them to your sister and brother. When there's no one left to recall past happinesses with, about the ones who've gone on ahead, you do indeed feel you have lost them.' She stopped, listened, crossed to the front dormer window, looked down. 'Oh, that's the whole crowd coming up from the S.S. *Earnslaw*. They've been to Glenorchy today.'

Lucinda picked up the towels. 'I take it there are two steamers?'

'No, just the one. It's huge, holds over a thousand passengers. It's a full day's trip, they're never in earlier than this. Why?'

'Oh, nothing much. I thought from something Giles said he thought he saw the Olivers coming back sooner. I—must have been mistaken.'

So Giles had pretended he'd thought it was them, as an excuse to kiss her. Naturally he liked kissing girls. Kissing didn't mean a thing in *his* life! A man to be wary of.

Lucinda donned the russet frock, slipped the long blue scarf through the slots, tossed one end back over her shoulder where it fell almost to the hem. She crossed to the mirror and wielded a styling brush, thankful for the thick dark brown hair that was easy to set. She back-combed it a little, piling the strands high in a sweep back from her forehead and allowing it to bell out at the sides. The long brown eyes met the mirrored eyes and a certain self-consciousness looked out of them, an unwelcome knowledge.

Giles wasn't a man to take seriously. Not a man to lose one's heart to. Lucinda almost took a step backwards, flinching from the unbidden thought. What a ridiculous thing to think! This was nothing but a masquerade, just a bit of play-acting—and he was a darned good actor at that.

She went downstairs. It was time she was with other people, not having stupid thoughts pop up from her subconscious.

The family meal had a quietness and serenity about it that was tranquillizing. Giles and Robert talked farming more than tourist business and of Robert's recent trip to Australia. Lucinda said, 'Oh, were you in Australia too? Did you join Kirsty

63

and Chris on holiday?'

She hadn't associated Robert Adair with evasiveness, but he said with less than frankness, 'Well, I was with them for a short time, but it was more of a business trip. Do you know Australia?'

'Not really, Mr. Adair. It's one of the few places we've not lived in. We've touched down a few times, that's all. I'd like to see it some time ... especially that glorious shoreline north of Sydney.'

It was an ordinary family dinner, cooked and served by Stella, from a small kitchen in this wing. 'We maintain the kind of family life we prefer, this way,' said Stella. 'That's why we keep this as a bed-and-breakfast place. And Chris and Kirsty started up the restaurant purely as their own venture. It caters for the guests who like to stay on the place, instead of eating in town.'

Robert said, 'By the way, you'd better call me Robert. I see you call Stella Star, no doubt on orders from Giles. He and I have worked together so long, we dropped the "Uncle". I take it we're going into the drawing-room tonight?'

Stella nodded. She turned to Lucinda. 'It's rather formal-sounding, but that's the way we distinguish it from the T.V. lounge. The motels on the ridge each have a T.V., of course, but the room guests make use of the public one. It would make less work to have just one main lounge, but I know if I were staying in a place like this, I'd want one room without television. So we use the drawing-room for just getting together. We don't go in every night. Sometimes we get personality indigestion and keep to the sitting-room, but Giles wants to be in there tonight, and those folk who came in at lunch-time, the Donaldsons, are keen for him to sing some Scots airs.'

Lucinda's eyes widened. 'You're a singer, Giles? You ought to have warned me. I could be expected to have known that.'

'I intended to do so before we went in. Star just jumped the gun.'

Stella said, 'He's got a marvellous baritone. Could have brought it to concert quality if he'd wanted to, but he couldn't bear to leave the land.'

'Spare my blushes, Star,' said Giles, grinning.

Lucinda said seriously, 'I can't imagine you even on speaking terms with a blush. I know you can redden with anger, but blushing, no!'

Giles looked askance at her. 'That sounds, for some reason, uncomplimentary.'

Lucinda giggled, 'With that ruddy sort of skin, you'd never notice one.'

He sighed. 'She's trying to water down that acid remark. No one ever regards me as a tender plant and I am. Very sensitive. So not so much bludgeoning.'

Stella laughed a laugh of pure happiness. 'We seem to be back to normal, as we were before that horrible business last year. We never seemed to banter the same. Life *should* be fun. All the joy went out of it last year. I did nothing but sigh.'

Lucinda pulled a face. 'To me it seems serious enough, this —a bit tricky. For instance, we could get caught out about Mrs. Haigie and the morning tea. You went to the airport instead, Star, and I didn't come out till the afternoon.'

Star looked aghast. 'Good job you reminded me. I threw that in for extra local colour last night and then forgot. Oh dear, to be a liar you need a good memory. Life is much less complicated when you stick to the truth.'

'That's what I meant,' said Lucinda.

Robert patted her hand. 'Enjoy it, love. You're young enough to get a kick out of a situation like this. Of course it's fun. No anxiety neuroses, Lucinda ... you're in the nature of a godsend to us ... let yourself go, lassie.'

Lucinda gave way to mirth. 'You're the most extraordinary family! Some families are so stuffy. I find this most refreshing.'

Robert said solemnly, 'It's that Giles. Nobody can stay stuffy with him around. Our three are nothing to him. We just pull him out of one escapade after another—the great soft-hearted thing!'

Lucinda told herself this was just sheer family affection, minimizing the fact that he was one of these breaker-of-hearts types. She thought they regarded him too indulgently by far. What of the girls he had trifled with? How did they feel? Mightn't some of them have got hurt in the process? Because even if you knew him for what he was, you had to admit he had a way with him. Nevertheless, Lucinda was not going to join their ranks.

CHAPTER FOUR

It became evident that the letter she was to write Harvey would have to be done late tonight, in the privacy of her own room.

The drawing-room was centrally heated, but it was a tradition at Drumlogie that on nights that were cooler, a fire was lit. It provided an aesthetic touch, Giles said, bringing in coal and logs.

The accent here was on the goldmining days, with glass cases of gold-bearing quartz, tiny dishes of gold-dust, and nuggets found in the area. There was scheelite from Glenorchy, samples of other minerals, and semi-precious stones made into fobs and pendants and bracelets; agate, chalcedony, jasper, jade, which was usually called greenstone here. There were scales for weighing gold, horn whisky glasses that had been brought out from Scotland, tent-pegs that made you shiver, thinking of men living under canvas in funnel-like gorges where the blizzards of winter must have cut them to the bone.

The old photographs interested Lucinda most, especially as they too had lists of names beneath them, but though she scanned them quickly there was no Mordred among them, neither the father, the mother, nor the son. Perhaps Mrs. Sylvester Mordred had taken her small child away from Queenstown when the scandal broke. That would be it; where no other child, in the cruel arena of the playground, could jeer at a small boy whose father was in gaol.

The phone in the office was busy, the girls were making sandwiches and savouries for the final cup of tea they would serve before retiring time. Lucinda pitched in to help. By mutual consent they did not discuss the situation; they accepted Lucinda as one of themselves and the girl in whom the boss had a romantic interest.

How swiftly they worked! They set the tables for breakfast, put things to hand for the busy morning schedule, the wrapped stacks of sliced bread for toasting, trays of eggs, cups and saucers, marmalades, jams, New Zealand honeys, from the run-of-the-mill clover to *manuka*, *kamahi*, and *rewarewa*. Everything was covered with organdie throw-overs.

Giles came through from the private wing bearing a spinning-wheel, one quite evidently not for show, but used, because there was homespun wool on it.

Rena said with interest, 'Why is Mrs. Adair's wheel going somewhere else?'

Giles grinned. 'It's to provide local colour for a song tonight. More than that I shall not tell you.'

Rena looked after him as he went through the door. 'I wonder what he's up to now? He had that look. I think we'll stay here tonight, Meg, instead of going over to our quarters. It could be interesting.'

Lucinda said, 'Does he mean to one of his own songs, do you think? Or to a record?'

'No idea. They're all good singers, it seems to run in the family. Chris has a good tenor. They keep mainly to the old-time stuff, the folk-songs and ballads. If the young ones want pop they can have it in the old barn. Giles had it done up for dances in the ranch style. The classical stuff or the old-time stuff suits the drawing-room better. Folk drift in and out, from various T.V. programmes, and Giles never overdoes it. Just two or three songs.'

At first it was an enchanted evening. The firelight flickered on the polished panelling, great tawny and yellow chrysanthemums were reflected in the flawless tops of small tables, nerines in coral tonings glittered gold-dust from their pollen-laden petals and a tall stone jar in the far corner held branches of maple and golden rod.

Even the sight of Arlene and Mark Oliver sitting with Giles could not spoil the magic for Lucinda. She had a feeling that now all would be well. Harvey and Janice would no longer know a burden of guilt when they saw her seemingly absorbed in Giles, and perhaps some day the old, sweet friendship with Janice would be the same. Beyond that she need not think or plan—yet. The sense of the loss of her future had departed and she was beginning to get accustomed to the idea that she was not Kenneth Darling's daughter.

Giles called Lucinda across to sit with him. He seemed perfectly at ease, asking the Olivers about their day at Glenorchy and Paradise. 'Lucinda's not been up-lake yet. As soon as things quieten a bit I'll take her there. If possible we'll spend a few days. I'd like her to see the scheelite mining, besides introducing her to my favourite mountain, Mount Earnslaw.'

Lucinda was surprised. 'Oh, Giles, surely you can't prefer any mountain to your very own ... Ben Logie! That amounts to treason!'

He chuckled, said to the other two, 'She's so attached to Ben Logie and now, of course, she can live with him ... it's framed in the back window of her bedroom. Thinks there's no other mountain to compare with it. Mother was the same. That was my parents' room. But, my love, Ben Logie is only a pimple compared to Earnslaw.' He grinned. 'I even feel Ben Logie is sadly misnamed. Oh, it was called that purely and simply because it was Logie's mountain, the first Giles's abode, but for a mountain to be called Logie is a contradiction in terms. In Gaelic, Logie means hollow. It's not so bad in the case of Drumlogie. Drum is ridge, so it could be the Ridge above the Hollow, which described it well. Its Maori name was *Kohukohu-raro-te-hiwi*, the hollow below the ridge, and my forebear therefore thought it was foreordained that he should settle here and attached the Drum to his own name for the name of the homestead. Oh, Lucinda, someone's asked Robert and Star to sing. They'll want me to play. Come on over with me.' He held out his hand.

He put her into a seat near the spinning-wheel he had set up. She was next to Meg. Suddenly John, who was on duty at the reception desk, came in, bent over Stella and said something. She excused herself, saying she wouldn't be a moment. The buzz of talk resumed. Giles looked up from talking to her as the door opened again to admit Stella and a stranger. 'Good lord, another guest! He left it a bit late to check in, didn't he?'

Lucinda glanced up and stiffened. She felt her mouth instantly parch. She swallowed frantically, clutched instinctively at Giles's hand, said in a faint, desperate whisper, 'Giles, it isn't a guest, it's Harvey!'

Giles whispered back, but vehemence was in it, despite its lack of sound. 'My God!' And there was no blasphemy in it, only feeling for her, and a plea.

He recovered quickly, he kept hold of her hand with a pressure that meant he was trying to infuse courage into her and to

68

warn her not to look aghast. He rose and no one would have thought it other than a casual greeting.

Lucinda, in a dream, her hand still in his, went with him. Robert was sitting in a chair a little apart from the others. turning some music over. Giles bent down, said, 'This is Harvey. We'll just play it cool,' and went straight on.

Stella's blue eyes were a little frosty, with apprehension at the back of the chill, but her voice was normal and she kept it low as they reached her. 'I thought your friend might as well come in, Lucinda, because I don't want you to miss one particular song of Giles's. You can have a word with him in the sitting-room afterwards if you like.'

(Harvey must have asked to see her alone and Stella, quick-witted, wanted to give her time to think. But she'd be wondering if she had done the right thing. If it would be a bit much for Lucinda, in front of this crowd.)

Lucinda had no idea what song Star had referred to, but responded automatically, 'Oh yes, Star, I'd certainly not want to miss that. Harvey, this is Giles Logie; what a surprise this is! Are you down early house-hunting? What a good idea. Giles knows everybody, he should be able to help you.'

She didn't wait for an answer, because she knew only too well that Janice must have insisted Harvey came down to see her, about the whole situation; about the fact that he had blundered badly in accepting this transfer when Lucinda wanted to stay here. So she rushed madly on. 'It looks like a general exodus to the south, doesn't it? Isn't it a dream of a place? And especially Drumlogie. It's not so crowded with tourists as right in Queenstown, yet you have the best view of any of the lake. And it's on the way to Coronet Peak and Skippers and Arrowtown. I haven't been to the Peak or the Canyon yet, but I'll see them soon.'

Giles's voice was smooth, creamy. 'You will, love. By next week, I hope. We've to go down to Alex for the children the day after tomorrow, and Mother and Father are hoping we'll take the whole day over it and go down to Roxburgh first for lunch with them, but next week will be more free, and I must take you soon to all my favourite spots ... Glenorchy, the Routeburn, Paradise, the lot.'

He turned to the somewhat winded Harvey. 'I'm so glad about your transfer ... it will be lovely for Lucinda to have some of her friends near her. I gather Janice is her best friend. Especially with Ivan and Trudy being overseas. She tells me you'll be getting married soon ... not a bad time of year to be house-hunting. In the height of the season it's impossible. I've a friend in the accommodation business, I'll ask him to help you out. But these people have have just asked for some songs from my aunt and uncle. Come away over here and sit with us, will you?'

Harvey managed to respond naturally and they threaded their way back to the grand piano. Giles let her hand go— Harvey couldn't have missed that. Lucinda sank back into her low chair feeling as if her legs wouldn't have supported her for much longer.

She was immensely grateful for the time and attention the music took. Giles sat down, his tawny hair and brown face glowing with health above a butter-coloured shirt with a wide-flowing orange tie, and his fingers strayed over the keys with the caressing touch of the born musician.

Robert and Stella sang *Ye Banks and Braes* and a woman from Massachusetts, who had stayed with them two years before, said, 'Mrs. Adair, would you sing *Robin Adair*? I love to hear you do it, and especially when I know your husband's name is Rob.'

Stella laughed. 'I suppose it does add meaning, and it certainly describes how I felt when he was away in Australia these last two weeks.' She began to sing:

'What's this dull town to me? Robin's not near.
What was't I wish'd to see? What wish'd to hear?
Where's all the joy and mirth made this town heav'n on
     earth?
Oh! all are fled with thee, Robin Adair.'

The clapping was most spontaneous. Lucinda said to the American woman, 'What a happy choice. I'm always keen on having the right sex singing songs. I remember reading once— no idea where—about some young girls getting the giggles because when the curate was asked to sing, he chose *My Mother bids me bind my hair*. Just imagine!'

When the laughter died down, Stella took Giles' place on the piano stool and played a bar or two of Burns's, *O my*

Luve's like a red, red rose. He said before he began, 'To me this is the most simple and the finest love-song in any language, of any age.'

When he came to the third verse his eyes sought Lucinda's. She had her face lifted to the singer anyway, because she always paid any performer or speaker the compliment of the uplifted face and full attention. Their eyes caught and held and everyone in the room must have noticed it. Lucinda was aware that Harvey had turned his head a little and was looking at her most intensely.

Oh yes, Giles Logie was a superb actor. But strange feelings stirred within Lucinda as he sang:

> 'Till a' the seas gang dry, my dear,
>   And the rocks melt wi' the sun;
> I will luve thee still, my dear,
>   While the sands o' life shall run.'

Someone said, 'We are having a Scots night, aren't we? I love it—such a flavour.'

Giles smiled, 'Oh, we sing lots of Welsh songs too, and Irish airs, but the one I want to finish with is none of these. It's a favourite of mine, especially lately.' The grey eyes rested briefly on Lucinda's face. 'It's by Samuel Rogers, who lived in the eighteenth and nineteenth centuries. My cousin Christopher set it to music last year. It's called *A Wish*.'

Chris must be quite a composer. Giles began:

> 'Mine be a cot beside the hill;
> A beehive's hum shall soothe my ear;
> A willowy brook that turns a mill,
> With many a fall shall linger near.
>
> The swallow, oft, beneath my thatch
> Shall twitter from her clay-built nest;
> Oft shall the pilgrim lift the latch,
> And share my meal, a welcome guest.
>
> Around my ivied porch shall spring
> Each fragrant flower that drinks the dew;
> And Lucy, at her wheel, shall sing
> In russet gown and apron blue.

The village church among the trees,
Where first our marriage-vows were given,
With merry peals shall swell the breeze
And point with taper spire to Heaven.'

There was a delighted murmur as he finished, with all eyes
turned in Lucinda's direction, as she sat in front of the spinning-wheel, in her russet dress with the blue scarf flung over
her shoulder.

Giles's chuckled. 'Lucinda was absolutely mystified when I
put her off wearing a purple trouser-suit tonight and insisted
on that blue scarf instead of the green one that goes with it.
But a trouser-suit isn't the right period for that song!' He
sketched her a slight, audacious bow. *How* audacious only the
family knew. For everyone else it was an idyllic interlude, a
part, for them, of an enchanted holiday in a place where time
stood still, seemingly; where overcrowded cities and the mal-
aise of the rat-race were forgotten, here in this enchanted lake-
land, a place where, they knew now, chivalry and romance still
flourished.

Harvey got the message. He couldn't have done otherwise.
Under cover of the conversation breaking out again, he said,
'Lucinda, that was for real, wasn't it? I mean, it has to be, I
think ... you seem to be accepted into the family, he was
talking of taking you down to meet his people ... what's it
add up to? I hope the answer is what I think it must be. You
deserve something like this. You've been such a brick. You
deserve a chap like Giles. Giles who? Is it Logie? Was that
the name you said? I'm slightly not with it at the moment.'

'Yes, Logie.' Lucinda even managed a sparkle in her eye. It
was very convincing. She said, 'It's been all rather sudden,
though of course I've been in Queenstown a month, but——'

'It's long enough, if it's a strong attraction. I don't want to
be too wishful—for my own sake, I mean, because I'd feel less
of a skunk, and it would be a miracle for Janice—but also for
your sake. When you said you'd fallen in love with Queenstown, I didn't dream you meant anything quite so personal and
wonderful as this. Look, I'd better get this out while Giles is
busy with that woman over there, because you may not want
him to know yet, about us ... I don't want to cause a rift in the
lute. We felt appalled when we got your letter, too late to

recall ours. My application was in and accepted, of course. One of those hideous and fiendish coincidences, as if the very devil gets hold of our lives and twists them.

'Janice was beside herself. I asked for a couple of days off, saying I wanted to house-hunt, but in reality to tell you—which is much easier than writing—that I'll see the management board and tell them I find I'm unable, after all, for family reasons, to accept a South Island appointment.'

Lucinda said softly, 'But now there's no need, Harvey. And I will so love to have Janice here, someone from my former life. Harvey, I'm only sorry now I didn't hint—it would have saved you and Janice so much anguish of mind. Only I was afraid you might think I was being caught on the rebound, even that I was doing it out of pride.'

(Heavens, it sounded so authentic she was almost believing it!)

Harvey said, 'I'm glad I came down. By letter I *would* have thought just that. But seeing you together is completely different. No one seeing you tonight could have any doubts at all.' He grinned. 'We were such good pals, Lucinda. Almost too good. I wonder if you know what I mean. We were so placid, never struck any sparks off each other. I think this was meant to be. We'd never have—quite—trod the heights. You've found in Giles, thank God, what I found in Janice. I wonder what it is. It's very hard to define. What would you put it down to, Lucinda? A touch of magic?'

She looked up at Harvey with the frankest of looks. 'Yes, that must have been why I asked for time to think it over. Without having ever experienced this ... this certainty, this reality ... I knew something was missing. But I've found it too now ... that touch of magic.'

She felt Giles's hand on her shoulder, exerting pressure. He laughed, said lightly, 'You two appear to be having a very serious conversation. Do you want to go off to our sitting-room to finish it? Sorry I can't come, but I must do my stuff with the guests. The personal touch they expect, and rightly. It's that sort of place.'

Lucinda said, 'Oh no, Giles. We were just discussing Harvey's future plans. I'm to be Janice's bridesmaid, of course. That means a trip to Wanganui some time. I don't suppose you want to wait so long now. No fun in being parted. Nice if

73

you could have got married before you start this job, Harvey.'

Harvey said, 'That's quite an idea. We hadn't thought of it, as yet, but now—yes, I'll put it to Janice when I get back.'

Giles came in with, 'Good idea. No point in taking a flat for one and then hunting for a bigger one. Lucinda, if you go up to be bridesmaid, you could pack up your treasures at the same time, couldn't you? Save two trips, and there's plenty room for them here.' He grinned. 'You can see which way the wind blows, can't you, Harvey? We've not announced anything yet. I'm all for doing just that, but Lucinda wants us to wait a wee while. Just in case folk think we've not known each other long enough. Lot of rot, but I'm going along with what ever she wants, though not indefinitely. By the way, where are you staying?'

'The motels nearest to the One-Mile. I'll be flying back the day after tomorrow. I rang Mrs. Millister at that address you gave me and she told me you were here, Lucinda. Sorry I didn't get here earlier in the day, but Momona Airport was closed with crosswinds and I had to come through the gorges by bus. I took a taxi out. I'll ring for another, if I may.'

Giles shook his head. 'No need. Stay for supper—the girls will be bringing it in soon, then we'll run you back. We get a bit bogged down with the guests here ... I'm all for a late relaxing stroll round the lake-shore, aren't you, Lucinda darling?'

Well, she had to hand it to Giles Logie, he was nothing if not thorough. She was grateful to him. At this rate, Harvey wouldn't have a doubt left. She caught Robert's eye and had difficulty not laughing.

She'd thought the stroll by the lake-shore was more spoofing, but Giles didn't take the Gorge road again, he turned along the lake. Lucinda said sharply, 'No need to go to these lengths, Giles. Harvey couldn't possibly see from his motel which way we took, and it's far too late for moonlight rambling!'

He chuckled. 'Lucy ... at times you sound so shrewish, and Lucy is such a gentle little name, such a darling little name. It sounds all sweetness and light. It suited that song ... the gentle Lucy, singing as she spun. Instead of sounding like an outraged virgin!'

Her voice was still cold. 'I don't see why virginity should be the butt of cheap jokes. You don't have to be prim because of it, but then neither do you have to indulge in any sort of light dalliance, if you've no inclination for it. It's late, it has been a rather stressful evening, and I'm so tired and tied up that that moon *couldn't* have any effect on me. I'd like to go back ho— to Drumlogie.'

He turned the car abruptly into the stone wall that bounded the lake and parked it. His voice was low but with an intensity of fury that surprised her.

'I know that perhaps it's not easy being a girl with high standards in this permissive age, but it doesn't mean to say you have the right to think every chap has wolfish instincts, ready to make the most of any situation! I think you're out of your mind. Save me from anyone as self-righteous as you are! Know what I thought? That you *were* tired, *over*-tired, and too strung-up to sleep. Many's the time last year when I walked off my sleeplessness and the ceaseless treadmill of my thoughts on the slopes of Ben Logie. I thought you'd go back to toss and turn, that you might want to put a certain measure of time, and good healthy physical exercise between saying goodnight to Harvey—the man you were going to marry—and bedtime. That a good brisk walk through the Government Gardens and along the lake-shore towards Frankton would do you good ... not sitting billing and cooing under the trees! Why, who said I——'

He stopped.

Lucinda felt all sorts of feelings rush over her. 'Why don't you finish that sentence?' she managed at last.

He turned to her, his tone savage. 'Because it's better left unsaid, even if you deserve it. Even if it's no worse than what you said. I'm supposed to be fairly easy-going, but by heaven——'

Lucinda knew he'd been going to say: 'who said I *wanted* to bill and coo?' and that she deserved his anger.

She turned to him and there in the faint light that fell on them from the lamp at the end of the sea-wall saw that indeed his face was a mask of anger.

She said, as calmly as she could manage, 'Giles, I'm sorry. Only—sometimes it's hard to be a girl, to know exactly how much a man expects. I—I don't *really* know you very well, do I? And I thought that because of the way you'd come to my rescue, you might ... that any man might ... expect to take a——' She paused, said, 'Oh, words are so inadequate. I don't want to make you more angry. Only—— Oh, I know so well lots of girls don't think anything of a little dallying underneath the moon, but—oh, I'm making a horrible mess of this, and you've been so good, even chivalrous, and I—I jumped to conclusions and you've every right to be offended and I——' To her horror she gave a hiccupping sob, and stopped, her hand pressed against her mouth.

In an instant he changed. She felt the rigidity of anger go out of him and he flung an arm round her shoulders. 'Oh, poor Lucinda! It's all been too much for you. Here, do you want a jolly good howl ... well, howl away!'

Lucinda took out her handkerchief, scrubbed furiously at her eyes for a swift moment, said, 'I will *not* howl! I never did. About the situation with Harvey and Janice, I mean. B-but I'm sorry, Giles Logie. That was idiotic. It—it was just you using that expression so flippantly, I think.'

She sensed the smile in his voice. 'You mean saying you sounded like an outraged virgin?'

She nodded. 'It was stupid of me. We all—these days—fling these expressions round right, left and centre. I apologize unconditionally. Will that do?'

He laughed. 'It certainly will. I'll forgive you on one condition, just to prove you don't distrust me. That we have that walk, a good, brisk, no-nonsense one. What was it you said once before? No hanky-panky. It will dispel any self-consciousness that may have arisen. We can't afford to feel like that, there's too much at stake. Besides, I feel in need of exercise myself. I can't say I'm enjoying having Arlene and Mark at Drumlogie. It's like standing on a bomb. I've not been able to fathom it, unless he wanted to see for himself if it was all over. Come on, Lucinda—I can't call you Lucy any more tonight. It's too incongruous when you're about as gentle as an active volcano yourself!'

Lucinda giggled. 'You ought to be careful, now you know what I'm really like! That could have set me off again.'

'That's much, much better. Nothing like a sense of humour to see you over times like this. I need *you* as a protection against Arlene, you need *me* as a smoke-screen between Janice and Harvey and yourself. Well, girl, let's extract the utmost fun out of the situation, and hang the lot of them! Now, out you get, and march!'

And march they did. As they moved under the arch that bore the names of the war heroes of the Lake County and into the shade of the immense English trees that fringed the shore, he said, 'This is my favourite thing ... just walking. I could tramp or ramble for hours and I get too little of it these days. Life has been hectic since we turned the sheep-station into a guesthouse.'

They walked along, crossed the murmuring Hotop's Creek by a little bridge and began to climb, the aromatic tang of Australian gum-trees all about them, their arms swinging at their sides, with Giles touching her only when the moon-bleached pathway beneath their feet suddenly revealed gnarled and dangerous roots. They came up into the more formal gardens, rose-scented, with a hint of lavender, crossed a stone bridge that arched over the lily-pond and went down through a little wood to the shore at the other side of the gardens' peninsula.

Here they were in a world of their own, with only the lake waters lap-lapping against the stones, and the cry of a little native owl in the spinney to give evidence that as far as other people were concerned, they had the world to themselves. Then they came through the trees and on to the road that bordered the lake here, where lovely homes overhung the black waters, some still lighted, and from one, a radiogram played a Viennese waltz.

A miniature headland ran out into the lake, tangled with willows that dipped down into the waters. They stood there, entranced, watching the reflections of the lighted windows and street lanterns of the new Kelvin Heights community on an arm of the lake.

Lucida broke the silence. 'An upside-down, topsy-turvy world. It looks so enchanted, but it's the wrong way up.'

'Things often seem the wrong way up, Lucinda, because reflections can be distorting. The perspective's all wrong. Your world may seem like that tonight, because you were in a strange house, and Harvey was there, but engaged to someone else, and you were pretending you'd lost your heart to me. My mother told me once that in her young days she took everything far too much to heart, till my father told her—one day when she thought things were quite unbearable—to try to think how small a thing it would seem twelve months from then. I thought that was pretty good. Mother seems—on the surface—so happy-go-lucky, but that night she told me she had learned to be gay for our sakes, that when you have children you have to control not only your temper but your moods and sadnesses.'

That night! Some particular night? One when Giles had felt something was unbearable?

'Giles, was that a night last year? When the trouble with Arlene blew up? Oh, you needn't answer that unless you want to.'

'Oh, it's no secret, it was all over town. I did take a pretty hard knock over that. Arlene had left her husband, but she became reconciled to him. That's the beginning and the end, but in between I got pretty badly hurt. That's all.' He bent and picked up a flat stone. 'Any good at playing ducks and drakes?'

That meant he didn't want to discuss it any more. Well, however unethically he had acted, he hadn't come out of it unscathed. One never did. Lucinda picked up a stone, aimed it at the surface of the water and was extremely surprised when it did five flips.

They walked on, cut up through a steep street and came out on to the Frankton road where there was still some traffic. They cut down off it again through the woodland path of Hotop's Rise, sweet with the murmur of a night zephyr in the trees, and back to the lake-wall. As they reached the car, Lucinda flung up her arms and stretched, 'Oh, thank you, Giles, I feel gloriously tired now.'

'You'll be between the blankets in half an hour,' promised Giles.

In which he was entirely wrong.

They came through the gorge road, dipped past the modernized tavern at Arthur's Point, rimmed with poplars that even in the moonlight shimmered goldenly, and over the Edith Cavell Bridge across the Shotover and beyond it, rising again. There, quite suddenly, the engine died on them.

They coasted on for a moment, then Giles drew in. 'Well, I'll be darned! I wonder if it's something electrical. Something's gone somewhere. Not to worry, I'm a fair mechanic.'

He got out a torch.

But not even a mechanic could conjure up petrol for an empty tank. It must have been siphoned out when they were rambling.

He cast a look of consternation at her, caught the light of laughter bubbling up in her eyes, and burst out laughing himself. 'If that had happened before we reached our understanding, Lucinda darling, you'd have smacked my face and got out!'

She sobered up. 'What a mean, horrible thing for someone to do!'

'I had it filled up today and the chap said the thread had stripped a bit on the locking-cap I have on the tank, said he'd fix it, and loaned me a non-locking one instead.'

He cast a comprehensive look round the dark contours of the foothills below the mountains and said grimly, 'Not a light on in any of these three homesteads ... that means we must knock someone up, poor beggar.'

'How far home, Giles?'

'All of three miles, even to the gate.'

'Well, why wake anyone up? We both love tramping. Let's just step it out. You can lock the car.'

'That's what I'd do if I were by myself ... sure you can manage it?'

'Of course. Let's go.' At first the breeze was cool, but they soon warmed up. Never a car passed them. Gradually the darkness seemed to become less intense, even though that fickle moon had gone behind a cloud. The barbed-wire fences gleamed silver in the starlight, the mountains were silhouetted darkly against it.

As they walked, Giles named every peak for her. 'We have the world to ourselves,' said Lucinda, and was amazed at the contentment that possessed her. Nothing mattered any more.

Alone, Lucinda knew she might have felt frightened and lost, dwarfed by the immensities of this Wharehuanui Valley. 'But to you, Giles, every paddock is part of some friend's farm. You know every bend in the road and, I daresay, the history of almost every gully, every crag.'

'Yes, I grew up here. It's part of me. Mind you, Lucinda, because of that, one also needs to get away for a spell. Mother and Dad wouldn't have had it otherwise. We were all encouraged to strike out for ourselves, to see a bit more of the world apart from our own blue-and-gold corner of it. Same with my sisters. They both went to England, free as air as far as the parents were concerned, and now they're both in Roxburgh with them. I had that three years in United Kingdom, working on various farms. Great experience—I feel so much the richer for it. So it's not just been all a sheltered, undisturbed existence.'

'Why do you say that? Did you think I was regretting our rootless life?'

'Yes, weren't you? I thought I detected a note of wistfulness.'

'In a way, yes. It's odd how one can suddenly become aware of having missed something. I think it must be wonderful to know so much about one's ancestors, to know you plough where they ploughed, sow where they sowed, look out upon the mountains and valleys they looked out upon. To be able to put a name to your great-grandparents. To hear stories about them handed down by word of mouth.'

He said rather curiously, 'But didn't you say you spent furloughs with your mother's folk in England? And if you were in India where you said she was born, you'd see the barracks, the frontier stations, and so on? And you'd meet your father's people here. You said he was a Kiwi, didn't you?'

She hesitated. She must be more careful. He meant Kenneth Darling, of course. 'They're gone now. But in any case they were city folk. It isn't the same.'

Inevitably they touched on the mining days, of the cosmopolitan mixture of the goldminers, still evident in foreign names here; of the ne'er-do-wells, the rogues, the women who followed in the tail of the rushes and provided doubtful entertainment in the saloons and out of them; the good, hard workers, who sent back their earnings to their families, and later, when conditions were not so starkly tough, sent for them. The tragedy of the many who won and lost fortunes overnight, or who gave up a claim only to have it turn out a bonanza.

Giles told her of the tragedies, the flash floods of the Shotover and Kawarau, pent in their narrow gorges, where men would seek gold when the river was low. Then the less rugged and less roystering days, when men gave up the hazards of the prospecting and turned to producing from the land; the mammoth tasks of making access roads, the perils of the bitter winters, the droughts of the summers, the way they learned to live together, these people from the four corners of the earth, united in the main, in their love of the beauty of Wakatipu and the shimmering mountains above her.

'It was a self-contained community,' he told her, 'cut off as it was with precipitous gorges and high mountains, and they had to be self-reliant too, in time of sickness and isolation. Not all its memories are of brawling and greed.

'There's a poplar over there,' he pointed across the valley, 'where quite a flourishing settlement was situated at the turn of the century. At the end of the Boer War, the teacher of the school gave the children a holiday, but first wanted a ceremony to impress it upon their minds, with a flag-hoisting.

'There was no flagpole, but off went the pupils to the stream to cut off a sapling and drive it into the ground. Only a few stones mark the school foundations now, but the poplar is like a golden torch every autumn, and is known as the Poplar of Peace.'

They passed a tumbledown hut. 'How long since anyone lived there?' asked Lucinda.

'Oh, that chap went off to the Boer War and didn't return. They called him old Step-a-Mile. Odd quirk really, he could step out a mile to uncanny precision, my grandfather said. Those old nicknames seem to have died out. There was another chap who was always telling fantastic stories. He——'

'Old Once-upon-a-time,' said Lucinda without thinking.

She became aware that Giles had turned his head and was looking at her curiously. 'How did you know that, Lucinda? You've only been with us a day.'

She hesitated, then said, 'Oh, but I've been in the district earlier. I was yarning to a storekeeper in Arrowtown and he mentioned him and a chap called Blue Duck Jake.'

'Yes, they were mates. As a matter of fact they lived in a miner's cottage up Red Spur Gully, where we first met. Did you notice a cottage just opposite the gate?'

'Yes, that's why I went up there. The storekeeper showed me an old photo of it. I thought the cottage looked picturesque and I took a look at it. It still had a pretty overgrown garden.'

He did not say who created the garden. She added, 'Has no one lived there since the mining days?'

'Well, the mining days lasted a fair time, so many stayed on fossicking after the big strikes were worked out. Especially during the depression. They won very little, though. Just enough to buy tobacco and beer and a bit of mutton and bread and syrup. They lived on rabbit when it wouldn't stretch to the mutton.'

Lucinda thought it wise to cease her questioning now. She must not appear too curious too soon. It might come out very naturally some time, where Sylvester Mordred's wife lived now.

What a strange night this was. She felt it couldn't possibly be early morning, that she could go on walking forever in this timeless emptiness. How friendly darkness was when there were no street lights. Nothing to cast a pool of light, beyond which the blackness always seemed hostile, rimming you in. But this was all magic.

They turned a bend past the shoulder of Ben Logie that sloped right down to the fence, and saw the rough-barked *manuka* gateway arch of Drumlogie. Only the drive lamps lit their way and finally, when they had climbed the steep hill, they took to the turfed edge and trod softly. Giles took her hand to guide her round some of the trees. 'We'll take the side door into the family wing.'

Before going upstairs he whispered, 'We'll have to go up and see if Aunt Stella is awake. Like all mothers she sleeps with one ear open till we're all safely in.'

That didn't sound so much like a gay Lothario, but like a dutiful and thoughtful nephew. Careful, Lucinda, these things are disarming. They trod gently on the thickly carpeted stairs. Giles paused at a room, softly turned the handle, opened it a crack and a voice said, 'Is that you, Giles?'

'Yes, did you wonder where we'd got to?'

'Well, I did rather. My imagination got the better of me, I thought the car might have failed to take the bend over the Shotover, but then I told myself you'd probably taken her for one of your mammoth walks.'

'Well, I did, but not intentionally. Someone siphoned the petrol out of the tank. It died on us about three miles back.'

A sleepy voice, Robert's, joined in. 'I thought you had a locking cap.'

'I have, but it's stripped, so I've got the loan of an ordinary one while they put a thread on it. Look, we're going to go down very quietly and get ourselves a hot drink, then get to bed.'

Stella said, 'I left something out for you, and filled a flask. Night-night, Lucinda and Giles.'

Down in the kitchen, sitting on the table and swinging their legs, munching celery-and-cheese sandwiches and drinking piping hot coffee, Lucinda had a feeling of incredulity. This might have been her setting for years. She felt as if she had known Drumlogie and its kindly hosts, Stella and Robert Adair, for ever. She didn't add to that list. Giles was someone to be wary about.

Stella had switched her electric blanket to low and there was a single red rose in a slim crystal vase beside her bed, and a pile of magazines. Not that Lucinda was going to read tonight ... it was almost dawn. But the thoughtfulness warmed the heart. What was it Dad had said once? 'In times of great loneliness, Lucinda, it's good to tell oneself there's always another view beyond the next hill, there's always another friend to come into one's life. Adventures can crowd thickly upon one, just when life seems most empty. As mine did, and that year brought me your mother.' He'd laughed. 'It's so foolish to want to protect one's children so much, but it is inevitable that we should want them to benefit by our own experience. When you're young, despair can seem incapable of being mitigated. But as the years pass, you know the truth and comfort in the saying, "This too will pass." That things do not stay at the summit of pain in the mental world, any more than in the physical one. Always remember that tomorrow may be full of the glad surprises of God.'

Lucinda was physically weary but, as always, the thought of Dad refreshed her. And one thing she knew, Kenneth Darling might not have fathered her, but he had loved her every bit as much as his own son and daughter and had in very truth thought of her as his own. She was his daughter in spirit. In it all, now, she could trace his desire to implant in her the philosophy she might stand in need of, if ever she discovered the truth about her parentage. Lucinda knelt down and said a prayer of sheer thankfulness for being Kenneth Darling's stepdaughter and for being brought here, to Stella and Robert Adair's rooftree. Truly, it was one of the glad surprises of God, finding a couple so like Anne and Kenneth Darling.

CHAPTER FIVE

GILES said next morning, 'There's one thing, in a day or two the Olivers will be gone and Harvey too, and we can relax.'

Lucinda grinned. 'I'm already more relaxed than I dreamed was possible, when I saw Harvey come in last night. But once that hurdle was taken, and he swallowed it hook, line and sinker, I began to think we might weather the storm and reach port safely. What on earth are you laughing at, Giles Logie?'

'Just the best example of mixed metaphors I've ever heard, but I know what you mean. I think Harvey was mightily relieved. No wonder. A chap wouldn't like to tell his superiors he'd changed his mind about the promotion he'd applied for and had accepted. He's going back tomorrow, isn't he? I expect he'll just ring to say goodbye to you, perhaps report on whether or not he's got himself board or a flat. I gave him the name of my friend, the accommodation officer. By the time he's back here, at least the Olivers will be away.' He looked at her keenly. 'I suppose you realize we'll have to keep this up for some time to really relieve your friend Janice's mind? I mean, don't have any ideas about flitting from here before they're married and settled in.'

Lucinda looked up at him gratefully. 'It could mean two or three months, then I'll fade gracefully out. I can make out that I've changed my mind about you. People will probably say Lucinda never really feels anything deeply, that she just isn't capable of a grand passion.'

She saw a strange look come into the grey eyes above hers. He looked at her searchingly. 'And are you?' he demanded rather than asked.

'Am I what?'

'Capable of a grand passion.'

She tried to hold his eye, to look nonchalant, but had to look away. 'I—er—don't know. I don't suppose one does know till one meets up with someone who inspires just that.'

'And you haven't . . . ever?'

'No, I've got to admit that. I just drifted, with Harvey. Anyway, perhaps it happens to some and doesn't to others.'

'That wasn't what I meant. I said were you capable of a grand passion?'

She frowned, didn't answer.

He made a sound of impatience. 'I'm sure you know what I mean. Everybody thinks about this. I think if you *are* capable of one, you long to meet someone for whom you'll feel just that.'

'I—I don't know if I care for someone so newly met to delve into my feelings like this, Giles.'

'Oh, tosh! We became involved in each other's affairs so quickly, Lucinda, you can't reckon our knowledge of each other in minutes and hours. We went headlong into a real scrape and you played up so magnificently at the Chalet. Time has nothing to do with it. It seems aeons ago. Well?'

Her almond-shaped eyes met his frankly. 'I'd like to think I was capable of deep feelings, Giles. To think I might some day meet someone I could admire and respect, yet feel irresistibly drawn to. Something I imagine Stella and Robert know. My own mother and father had it. Harvey was right about that last night.'

'Harvey? Then you *did* have a serious conversation last night even in a crowd like that?'

'Yes. A crowd can isolate you and we kept our voices low. It was after you finished your song about Lucy at her wheel, singing. He——' She went vividly rosy.

Giles looked intrigued. 'Come on, he what?'

'He told me that this time he thought it was for real. That I—that I——'

'Come *on*, Lucinda!'

'It sounds so stupid when you and I know there's nothing in it at all, that it's just that you're a superb actor—he said I deserved a man like you. He went on to say we—he and I—had been rather too much of the good pal touch. That we hadn't struck sparks from each other. That we'd—we'd never have trodden the heights. That he'd found that in Janice and he knew I had found it—in you.' This time she managed a laugh to cover her embarrassment. 'And he wondered what it was and said it was hard to define and—well, then he asked me would I put it down to a touch of magic?'

She rather dreaded mirth, thinking Giles might find it hilarious because it was all pretence, but the grey eyes in the

85

brown face remained serious. 'I certainly think that about sums up Star and Robert's relationship, and if ever anyone deserved it, it was Aunt Stella. She didn't have an easy younger life.'

Lucinda was surprised. 'Didn't she? I'd have thought her one who'd always known happiness. There's a certain serenity.'

Giles said slowly, 'That's not always the sign of an uneventful life. I remember once hearing Uncle Robert pay Star a terrific compliment. It was before they lived here, but they were visiting us. They didn't know I was in the window alcove of the library and I had enough sense—even in my teens—to keep quiet.

'They came in, and Uncle Robert was saying as they entered, "I can't wait to show it to you. It fits you so exactly. I would have written just such a poem to you, if I'd been a poet. The writer called it *A Portrait*. I would have called it *Portrait of Stella*." The poem is still there, in that book, Lucinda, and I think Stella must have read it often, savouring that compliment. It falls open at that page. Come along.'

There was no one in the library. Guests were free to wander in and browse, but they rarely did in the mornings. As they entered Giles shut the door and turned the key. 'I don't want Star to catch us.'

He crossed to a set of shelves. 'Listen, Lucinda. . . .

> ' "*They wonder at her still serenity,*
>   *Her little air of wisdom, quaintly worn,*
> *But I—I wonder not, for I have seen*
>   *That deep tranquillity by tumult torn.*
>
> *The shallows know the fret and fuss of tides,*
>   *The ceaseless urge of waters to the shore,*
> *But out beyond the breakers' foaming line*
>   *The ocean depths are stirred by tempest more.*
>
> *So, when I see that patient brow of hers*
>   *Steeped in its mask of still serenity,*
> *I know it for the crown of peace regained*
>   *. . . The aftermath of cruel storms at sea.*" '

He stood with the open book in his hands, looking down on Lucinda. She said slowly, 'Robert felt this fitted Stella? Isn't it odd how blind we can be? I thought her lines must always have fallen in pleasant places. Perhaps this beauty around us, the blue of the lake and the sweep of the hills blinds you to the fact that there can be heartbreak and loss here too. A few weeks ago, I'd have found it hard to believe any sadness could lie behind Stella's gaiety, but I—came across an instance of this sort of thing recently. Someone whom I recall as so gay, so light-hearted, yet——'

At that moment there was a knock on the door. They both swung round, looking at each other rather self-consciously. Then Giles laughed, said, 'Coming' and with the book still in hand, turned the key. Robert entered, a surprised expression on his face.

Giles burst out laughing. 'It's okay, Robert. It's not a case of hanky-panky, as Lucinda puts it so aptly, it's just that I brought her in here to read poetry and didn't want to be interrupted. But seeing it's you, it's all right.'

Robert shook his head at them. 'I feel it's out of place in the morning, Giles. Night-time is much better for reading poetry. You can have our wee sitting-room upstairs any night you like.' He turned to Lucinda. 'Guests never go there.'

She found herself without a word to say. They were almost taking this for real. As if she and Giles really wanted to be alone.

Giles queried with real interest, 'Why not the morning, Rob?'

'Oh, it's a bit prosaic. You have to come down to earth so soon after building up a mood.'

Giles said, 'You crafty old so-and-so! I'll have to come to you for hints on courting. Who said middle-age isn't romantic? Anyway, I'm skipping some of the chores for a while. Lucinda and I are going away to free her hare. I want to release it near where she found it. She thinks it may be a member of a family! Come on, my gentle Lucy!'

She said, 'How are we going? You haven't got your car, and I saw Neill off in the Land-Rover.'

'On the horses.'

'But, Giles, I don't ride.' She started to laugh. 'What a blessing you didn't say this in front of the Olivers! I'd have had to assent and I'd probably have been bucked off in the first five seconds.'

'Gosh, what pitfalls yawn in front of us! Well, I tell you what, you can come up before me. It will give you the feeling of movement under you and we'll start lessons very soon. Run up and get some trews on.'

The hare was certainly well enough to be released and was strongly objecting to treatment and confinement now. If it escaped here the dogs would make short work of it. Giles was badly scratched by the time he got it into an open but finely-meshed bag, and held it for Lucinda to tie.

They met the Olivers as they went to the stables. Mark put a gentle hand on the hare's head, covered with the mesh, and soothed it. He seemed perfectly at ease. Arlene didn't, particularly, but you could hardly expect that, in company with her husband and the man she had dallied with when separated from him. How far had it gone? Lucinda clamped down on the thought. It was no business of hers.

'We're going up Coronet Peak today,' said Mark, 'then on to Arrowtown. Care to join us?'

'Sorry, too busy. We're releasing this animal where we found it, then going up the gullies to see how the cattle are coming along. Tomorrow is our day off, and we're going to Roxburgh.'

He saddled Rufus and brought him out. Before he helped her up, he asked, 'Are you nervous, Lucinda?'

She shook her head. 'Not at the moment. But maybe I'll know better when I'm up.'

But she wasn't. She was annoyed with herself instead for being so acutely conscious of him, his warmth against her, his arms about her, of her assessment of the strong hands holding the reins. They had tawny-gold hairs on the back of them, springing up wirily. Then the hare began to struggle and she had to concentrate on soothing it. Giles's chin was over her shoulder, his breath warm on her cheek.

A *tui* sang from a *kowhai* that drooped pendulously over a creek that provided the incomparable song of running waters on a pebbly bed, to enhance the delight of the day.

Rufus picked his way carefully till they were clear of the valleys and they came to where the hills widened out into a flat, with beyond it a plantation of pines and larches, and the pocket of native bush where she had stampeded the cattle.

Giles turned Rufus towards the five-barred gate that led

into the Red Spur Gully road and dismounted. 'Hand me Master Hare ... do you think you can dismount yourself? Rufus will stand quite still. Steady, boy!'

She managed it quite neatly. 'I'll have those lessons if you can spare the time. How marvellous to be free of the need for motorized transport, yet be able to go further and quicker than on foot.'

They stroked the hare, set it down by the willows at the gate and it lost no time diving into cover, waited for a few moments, then they saw it streaking uphill.

They leaned on the gate, revelling in the warmth of the autumn sun, the gentle zephyr that fanned their faces, the utter gladness of the morning.

They looked across at the little cottage, its flowers massing over it. Lucinda said, lightly enough, 'Someone loved flowers, even if it was long ago.'

Giles's voice was harsh. 'It was all she had to love—almost. A lot of heartbreak went into that garden and worked itself out. Nothing like hard work for stopping you brooding. I found out that for myself last year.'

So Giles knew the story of the woman who had lived there, Mrs. Sylvester Mordred. He might even have known her little boy, or was he too young? Lucinda must be careful, she didn't want to give herself away, because if that woman still lived in Queenstown, she would not want the old scandal revived. Giles might say more some day, without probing.

Her mind switched to his last sentences. He'd found hard work remedial last year. It had kept him from brooding. He must have taken it hard when Arlene had gone back to Mark. But evidently he would not break a marriage up. He might be, as Marny had said, a womanizer, but he had certain principles. Or was that right? ... did she just want to think that? It could be he wanted his fun but no responsibility.

Giles said, 'Can you take a bit more? I'd like to have a look up that far gully and work round another way home. But only if you feel you can.'

'Oh, I can take it, if Rufus can.'

It was idyllic, with snowy-fleeced sheep against the ochre of the tussock and the cattle were Herefords, the sun on their chestnut flanks striking iridescent gleams from them. Their broad white faces seemed friendly.

'Such a land of plenty,' said Lucinda, 'even if prices aren't what they were. It's so spacious. Nothing of the small, thickly populated areas of Asia, with people striving so hard to wring the tiniest returns from the soil, where water is so precious, not going to waste as here.'

Their problems receded. They might have been friends of long standing. They came up to the Two-mile Hut, just a rough stone shelter with a corrugated roof and a chimney made of boulders from the hillside. 'There are supplies here, we can make ourselves some tea.'

It was musty inside, and had a dirt floor and a couple of rough bunks at one end. 'We'll eat outside on that bench,' said Giles.

He took the blackened kettle, rinsed and filled it at the creek, brought it in to set upon the trivet, and put a match on the heaped-up brushwood that, tinder-dry, leapt into crackling flames.

Lucinda helped him carry out the cups, dusted them out with a clean tea-towel stored in a tin. Giles said, 'Can you take your tea black? I ought to have brought some milk, but I thought you'd have had enough by the time we got to Red Spur Road.'

'I quite like tea black. It's refreshing when you're thirsty, as I am right now.'

He brought a packet of gingernuts out of another tin, threw in a handful of tea-leaves on top of the boiling water in the kettle, waited for them to settle. Never had a brew tasted so good.

Lucinda said, 'I've a feeling I'd like to stay here, spiders and all. Not so many problems as at Drumlogie. It's awful having to watch every word you say.'

'Oh, I'm enjoying it. Serve the lot of them right. Not to worry, Lucinda. Tomorrow we'll be away all day.'

'Do we have to go, Giles? I thought you'd thrown in the visit to your parents just as local colour. I mean, the more who know, the harder to deceive.'

'Oh, Mother's right in it. I talked to her on the phone. She said I had fool's luck all right, meeting up with someone ready to play it my way. What happened last year wasn't the sort of thing any mother would relish. If we hadn't told her and she'd heard Arlene was here again she'd have been in a real flap.'

They came back to Drumlogie for lunch, a family meal, and it was a relief to be just a small circle, with no play-acting.

Stella said, 'We've had word from Chris and Kirsty. They're coming home day after tomorrow.'

Giles was outrageously attentive to her that evening in the drawing-room, talking openly of the fact that he and Lucinda would be away all day tomorrow, and the next that they would be off for Glenorchy. 'Lucinda hasn't met Annabel and Gideon Darroch of Mount Carmel.'

He had prepared Lucinda for this. 'I feel if the Olivers think we're going to be away, Mark will have no trouble persuading Arlene to take off for Milford Sound.' Lucinda was all in favour.

Halfway through the night Meg came in to say Lucinda was wanted on the phone. 'It's Mr. Renfrew.'

She sent a swift look to Giles. 'Like to come with me? He may want to speak to you too.'

He rose immediately. In the hall he said, 'Don't look so white, Lucinda, it will just be to say goodbye. After all, you said it wasn't a grand passion.'

Her look was a little pitiful. 'It isn't that. It's just that if I've been convincing enough, I may have Janice back as a friend. She's such fun. She's so dear to me. Giles, she's the only link I have in New Zealand with my mother and father. Trudy and Ivan are half a world away.'

He caught her hand. 'Of course. I'll back you up, they'll never guess. Now . . .'

She was amazed to hear her voice so crisp. Harvey came to the point at once. 'Lucinda, I've found a house to rent. I've got an option on it for three days. I'd like Janice to see it, and she's pretty sure she can get Friday afternoon off, and be here for the weekend. This is frightful cheek, but I wondered if you could put her up at Drumlogie.'

Lucinda said, 'I'm not sure how bookings are—just a moment, I'll find out.'

She bit her lip. They'd have to keep up this pretence. Before she could put the phone down, Harvey added, 'Besides, Jan wants to see for herself if what I've told her is true. She doesn't really trust me over it. Says it might be just wishful thinking on my part. I said: "If you could see her with this boss of hers, you'd have no doubts." So it would kill two birds with one stone.'

Lucinda put her hand over the mouthpiece, told Giles. He had been standing close to her, listening. He put a hand over hers, clasping it tightly over the phone. 'I got all that, anyway. I can understand Janice feeling this way. Let her come. In fact, let me speak to Harvey.'

Giles said, 'Hi there, Harvey. I was right beside Lucinda. Of course it will be okay. Nice for Lucinda too. She's got hardly anyone in New Zealand, bar me. If we can put you up too, we will.'

He put the phone down. The grey eyes were sparkling, impudent and carefree. 'I'm going to use this as a prod to get the Olivers on their way. It will be just that much less tricky with them out of it. It would take only one hint from Arlene re my murky past—and believe me, she's capable of anything—and Janice would wonder if you were, after all, getting a matrimonial prize!'

Later in the evening he picked up a dish of savouries, said to Lucinda, 'Bring those sandwiches with you, will you, and come to the Olivers?'

He bent over them, serving them, said, 'By the way, you know you said you might be moving on to Milford? Mark, without wanting in any way to appear to put the skids under a guest, mind if I ask you if you'll be away by Friday night? Lucinda has a friend coming down—who's engaged to that chap, Harvey Renfrew, who came out to Drumlogie last night. He's getting a transfer here, and wants his fiancée to come down to look at a house to rent. It would mean a lot to Lucinda to be able to offer them both hospitality, and we're chocker at the moment.'

Mark said promptly, 'We were going to tell you tonight. We've decided to travel on tomorrow after lunch, so that will suit us fine.'

Arlene said, 'And of course the Milford Hotel is the last word in elegance and comfort. I'm looking forward to it.'

Lucinda saw Mark redden a little. He hadn't missed Arlene's slighting reference. She was sorry for the man's embarrassment and said quickly, 'I've never been to Fiordland, though Milford Sound is so familiar to me through the New Zealand calendars Janice sent us faithfully each year.'

They moved on with their plates to other guests. Later on,

washing up the huge stack of dishes, Giles said, 'What did I tell you? Lucinda, I shall never cease to be grateful to you for saving me from the consequences of my own unspeakable folly last year. Mother will be, too.'

Lucinda knew she would be glad when the Olivers were gone, and not only for the reason that she was conscious of tension, afraid she might betray their plot. No, it was because when Arlene was around, with her too-knowledgeable eyes, her way of trying to lock glances with Giles, a great distaste for the whole thing filled Lucinda's spirit.

But the next day it was so hard to recapture that uneasiness. It was such a happy family sort of day. They went through Speargrass Flat instead of through the Gorge Road, and came out on to the highway past Lake Hayes, which lay there dreaming like a sheet of mirror glass, rimmed with gold, and with the lavenders and blues of distant mountains reflected symmetrically on the far rim.

They were quickly into the gorge where the Kawarau River, emptying Lake Wakatipu, had carved out straight-sided clefts, through which it flowed, snaking along like a vivid peacock-blue-green serpent.

At Cromwell, the Clutha, emptying Lake Wanaka, joined it, the waters meeting with such velocity that they did not mingle for a terrific distance, then hurtled down the Cromwell Gorge to Clyde. Everywhere in tailings from dredges and remains of old sluices, in caves blocked with loose stones to provide dwelling-places in the doughty days of a century ago, were evidences of the gold-fever that had swept Otago. Now the wealth of the country was in the vast sweeps of fruit orchards, hives of activity for the moment, with ladders and pickers, trailers of cases, and golden-hued and russety apples and pears hanging from laden boughs. Planes were taking off, for the markets of the north and overseas.

Alexandra lay in a pool of sunshine, girdled with the brightest gardens Lucinda had ever seen, in contrast to the ranges of jagged rocks, bare and pitiless, that ringed it round. Almost all the way the river followed the road, right to the big dam at Roxburgh. Here the colours were so bright they almost hurt the eyes. Had there ever been an autumn such as this? Giles turned the car up a quiet road under Mount Benger and drew to a stop in front of a gabled house with an orange-tiled roof, set against the lower slopes, a house with sparkling, wide-open windows and a long narrow orchard at one side.

'That orchard gives Dad an interest, now he's retired,' said Giles, 'and is reasonably profitable too.' He put his hand on the horn. Like a shot from a gun a door burst open and out flew not the tall, matronly figure Lucinda had expected, but a tiny, slim one, running down the path as if she were practising for the Olympic Games, as Giles said, laughing. 'She's a miniature tornado, a whirlwind.'

Lucinda said, 'Then no wonder you are. The way you erupt into a room, I'm always expecting a crash in your wake.'

Giles got out and suffered his mother to hurl herself on him with cries of delight. 'Hold off, you madcap! I saw you just a fortnight ago. Oh, hullo, Dad, how are things? Now, you two, this is Lucinda, an answer to prayer. She has the knack of popping up at the most felicitous moments and is quick on the uptake too.'

Marguerite Logie giggled—there was no other word for it. 'If only I could have been behind a pot-plant at the Chalet! Lucinda, dear, how good to meet you. How you caught on so quickly, I'll never know.' She embraced her. 'I'm eternally in your debt. Giles will have explained everything to you. We were nearly out of our minds with worry last year. But come on in. I've been papering the sunroom and I'm dying to show it to someone. Angus is *so* unsatisfactory at oohing and aahing, though I should know, after more than thirty years of being married to the brute, that his "Aye, it's no' so bad," is the highest of praise.'

Angus grinned. 'Well, Lucinda, we strike a balance. That's nature for you. I never see the need to say ower and ower that she's done a good job. But I'll hand it to her, she has. I was fair aghast when she started these capers again. I'd rather have a tradesman in, any time, but for once she managed fine. Didn't get a single piece on upside down. I couldn'a believe that this time I wasn't to be press-ganged into sloshing water on the walls and scraping off upside-down wreaths and garlands.'

Marguerite led the way in, straight into the sunroom. Giles burst out laughing. 'Poor Dad, I don't think it's dawned on him yet that even Mother couldn't get this one on upside-down

... it hasn't got a pattern, man!'

But Mrs. Logie wasn't just a chatterbox. She had a lovely meal set out for them in a dining-room at the back of the house with a corner window that looked right up Mount Benger. She had green fingers too; maples were bright scarlet against the hill, and sumacs. Birches moved in the breeze so goldenly that you expected the leaves to tinkle against each other like strung sovereigns, and dahlias glowed with jewelled colours.

They talked of the encounter at the Chalet, the earlier one with the hare. Mrs. Logie said, 'And you called him Farmer Giles! How funny! I could just see the two of you blazing away at each other! You'd certainly never dream that by that night you'd be as good as engaged to each other!'

Lucinda said quickly, 'Well, in a sort of way. I mean, it's just pretence.'

Mrs. Logie's eyes met hers with a quizzical expression and suddenly Lucinda's cheeks were hot. She said hastily, 'We let the hare go yesterday.'

As a red herring that hare was a non-starter.

Mrs. Logie continued straight on, 'It was so absolutely right ... the perfect solution. I couldn't have thought of a better myself.'

Giles choked. 'Hark at her! She's saying that in tones of the utmost praise. My dear, dilly mother, if it had been one of your hare-brained schemes, it would have come unstuck at the seams long since.'

Lucinda said, 'Don't say it, just don't say it! I feel I walk a tight-rope as it is. It's so easy to say something inadvertently. Thank heaven the Olivers are moving on. With the Olivers thinking we met in Wanganui, and Harvey knowing we didn't, plus the fact he thinks Giles and I have known each other for the best part of a month, I feel the sword of Damocles could descend upon our heads at any moment. Talk about Scylla and Charybdis!'

She broke off, glared at Giles, 'What's so funny? Oh, I'm at it again, the mixed metaphors.'

Marguerite Logie joined them in the laughing while Angus merely looked puzzled. Marguerite wiped her eyes. 'Oh, you'll do our family fine, Lucinda. Giles will have someone to poke fun at besides me ... I do the same. And it doesn't matter, does it? It makes conversation so much more colourful.'

Lucinda noticed that for all Marguerite seemed to jump madly from one subject to another, on one thing at least she had a one-track mind. She'd made it up ... it was time Giles settled down and stopped flitting from one girl to another. The Arlene affair had really shaken her and she was intent on making this bogus attraction real. Possibly she thought a missionary's daughter sounded safe and sensible!

Lucinda took another helping of salad and said calmly, 'Yes, the best thing we can do is to urge Harvey and Janice to settle quickly on this desirable house and persuade them that it would be ridiculous not to get married right away, then when they're well entrenched Giles and I can stage a gradual breakdown in our relationship, drift apart and eventually I can go back to Wanganui.'

Mrs. Logie's face was a picture—just like a disappointed child's.

Giles looked up from his plate, caught it, and burst out laughing.

'Look at Mum's face! She never likes *non-sequitur* endings. They've just *got* to follow through to a logical and satisfying finish. Lucinda, you're disappointing my dear mama.'

Lucinda said quickly, 'Well, real life can't always follow right through to happy-ever-after finishes.'

Mrs. Logie looked even more let down. 'Oh, Lucinda, you aren't one of those horrible creatures who pretend they don't like happy-ending books, do you? I mean, they babble about realism and artistry and I don't know what, and when I read a book like that full of frustration and what-have-you, I toss and turn all night trying to work out what *should* have happened. And there are so many happy endings in real life. Mine, for instance, and Christopher's, and Stella's. Who could have thought, at one time, that Robert would have come into Stella's life? And there he was, all the time, waiting to emerge. And as for me, I nearly made a horrible mess of my own life. I so nearly married an irresponsible glib-tongued rascal. And it was all because Angus wasn't very articulate and I thought he didn't love me!'

She cast Angus a glance and his answering look was eloquence itself. Lucinda knew a pang of envy that surprised her. How wonderful to have one's life so settled, a life-partner like Gile's father. Never to know that loneliness of the spirit that

96

came from not having someone to share one's gladdest and saddest moments. Yet, evidently, they all had had to win through.

Mrs. Logie removed the salad platters and brought in a lemon chiffon pie, but it hadn't broken the thread of her thoughts. 'Of course, to really convince Harvey and Janice, to dispel any lingering doubts, Giles, you ought to buy Lucinda a ring.'

He lifted a rueful eyebrow. 'Mother ... just give me time, will you, please? I've only known Lucinda a few days.'

Lucinda said quickly, 'There's no need to go as far as that, or waste money. Lots of couples think of marriage and act as if it were a natural outcome of their courting, long before they get engaged. We'll be one of those.'

Angus unexpectedly backed her up. 'I think that's wise. A broken engagement always causes a deal of speculation and Giles has got himself talked about too much as it is. Lucinda has her future to think about too. She might find it very hard to explain an engagement away as a pretence one when, as is more than likely, she finds someone she can really love.'

Marguerite looked like a child who has been put in the corner, but she made no protest. Lucinda thought Angus probably managed her beautifully. They didn't linger after lunch. Giles said, 'Fergus and Mhairi will have had their bags packed since the crack of dawn, and will be driving their grandparents mad running up and down to the gate looking for us. Mr. and Mrs. Ramsay said last night on the phone that they're wildly excited about having their mother and father back. They can sleep at Drumlogie tonight and go across to Leith Lodge after Chris and Kirsty arrive.'

Angus said, 'Has everything turned out satisfactorily for Chris? No hold-up? After all, he's entitled to it, if only he can get over his distaste for the whole thing.'

Giles said hastily, 'Well, we've just had short notes from him. And only one since Robert came back. But we'll hear about it when he gets here,' and she had the distinct impression he gave his father a warning glance. She didn't want to know anything ... it was probably something to do with the ins and outs of the tourist trade.

Away they went to Alexandra. Sure enough, two heads were hanging over the gate, one as tawny and sun-bleached as

Giles's, the other a pony-tailed black. As Lucinda got out of the car, the pony-tail turned over, completely somersaulted with a thump on to the asphalt, and righted itself before the tawny fringe had opened the gate and emerged. Then Mhairi flung herself on Giles. He hugged her back, but protested, 'You're strangling me! Stop it, you thunderbolt! Hullo, Fergus, spots all gone, I see. Well, your mum and dad will be back tomorrow. This is Lucinda, and her last name is Darling.'

'Good gwacious,' said Mhairi, sliding down his legs and subjecting Lucinda to a candid appraisal, '*Another* girlfwiend!'

They both burst out laughing, apparently to Fergus's relief. He said to Lucinda very earnestly, 'She always says what she thinks. It's very embarrassing at times. But then she's very young.'

'And time will cure that,' said Lucinda solemnly. 'And it doesn't matter, Fergus. I know he's had dozens of girl-friends.'

Giles looked outraged. '*I* should be the one to be embarrassed. What man ever deserved such relations? What with Mother——'

Lucinda giggled. 'Don't panic, Giles. I didn't take her seriously. Mothers are like that. Mine was. As soon as some safe, secure young man arrived on my horizon, Mother got a certain look in her eye. She did with Harvey. And I expect, with your recent peccadilloes, your mother could think I was reasonably uncomplicated.'

Giles looked even more outraged. Then he grinned. 'I trust, Miss Darling, that your choice of words is due only to the hope that the younger generation won't understand what you're talking about. Now for the kids' grandparents, and more involvements. I clean forgot to ask my mama what she'd told them.'

At that moment the Ramsays appeared. It was quite evident that Giles was a favourite and it seemed as if they knew little more than that Lucinda was Giles's latest girl-friend.

'Come awa' in and have a cup of tea before you set out through the gorges. The bairns' things are all ready. I'll be that grieved to see them go. I'm glad it's so warm a day. I'm always a bit afraid of ear trouble after measles. Tell Kirsty when you see her tomorrow to keep that wee bit o' cottonwool

98

in for a week or so more. We want no complications now.'

'I'll get Star to pass that on, Mrs. Ramsay. I'm taking Lucinda up to Glenorchy tomorrow. We won't see them till night.'

'Oh aye. Good idea to go up there while the weather holds. Well, it will be grand to have them back and mebbe now there'll be a bit of capital to put into the place. I'd like fine to think Chris benefited at last.'

'That's so,' said Giles hurriedly. 'I was wondering what that was over there—it looks like an arbour. Some of your work, Mr. Ramsay?'

'Come away ower and see it, lad. Meg thought she'd like one to follow the sun. Said what was the use o' having an engineer for a husband if he couldn'a make a summer-hoose that worked on a turntable. It's no' finished, but likely will be by the time you visit us again. I've used *manuka* in its natural state. Mebbe Lucinda would like to see it too.'

Just before they got in the car Fergus said gravely, 'Uncle Giles, would it be all right if Lucinda sat in the back with us so we could ask her all sorts of questions?'

'Heavens! Sounds like an inquisition. Only if she wants to.'

'Well, you see, when Aunt Marguerite rang Grandma Ramsay, she said Lucinda had had a very exciting background, that she'd lived all over the world. I thought if I could get in now with some questions when not too many people are round, I could do an essay on her for school. There's a kid at school who has an aunt in New Guinea who's always having terrific adventures, and all our family seem to stay put and don't do anything exciting.'

Lucinda laughed, 'But your mother came from Scotland.'

'Yes, but you don't have head-hunters there, or swamps, or snakes, or elephants and tigers. I thought you could have had all sorts of adventures like terrorists attacking, or being rescued from floods or——'

Giles said quickly, 'Those things aren't always such fun when they're actually happening, Fergus, and——'

Lucinda touched his hand, stopping him. 'It's all right, Giles. I've plenty to tell them without touching on the last flood. But thank you.'

They got settled, drove off. 'When we were in India once, Dad had a friend who happened to be a Maharajah, and he took Dad on a tiger hunt. Dad didn't like killing things for sport, but he just had to be a good shot, because sometimes leopards and tigers did frightful damage in the villages. This tigress was a real man-eater. They went on elephants, of course, and . . .'

She had a rapt audience. Lucinda threw in plenty of description of the luxurious surroundings, but didn't forget to stress the terrific problem of improving conditions so that, in aid for digging wells and irrigating, the people could be assisted to produce more.

There were stories of Korea, Hongkong, and of a year on a tiny fishing village on an island offshore, where families once crowded in terrible conditions on fishing junks were now housed in a place to which the men could return frequently, knowing their children were being educated and were within reach of a doctor, Lucinda's father.

'But one of the most scary things that ever happened to us,' said Lucinda, 'wasn't really an adventure at all. We lost my little sister Trudy, when she was only two and a half, for a day and a night and half the next day. It was in Singapore. We were only passing through and there was a procession in celebration of something or other. A baby elephant, shambling through behind its mother, got suddenly frightened with all the noise and took off, right into the crowd, scattering it in all directions. Trudy's hand got knocked out of my mother's and she became completely lost. It's my earliest vivid memory. My parents were almost demented. A terrific search was instigated. And you'll never guess where she was found—but not till well on into the next day——?'

They guessed all sorts of things, but Lucinda shook her head to them all. 'I was with them. They found her with an old snake-charmer, curled up on a mat among his baskets and snakes. He had been so kind to her, she wasn't a bit upset. She'd wandered off, well away from the search area, and had found him camped under some trees. He couldn't speak more than a few words of English that he knew by heart, to say to the tourists, and he had let her curl up beside him, and had fed her.'

'What a beaut story,' said Fergus. 'Boy, what an essay it'll make!'

By the time they were over the Shotover and into Queens-

100

town, Lucinda felt as though she had known the children all her life. It was quite impossible to believe that a week ago, she hadn't known any of these people had existed.

There were quite a few new guests on the loggia, replacing this morning's departures, and there was a great sense of freedom in knowing that tonight they would not have to watch their step because of the Olivers.

Mhairi's arms were full of toys, two dolls, a furry rabbit, a monkey called Boko, and a selection of puppets. As they crossed the loggia, smiling to the guests in a general sort of way, Mhairi dropped a puppet. A strange woman picked it up, handed it to Lucinda, said, 'I think your little girl dropped her Pinocchio.'

Lucinda chuckled, 'Yes, it's hers all right, but she's not *my* little girl. I'm still single!'

The woman stared, then chuckled. 'My goodness, and as you came up the steps, I said to my husband, "The wee boy's the image of his father, and the little girl is just her mother over again." That shows what imagination can do for you!'

Giles chuckled too. 'Yes, I often think these family likenesses are fifty per cent imagination. By the way, I belong here. I'm Giles Logie of Drumlogie. But the boy isn't mine either, but in this case it's a genuine resemblance. He's my cousin's youngster. Mr. and Mrs. Adair are their grandparents. The children's parents run the restaurant, Leith Lodge. And this is Miss Lucinda Darling.'

The children gave their grandparents rapturous hugs.

Stella said, 'Well, we'll not go into the drawing-room till later tonight, Giles. I'll get the children well settled first. And I don't want to banish them too soon, it's so lovely to have them back.'

Mhairi was giggling, 'That lady out there thought I was Lucinda's little girl. And that Uncle Giles was our father.'

Giles said, 'She thought Mhairi was the image of Lucinda. Must be the colouring—brown eyes, dark hair.'

Robert Adair looked at them both, said, 'Well, I'm blessed! That must have been what I noticed. Remember, Lucinda, how I said you reminded me of someone and pushed your hair back. But I couldn't quite click on. That's it, a chance likeness to Mhairi.'

Lucinda nodded. 'I thought when you did that, I must remind you of some man. But you were really wondering what I'd look like with a pony-tail.'

Stella took Lucinda's hair, gently pushed it back with both hands, holding it tightly, then looked from Lucinda to Mhairi. Then she quite abruptly let it go. 'I'm sure we're embarrassing Lucinda. Isn't it awful to suddenly find yourself the centre of attention? Well, children, now to wash up for dinner.'

The children had a fair innings later, and Fergus couldn't resist telling about the tiger-hunts and the fishing-village. 'But Lucinda says their worst fright was in Singapore.'

'Singapore? Did you live there too?' asked Stella.

Lucinda shook her head. 'Dad was never stationed there. We were passing through when this happened. Though I was born there, my mother's people were in the Army, and I was born at their home.'

She was conscious of feeling a little hot. It was true enough, but she must be more careful. She might want to find out about Sylvester Mordred's wife and son, but wanted no one to link her with them.

Fergus got impatient. It was his story. 'Nanna, I wanted to tell you. Lucinda can just remember how awful it was. Her little sister was lost for a day and a night and another half-day. Trudy was only two and a half and . . .'

They let him finish, oohing and aahing enough to satisfy Fergus, and Mhairi didn't interrupt, she was so busy turning her Teddy-bear from a girl into a boy, she had announced. Lucinda had looked rather startled, but Giles said solemnly, 'It's okay. It will never reach the headlines . . . it's just a matter of removing that frilly dress, and putting on shirt and shorts. And changing the name from Pwimwose to Woderwick!'

Mhairi looked at him scornfully. 'You aren't saying the names wight. That's baby-talk! Would you do this button up, please, Uncle Giles?'

Stella seemed to have gone into a trance when Fergus finished. Then she came out of it, said, 'How odd. I hadn't realized the twins were younger than you. I expect that was because Trudy was married. I assumed she was older.'

'No, there's more than four years between us. Trudy married quite young. I'm glad she did, because we had the happiest of days. Mother and Father were still with us. She met

Gordon on our last furlough. Gran—Mother's mother—was still alive. Trudy was married from her house in the Lake District. They retired there when Granddad left the army.'

'Whereabouts in the Lake District? Robert and I spent a month there once when we had a year in Britain.'

'In Grasmere, not far from Dove Cottage. A very romantic spot.'

Robert said, 'We were at Ambleside—how close! We spent a lot of time at Grasmere and Rydal, treading in the footsteps of Wordsworth. I must show you our slides some time.'

Stella came across to the couch to pick up Mhairi's dolls from it. She looked at Lucinda's right hand, said, 'Oh, what a lovely ring! I love opals. Let me see it.' She took hold of Lucinda's hand and laid her own underneath it. 'That looks a very good opal.'

'I expect it is, Star. Dad gave it to me for my twenty-first and got it in Colombo where they're very reasonable.'

All of a sudden the hand under hers gave a little twitch and Lucinda had the distinct impression that Stella was about to say something, but had checked it. She looked up to surprise a really strange look on Stella's face. It looked like embarrassment.

Stella moved swiftly away. 'Now, come along, children ... by the time you're bathed and bedded, it will be quite late.'

Robert said, 'I'll give you a hand. I'm sure Lucinda and Giles will do the dishes.'

Suddenly Lucinda knew what Stella had bitten back. She had probably noticed her littlest fingers. She glanced down on them now as she scraped a plate. They each lacked the top joint. Most of the time they went unnoticed because they were still perfectly proportioned as to length but lacked the top bend. Stella might have thought Lucinda was sensitive over them.

When Robert came downstairs he said, 'You two can hold the fort in the drawing-room tonight. Stella's tired and doesn't feel like singing. It's a good thing Chris and Kirsty will be back tomorrow.'

Lucinda said quickly, 'Perhaps Giles and I ought to postpone our visit to Glenorchy. After all, we've had a day off today.'

Robert shook his head. 'Stella wouldn't rest anyway, with

them coming home. No, a good night's sleep will put her right.'

But even next morning Lucinda felt Star had dark shadows under her eyes.

CHAPTER SIX

HAD it not been that Lucinda had been used to ill-formed and dangerous roads all her life, the Glenorchy road might have scared the life out of her. It led up-lake from Queenstown and was extremely narrow at the beginning, skirting implacable rock faces and edging out over the lake far below.

This was the old road, Giles explained, that for many years had gone for only a few miles, till the residents of Glenorchy, weary of promises and tired of their years of access by water only, had banded together and had begun the road from the Head-of-the-Lake themselves, raising the money somehow.

'By bazaar efforts, even. In fact one resident up there put it very pithily when she said the first miles were built on aprons ... they made and sold hundreds of aprons. Then the Road Board went ahead with it. It's a magnificent undertaking. Now it's to become a major tourist project, like the Haast Road was. The Dart River at the Head is to be bridged, giving access from here to the far side of the Lake, and right through to Milford Sound. That will cut the time of the journey from Queenstown to Fiordland—which at present has to be via Te Anau—fantastically.

'One thing about a road like this—everyone, or almost everyone, takes care.' He sounded his horn at the blindest of corners, then had to stop because a huge, articulated sheep-truck was just round the bend. He managed to reverse on to an extended area on the edge. 'Usually the one on the inside does the reversing, but in this case it's over to the smaller vehicle.'

There were only two great homesteads on the way, Close-burn, where once the road had stopped, and Mount Creighton. Sometimes the trees gave way to sheets of tussock, blowing silver in the slight breeze off-lake. Now and then they caught a shimmer of distant snows, away back-in, that even all the brilliant summertime and golden autumn heat had failed to thaw.

Giles told her of Glenorchy's Biblical names, Mount Judah, where they mined for scheelite, the Bible Terrace, Heaven's Gates, the Jordan River, and the Rees River, whose bed had been called Purgatory by the early coaching parties, but which had now been bridged. After that lay Paradise ... the road's end.

'But I'm not taking you quite to Paradise today. We turn off at Canaan. We'll have lunch at Mount Carmel Station. By the way, I haven't told them there what we're doing. They're such close friends I was tempted, but Stella thought if too many know it might get out. Harvey's duties as a tourist officer will take him up there.

'Gideon and Annabel Darroch would think it great fun, of course, but it's safer not to. Gideon has been a mate of mine from schooldays on. And he was in England when I was there. He engaged a girl he met at New Zealand House to come out to Glenorchy to help his stepmother run her guest-house, Olivet, next to Carmel. He had no idea, but Annabel had been trying to get information about Paradise, to see if she could trace her people. She was a victim of the blitz, her mother was killed and the child's identity was unknown. She'd only a snapshot with Annabel Lee scrawled across it and a remembered song about Paradise.

'She told no one, because she thought she might have been an illegitimate result of the war years and didn't want to embarrass anyone, but quite suddenly, and dramatically, she found her father.'

He glanced at Lucinda a moment later because she had made no response, then said, very quickly, 'Oh, sorry. I hadn't realized these bends were getting you. I'll run in to the side on the next bluff. Hang on.'

It was only a few yards and had a magnificent viewpoint. He opened her door. 'Out you get, and put your head down between your knees. You're as white as a ghost.'

She permitted him to push her head down as she sat sideways on the seat, her legs out of the car. She didn't particularly want to look at him just now. How stupidly one's physical reactions could let one down sometimes! It was just the strangeness of knowing another girl had come to these parts seeking her own. Only she, Lucinda, wanted to find and leave—her half-brother. And to somehow satisfy herself that the half-brother's mother had, during the long years, found some sort of happiness.

She brought her head up, said, 'How stupid of me. I've been on much worse roads than this, on greater heights, and in a much less road-worthy vehicle. I'm okay now, Giles. What bay is that over there?'

'Elfin Bay, only access by steamer, as they all are that side. Sit down for a bit on the grass.'

'No, truly I'm all right. I'm glad that story had a happy ending. How courageous of her to come all that distance, alone.'

'Yes, and she was prepared to go away, still unknown, if she would have embarrassed her father, or his subsequent family if he had married. Which was fair enough. Ghosts from the past can be most unwelcome. Even ancient sorrows are sometimes best unresurrected.'

Lucinda felt as if a knife turned in her heart. Yes, Annabel had been brave, had taken a big chance and won, but there was no question of that with her, no mystery. She was merely the result of a bigamous union. *Nobody* would want *her*.

Mount Earnslaw came into full view soon, the most individual mountain Lucinda thought she had ever seen. It didn't have the shapeless mass of some, or the anonymous cone shape of perfection. There were two great peaks, East Peak, West Peak, and supporting them, the massive shoulders of the mountain, upthrusting, Big Turret, Middle Turret, Little Turret. Over to the left of it lay Paradise, but to the right, up a narrowing road, the valley of Canaan.

Mount Carmel homestead was spread out on a terrace down which aubretia and gentians flowed in a blue tide. There were pansy-faces everywhere under huge clumps of daisies of all colours, and dahlias were flaunting their last triumphant colours before the frosts would blacken them. Round the bend, beneath silver birches, came a long-legged girl riding a donkey the colour of a Siamese cat.

'Here's Annabel and Balaam now. What a girl she is for riding the donkeys!'

Annabel was off Balaam in a trice. 'I was on my way to look for you. Frances is with Granddad Bell, and Luke the Less is down for a nap. Balaam is getting fat and lazy with too little exercise.'

Her golden-greeny eyes came up to Lucinda's brown ones, searchingly—she may not know the story, but she's frankly curious, Lucinda thought. Annabel smiled a wide, crooked smile as if she were satisfied. Ah, they all want to see Giles the charmer, the rover, settle down. They'd be glad to have him finished with his sowing of wild oats.

It was an idyllic day and Lucinda knew a real regret that her ways would not lie for ever in this enchanted mountainous land. Wakatipu was like that. It put a spell upon you. Some alchemy ensured that you were never quite the same again.

After lunch, Gideon and Giles, Annabel and Lucinda all went riding on the donkeys, to explore the valley, Lucinda professing she had less fear of them than of horses, and the men saying resignedly that in that case, they'd have to ride the donkeys too, or they'd hopelessly outpace the girls.

Lucinda and Annabel were helpless with the giggles at the sight of the long legs of the men dangling right to the ground and brushing the grasses.

Giles turned round threateningly. 'Lucinda, if you poke fun at me like that, I shall clobber you, so help me if I won't! I've told you I'm a tender plant. You'll give me all sorts of complexes.'

He turned back and Lucinda said to Annabel, 'I'm afraid I can't even imagine him on speaking terms with a complex. He's far too brash for that.'

Annabel looked at her seriously. 'Is he, Lucinda? Or does he just whistle in the dark?'

Their eyes met and in that moment a friendship was forged. It was true, that you never knew, as Kenneth Darling had said long ago, what gifts a year would bring you. The friendship she had known with Janice was hardly likely to ever be the same again—quite—but here was a new friend.

But for how long? Because when she and Giles had played out this farce to the end, she would have to leave Wakatipu, leave Queenstown with its darling gaily painted houses snuggled into the curve of the lake that was delphinium blue today; leave the Half-Million, leave Annabel Darroch, Star, Robin Adair . . . Giles.

Yet when they had traversed the hazardous miles home again, Lucinda knew only a warm content and the feeling that she would not—yet—look too far into the future.

Giles said, 'You can meet Chris and Kirsty tomorrow morning. The lights are on in their place, so we won't disturb them. Neither will we go into the drawing-room yet. They can get on fine without us and it's such a relief not to have the Olivers here.'

'You mean,' said Lucinda, and to her horror, she thought her voice sounded piqued, 'it's a relief not to have to continue playing a part. Well, I couldn't agree more. It *is* a strain pretending to an affection you don't feel.'

She'd looked upon him as such a philanderer she was surprised to hear his voice so rough with anger. 'Thanks *very* much! I thought today that we'd become—well, at least pals. But I can see emotion simply doesn't touch *you*!' He paused, flung out, 'You seem to have no good, honest warm feelings at all!'

Not warm? Why, what surged up in Lucinda now was red-hot and spilled over in burning words. 'How *dare* you say a thing like that to me! What colossal vanity! You must be a real bighead! Surely to goodness you haven't got the nerve to fancy that on the strength of this—this enforced relationship— I *am* falling for you. That's the trouble with men like you— you think you're irresistible, think no woman can help being flattered by you, moved by you!' She actually stamped her foot.

Unforgivably, he laughed.

She turned swiftly, to leave him, but his hands shot out to her wrists, bruising them. She was powerless, so she said through gritted teeth, 'If I scream, here in the garage, it will sound well, won't it? So let me go!'

He kept a firm grip on her despite uncontrollable laughter. 'Lucinda *darling*, you'll be the death of me. No, I won't let you go, and you know damned well you won't scream!'

The next moment he'd let her wrists go and had managed to clamp one hand over her mouth just as she opened it to full extent. The scream died a natural death as her teeth met over his thumb. So it was Giles who uttered a yelp, albeit a quickly strangled one.

Lucinda leant up against the car and gave way to her mirth. She was grabbed and her hands twisted behind her back. 'Fancy naming you Darling! You—you termagant! You shrew!'

She said, still shaking, 'Well, if a man uses force on a woman, he asks for her to use what weapons she has. You didn't think I'd retaliate, did you?'

'Not a missionary's daughter!'

'Perhaps there's bad blood in me despite that,' said Lucinda lightly, and caught her lip between her teeth as the truth of that statement hit her. There *was* bad blood in her. Her father had been a gaolbird!

Giles said, 'You could have had that whole roomful of guests rushing out, thinking someone had attacked you.'

She said airily, 'Oh, I'd just have said a big creepy-crawly *weta* had dropped down on me from the rafters.'

But the tension between them had gone. She said, 'If you don't want to face the crowd tonight, I expect you're just going to your room. I'll do the same and have a long read in bed.'

'Oh no, you won't. Everyone would suspect a quarrel. I'm going to show you the best view of all ... the moon is just perfect tonight, see, it's rising behind that bar of cloud. Let's go through the moongate.'

'The moongate?'

'Yes, this way.' He took her arm. How absurd to be so conscious of his fingers, cupped about her elbow. It was nothing but this place, and its spell.

Giles's voice was soft. 'My father built it for my mother, to frame her favourite mountain ... Walter Peak.'

They skirted the place they called the United Nations Garden, where trees and flowers of so many countries grew, threaded through the larch grove and rounded a small, conical hill. On the other side was a ridge, planted out with sweet-smelling herbs and flowers with a path winding through it. They turned a bend and there, framing the lake through a cleft in the mountains this side, was the circular moongate, set in a wall that cut across the path. The beauty of it halted Lucinda in her tracks.

She stood, one hand on the stone curve, looking through. The ridge widened out through the orifice, and here Angus Logie had made a mountain garden, intersected with paving-stones brought from the Arrow month after month, year after year, for his Marguerite. Giles said, 'He planted mostly white flowers so they could be seen at night, and the aromatic ones that would make their presence felt, even when there was no moon.'

There were white roses, with petals spilled all over the ground, marguerites, of course, with great moon faces and dark centres, white alyssum, snow-in-summer, white petunias with, could she but have seen them, purple streaks at their hearts. There were tiny white chrysanthemums, and in spring, Giles told her, native clematis wreathed its white stars round the moongate, and white violets peeped out from the rocks. And everywhere, at every season, spilled the pale beauty of the alpine flowers of New Zealand, brought here from remote mountain fastnesses, where no roads led. They had been brought down in Angus's knapsack on countless foraging expeditions.

They sat down on a bench formed of rough-barked *manuka*. The stone wall at their back still held a little warmth from the heat of the day.

Lucinda said softly, no termagant now, 'Your father didn't need to be articulate, did he, Giles? Not when he can be as eloquent as this with his hands . . . something he had to dream up first. It's a poem in stone and flowers.'

'Thank you, Lucinda. Very nicely put.' All the tension went out of her. If he had moved towards her in the intimacy of that moment it would have spoiled it for her. She would have recognized it as the sign of the incorrigible flirt, taking advantage of her softened mood.

The peace of the evening seeped into them. The radiance of the stars was brightly silver, it outlined the symmetrical angle of Walter Peak as it brooded over the darker waters and looked down at the golden cluster of lights where the homestead windows lit the water's edge. The pungency of the bruised lavender came up to them, and the sweetness of night-scented stock. The space between them did not diminish. When they did move, it was with a shared and regretful sigh.

They came in to find the private sitting-room lights still on. Stella and Rob looked so relaxed, reading. Stella said, 'I'm glad you came in. There's some mail here for you, Lucinda, forwarded from Wanganui.'

Lucinda was glad to see it was not from Janice. It had her lawyer's address on the back. Just a statement, she supposed.

She slit the envelope, drew out the enclosure, read the short letter with one comprehensive glance, glanced at the sealed letter it was clipped to and turned as white as the roses by the moongate.

Stella crossed to her immediately, took her hand. 'What is it, Lucinda ... not bad news?'

Lucinda managed to swallow, shake her head. 'No, Star, it's not bad news. It's something almost too wonderful to be true. Something I'd thought never to see again ... my mother's handwriting. She read out what was written on the envelope: 'For Lucinda, from her mother, on her twenty-fifth birthday.'

They shared her joy. Stella had tears in her eyes. She said gently, 'When is it, this birthday? Soon?'

Lucinda's smile was radiance itself, though wobbly. 'It's today. Oh, how glad I am that I got it on the very day itself!'

Rob said, 'I wish we'd known. We'd have had a celebration.'

Lucinda said slowly, 'I couldn't have had a lovelier day ... the trip to Glenorchy, meeting Annabel, then tonight I had my first glimpse of Walter Peak through the moongate. And now *this*!' Her colour flooded back.

Rob rose and held out a hand to Stella. 'I think, in these circumstances, you'll want to be alone. We'll be off to our beds.'

Giles said, 'I'll go too. I'll leave a flask out in the kitchen for you, Lucinda.'

They went out, leaving Lucinda with her birthday greeting from the past.

It was the most bitter-sweet moment of Lucinda's life to date. The anticipation was so wonderful and so terrible. Because she knew beyond doubting that although an aura of love would emanate from these pages, there would also be truth, a truth that must have caused her mother much agony in the writing. All of a sudden she felt just as if Kenneth Darling's hand engulfed hers as it had done so often when she was a child. Warmth flowed into her. As if he said, 'Take the sweetness out of it, Lindy-Lu ... it's not given to everyone to have a loved voice, long stilled, speak to them out of the past.'

So she *would* savour the sweetness of it to the full. There would be a greeting for her birthday. It had been the strangest birthday of her life, with no word from anyone. Oh, gifts

111

would be on their way from Trudy and Ivan, but they would have been sent surface and long ago, and would be still following her around. But this greeting from Mother . . . to be able to read words penned by her again was the greatest gift the day could have brought her. Except that——

The first two pages were delightful, full of fun, loving, tender. They recalled the years they had spent together. What a madcap family they had been! Then Mother had got to the point. 'I am hoping to come to New Zealand for your twenty-fifth birthday, dear, to tell you this, but if you are reading it, it means I've not been able to make it, for one reason or another, and our lives have been such adventurous ones, one never knows. Though if anything should have happened to me, Kenneth will tell you. But I must guard against all eventualities in case he too is not able to come to you.'

Then Anne Darling had gone on to tell her that which she knew already. But some of it was news to her. She learned that Sylvester had deserted Anne and her tiny daughter just as he had deserted his wife and son in Queenstown, New Zealand. It hadn't been that he had feared exposure . . . that had caught up with him later, it had just been that he was a lightweight, immature in spite of his years, unable to bear family responsibilities. Not for him the ordinary cares of domesticity, the bind of having to get a babysitter in so they could go out to dinners, theatres, dances, all the gay life of Singapore. He'd wanted life to stay on a courtship level, a honeymoon level, so he had gone without word or trace, and the disillusionment had been severe.

Worse still was to come, when the full horror of knowing it had been a mock marriage came out. Anne didn't dwell on the poignancy and drama of that moment when the police came to her door to make inquiries, but on how wonderful her parents had been to her and to her child. Then she asked Lucinda's forgiveness that her judgement had been so at fault that she had fallen for a man like that and so robbed her daughter of a name, of a birthright.

Then the tempo and atmosphere of the letter changed. In five short words: 'Then, darling, I met Kenneth! If I hadn't picked a good father for you, dear, at least I gave you the finest stepfather any girl could have had. You were as close to him in kinship of spirit and interests as if you had indeed been

112

flesh of his flesh and bone of his bone. I have a sure and certain faith that his philosophy, his outlook on life, is so imbued in you that you will not let this knowledge I have had to pass on to you, in any way tarnish your happiness, or make you feel any sort of shame. Nor do I ever want you to look for faults in yourself, for weaknesses that could be attributed to your father. You have all his sweetness, but none of his instability. You have a strength of character that you must have inherited from his mother. I'd thought he was an orphan, but when this was made public, she wrote me from Australia, and I took you to see her. She had not known for years where her son was. When we left her, after a very healing month, for me, she put her hands on your head and gave you her blessing.

'In some way she removed from me the stigma I felt, helped me to face life again. She died a few months later—of a broken heart, I felt. Your father—though I mean Kenneth, of course—has put in a couple of pages for you too. But, if you're reading this, it can only mean that we've both gone on ahead to a world where there is no disillusionment, and where all things will be made plain to us.'

Kenneth's letter was even more wonderful than she expected. Even before reading it Lucinda would have had no doubts of his love for her, but in case she had thought it had made any difference, he assured her that his three children had an equal place in his heart, and that in kinship of spirit, she had been nearest him. When she had read it, Lucinda shed the tears she had not been able to weep when she had read her mother's. Those tears washed any bitterness and resentment she had known out of her heart. The only anguish she knew was for that young girl who had been Anne Sellaby, who had loved, and trusted, and lost. She looked back at a phrase: 'You have all his sweetness.' So it hadn't been all sorrow. Her mother had retained *some* dear remembrance of her springtime love.

Lucinda carefully refolded the sheets, put them back into the envelope. She would put them into the fire-proof cash-box where she kept their other letters. Now she would go and have that hot coffee Giles had promised to leave for her. But when she came into the kitchen, it was lighted, and he was there at the table, reading.

He said, 'If you want me to go, I'll make for my room right

113

away, Lucinda, because you might just want to read that letter over and over and not have any other contacts to overlay it for tonight. Nevertheless, I couldn't bring myself to go to bed and leave you up alone. I guess it must have brought back your loss. I know it would me had it been from my mother in these circumstances.'

Lucinda smiled at him mistily. 'I'm glad you waited up, Giles. Thank you. I need to come down to earth now. Reading those letters—there was one from my father too—has been a deeply emotional experience I wouldn't have wanted to forgo. In fact, I wish everyone who suffers sudden bereavement could have that experience. I feel as if a curtain has been lifted. They wrote those letters knowing I would only read them if they'd gone. So it's as if they stretched out a hand to me.'

Giles nodded. 'Are those letters to be shared with your brother and sister?'

'They're to have theirs. On the same day. I imagine they'll be different, which is right and proper.' Oh yes, very different. Anne Darling had said: 'It would be too painful for you to tell the twins, so we've told them. They have their letters, sealed, in Ivan's keeping, for them to read on your birthday.'

Giles began to pour the coffee, hot, aromatic. He knew how she liked it by now—black, sugarless, with a blob of cream on top. He drew a plate of buttered toast out of the oven. Lucinda was surprised to find she enjoyed it. She bit into it with obvious relish and saw a gleam of something that could have been respect in Giles's eyes. They were more blue than grey in this light. When he was angry they were steel-grey, cold, hard. Then what emotion made them blue? Oh, what an inconsequent thought to have on this momentous night, but then life was like that.

They went on to chat about other inconsequential things. He was really very—well, kind. She was aware that he was trying to loosen her up, to dispel tension. Much better than a sleeping-pill. He was perceptive, almost like Kenneth Darling in his understanding. Some of his stories concerning characters among the guests were irresistibly funny.

Then suddenly, just when they were on the point of turning in, he seemed ill at ease. As if, once they stood up from the table, he was uncertain about something. She looked up at him inquiringly, her chin tilted on one side, and her lop-sided dimple flashed out, turning her face immediately from a certain sadness of expression to an urchin mischievousness. 'What is it, Giles? I've never seen you at a loss before.'

He grinned back, a relieved blue flash in his eyes, creasing at the corners. 'Well, let's admit it. I'm afraid something I'd like to do might seem a little clumsy and obvious in the circumstances.'

Lucinda burst out laughing. 'I bet I know what it is—you'd like to wish me a happy birthday, and feel it wouldn't—quite —be the thing! Oh, do go ahead, Giles. I'd feel very flat if you didn't.'

He laughed too. 'You've hit the mail on the head. That's it.' He put his hand in his pocket, fished out a twist of tissue paper. 'I don't know if you're aware that the gemstone jewellery we sell as souvenirs in the restaurant is my work? It's a hobby. Wakatipu is famous for the variety and colour of its stones. This one I was particularly fond of because it was perfectly shaped. I found it in the Ros Scuir, the river that runs through Red Spur Gully. It's a bit of red jasper. I feel the colour is just you.' He was unwrapping it as he spoke, and held it out to her in the palm of his hand. It was a pendant, set in the gilt clasps she had seen in the souvenir showcases, and it was strung on a fine gilt chain. It lay in her hand, glowing like a ruby. She could imagine it embedded for centuries in the mountains back of Red Spur, till gradually, but remorselessly, it was trundled down to the lower reaches, ground to this perfection of shape by aeons of glacial and water action. And here it lay in her palm, as a token of kindness from a stranger.

She looked up at him with eloquent eyes. He said whimsically, 'I'll not be banal after all and say happy birthday. It's too prosaic. What ever we say, in any case, my Maori cobbers say better. *E iti noa ana, na te aroha.*'

Lucinda said almost beggingly, 'But you'll tell me its translation, won't you? Because I know only the odd word or so of Maori.'

He laughed teasingly. 'That I will not, it might make you vain. Or—well, let's leave it at that.'

She put out a hand, clutched his sleeve. 'Oh, please? Well, at least say it slowly, so I can find out some time myself, Giles?'

But he wouldn't. It was both intriguing and exasperating. So, laughingly, at the foot of the stairs, they parted.

Lucinda stood a long time in her room, staring down at the pendant in her hand. It had been a nice touch. If he had put an arm round her, kissed her, even lightly, she'd have put it down to his fondness—even weakness—for women. His gay Lothario ways had brought him almost to the divorce court, but this, somehow, had been a comfortingly brotherly gesture. A brother? She had no true brother now, just two half-brothers.

She wondered if she could have liked her Mordred half-brother as well as Ivan. She ought to be getting on with her quest, finding out if Sylvester Mordred's wife was in need of money. Because if so, Lucinda would like to try to have her share go to her. But if her son was a good son, and inherited as next-of-kin, he might share it with her. But if he wasn't, if he was as selfish as his father, Lucinda might just have to reveal herself and try to have the money turned over to that woman who had been so deeply wronged. Some time she must seek legal aid on it. She had a strong suspicion that in the event of no will being found, nothing would go to the boy's mother, seeing she was divorced. So Lucinda dared not—yet—burn that will, as had been her first impulse.

She put the pendant down and picked up her letter again. Her mother had said, 'I felt so terribly sorry for the first Mrs. Mordred. Oh, I was never the second, but it was, after all, the name I bore, unknowingly and falsely, for two years. But *I* was now free of him, and besides the scandal and the case, *she* had to face the machinery of the divorce court too. I wrote to her, in case there was any way in which my evidence could assist her in this, but she never wrote back. I felt I had done her a great wrong—however unwittingly. I said I quite understood if she didn't wish to answer. She must have felt that way, because she didn't. I've always hoped that somewhere, some day, she found the sort of happiness with someone that I found with Kenneth. I hope that when your father served his sentence, he did repent, and that he wrecked no other woman's life. And I hope he went straight and found a measure of happiness. Even if I had no right to take marriage vows, I *did* take them, and said for better, for worse. Though now, of course, I had no right to share those things with him. Well, darling . . . I think you'll forgive me for being such a poor chooser, but because of that, and because it's so easy to fall for the charmers, I'm going to ask you to be very, very careful into whose hands you commit your own future.'

Lucinda wondered why it was the last sentence that stabbed the most. Was it because her mother had written it against this very hour her girl was facing now? As if she didn't want history to repeat itself?

Lucinda turned away restlessly from the thought. Her eyes went to the pendant. Yes, there was a certain sweetness in Giles too, something that made you reluctant to believe he was a trifler. Because trifling with a married woman *was* nasty, no matter how much you tried to gloss it over in your thoughts.

Giles always said the right thing at the right time, made the right gesture, had the correct touch, knew, perhaps by instinct, what a woman's mood was. But had he in him anything of faithfulness, of true integrity, or was he just such another as her father, taking the delights of loving, never the responsibilities or the consequences? Well, she'd been warned right from the start.

She took out the big deed-box that held her treasures. There, under the photos, was her mother's scrapbook. She had been a great lover of poetry. Lucinda always felt near her when she dipped into it. She flicked it over now. Her eye lit on a page where her mother had put an exclamation mark beside a poem cut out from a magazine.

It was just as if her mother had endorsed these sentiments. When first her mother's things had come to her, Lucinda had wondered at this, because then she had not known her mother had loved anyone save Kenneth Darling. It was called *The Bell* and was by a Tasmanian poet, Norma L. Davis, but had been published posthumously. The first two lines riveted Lucinda's attention now:

> '*You have such charm of manner, and you know
> The potent power of a word, a touch....*'

She read on. Yes, no doubt it could have described one Sylvester Mordred and Anne had recognized that. The last lines came up at her:

> '*Your clear eyes glow so steadfast and so true
> It seems sheer sacrilege to harbour fears;
> And yet, and yet, each time I think of you
> Some dark bell peals dire warnings in my ears.*'

The recollection of a pair of concerned eyes, eyes that were sometimes grey, sometimes blue, came up at her. How well he had known what to do tonight. He had ministered to her gently. She had felt there was a depth of understanding in him. But——

Her mother had done well to time that dark bell's warning in her daughter's ears. Yet a desolation greater than the first anguish of knowing she was not Kenneth Darling's daughter swept over her now.

CHAPTER SEVEN

LUCINDA was glad of the return of Christopher and Kirsty Adair. What fun they were! Christopher had clapped her on the shoulder at their first meeting. 'What a great girl you are, Lucinda. Mother and Dad put us in the picture right away. How I wish I'd been there to see that Arlene get her come-uppance! You must be very quick on the uptake. It's about time someone like you took my poor little cousin Giles under her wing and saved him from himself! For all he's such a great hulking brute, he hasn't a clue how to extricate himself from such affairs. The minute we see him getting involved with someone else, we keep our fingers crossed till it's over. He can't help heading into these things—he's been like it since schooldays—and they all take him seriously.'

Lucinda said to herself, 'Except me. I was forewarned.'

Aloud she said, 'Well, that makes two of us. He's helping me out of a difficult situation. I suppose your mother told you, did she? Because you'll have to know when Janice and Harvey come here.'

Christopher nodded. 'I take it, from what Giles and Mother told me, it hadn't gone too deep, anyway? So I don't need to proffer sympathy, do I?'

She laughed. 'No, I grieved more over the fact that Janice felt so awkward about it, she assumed I wouldn't want to see her ever again. So I think realizing that this had hurt me more than losing Harvey put it into right perspective for me.'

'Good girl! So now it's behind you and you're looking forward into a new future. I only hope—from what Mother's told

118

me—it's here. We could do with someone like you round the place. Mother tells me you love the garden. It's taken some of the responsibility off her shoulders. She hates to see it slipping back. It did a bit this year over Christmas. Our regular chap took ill, and this new one, as you know, isn't full-time. He can only just cope with the maintenance, and barely that in the growing season. I could see she was more relaxed as soon as I got home, just at the thought that you'd offered to work in the garden instead of the house. Of course apart from that she worried terribly over Giles last year. Said the mud might stick if it got into the courts. Some has, of course.'

Lucinda thought with resentment that Giles had no right to have worried Star like that. It was not enough to be fond of people—you also had to keep worry from them, on your account.

Christopher was like his mother, tawny-haired, with blue eyes, and Fergus was like both of them, plus Giles. Mhairi must be like her mother. She wasn't. Christopher whisked Lucinda over to Larch Lodge to meet her. Kirsty was a Scandinavian type. 'Takes after her mother's mother who was a Stanger from Orkney,' said Chris, tweaking the snowy-blonde locks.

Lucinda laughed, 'I'd imagined you a second Mhairi.'

'Oh, Mhairi's like my father,' said Chris. Lucinda couldn't see it, but was tactful enough to just agree. Certainly Robert Adair was dark, but there the resemblance ended. Maybe Chris didn't want his father to feel left out.

Despite Kirsty's decorative appearance, she was a ball of energy and practicality, had a flair for organization and managing staff, and the harmony of the restaurant atmosphere was largely due to her.

Finally Lucinda excused herself. 'I've had so much time off, I feel I'm not earning my salt. I've made up my mind that terrace rockery must be weeded today.'

She ran up to her room and got into blue jeans, with a scarlet jersey pulled over them, and was soon at it. What a lovely family they were, the Adairs. She must be careful not to put her roots down too deeply. Otherwise it would hurt too much pulling up the tent-pegs. More mixed metaphors! She laughed out loud as she yanked out some tenacious bindweed.

'I like a woman who laughs when she's all alone,' said a

voice above her. Giles.

'I'm not alone,' she pointed out.

'But you thought you were. What amused you?'

'I was mixing metaphors even in my thoughts.'

'Such as?'

She shook a reproving head at him. 'Thoughts aren't always meant to be shared.'

'Are you good at that, Lucinda?'

'At what?'

'At sharing? I've an idea you aren't.'

She jerked her head up to stare at him. 'You've got to be joking. Of course I'm good at sharing. We were brought up that way ... and not just sharing between each other, but sharing with everyone. Why, Giles Logie! When you work among refugees all your life, that's the keynote ... sharing, so what *do* you mean?'

He didn't look abashed. His eye was cool and steady. 'I didn't mean sharing *things*. That's not the hardest to share. I meant sharing yourself. You have a reserve in you that I don't quite appreciate.'

'Does that have to matter? That *you* don't appreciate it?'

'Yes. It does.'

She dropped her hand-fork and stood up, measuring glances with him. 'I can't think why. We are just ships that pass in the night.'

'Hardly.'

She spread out her hands in a gesture of helplessness, as if he could not, would not understand what was so plain to her. 'Well, if you want to split hairs ... a *few* nights! Listen, Giles, once we were on a ship in mid-Atlantic. We took a sick seaman off a merchant ship that carried no doctor. Ours operated, and we put the lad ashore at Panama and he was flown home. So we'd given him what aid he needed and then parted. *That's us.* I saved you from a few moments' embarrassment, and perhaps helped preserve a marriage. In return you're saving my face with regard to Harvey and Janice. When they're happily settled here and it won't appear obvious, I'll break it up with you and move on.'

'If you're allowed to.'

A line appeared between Lucinda's beautifully arched brows. 'I can't think who'd stop me.'

120

'It might not be a *who*.'

She stared.

He laughed. 'I've a feeling the lake will never let you go. That you're bewitched. It's cast its spell over you—plus the fact that you saw the moon at the full through the moongate. If legend is true, you'll never be the same again.'

She was intrigued in spite of herself. 'Legend? But that gate isn't old enough to have a legend. You said your father built it for your mother.'

'All moongates are involved in the same legend. It belongs to the mysterious East. I wonder you didn't know of it. You spent a lot of your life there.'

'Then what does it mean, this spell? What does it do to you?'

'It means that whatever scene you see through the moongate when the moon is full remains for you the one spot beloved over all!'

Lucinda said most suspiciously, 'That sounds much more like Kipling than a legend out of the East. I think you're making it up. Kipling was speaking of his beloved Sussex. I know, because Dad knew most of Kipling by heart.'

'And was there any poet who knew the East better than Kipling? I expect that's where he got it from ... that phrase. So I do *not* think you will be going from us in three months' time. You'll be here still when your hair is turned to silver.'

Her voice was harsh, because she knew by now that the moongate *had* worked its spell, but she was going to benefit by her mother's experience. 'Then it can't work with everyone. Maybe this reserve you talk about makes me immune to its magic ... and I'd like to get this patch done before lunch, Giles. So, if that's all you came out for, then——'

'Oh, it wasn't. I had a phone message for you, from Wanganui. Harvey. He's managed to satisfy Janice that everything is right with you—because of me. So she isn't coming down. Says if he likes the house, she's sure she will, and would rather save the money than have an expensive air-trip down. Fair enough. They're advancing the wedding date—next month, the fifteenth—and want to know if it will suit you to be brides-maid then. I said you'd ring them back to discuss things to-night. I didn't want to hold him on toll too long. Silly chump should have made it a person-to-person call. I said it would suit us fine. We'll fly.'

'*We'll* fly?' repeated Lucinda. 'What——'

His eyes danced. 'Harvey has asked me to be best man!'

Lucinda sat down on the rocks, winded. 'Why you?' she asked, when she recovered.

'Well, for a start, his best friend won't be there on the earlier date, he'll be on vacation in Australia, and next, he thinks this will scotch the tongues wagging up there. He's convinced that all your mutual friends, once they see the two of us together, will stop saying "Poor Lucinda" and looking daggers at him and Janice. You'd better consent, Lucinda, because that poor chap feels no end of a heel, you know. And you played your part very well when he was here, even if you seem to be slipping a bit since.'

She said slowly, 'I suppose we'll just have to go through with it. But, Giles, isn't it disrupting for you, besides being expensive? I've an idea if I offered to pay your fare, you'd be offended and say I was not only reserved but devilishly independent to boot.'

'And you'd be right. Now listen, girl, take that too-serious look off your face and get a bit of fun out of the situation. No one is going to bludgeon you into marrying me, you know. I've an idea that the calculating looks all my loving relations have been casting upon you, have scared hell out of you. I go up to Wanganui every couple of years or so to visit Aunt Caroline, Dad's sister anyway, and it's eighteen months since I saw her. We'll take about five days off. Janice wants to talk to you about the dress tonight. I told Harvey to tell her we have a rattling good dressmaker here if she sends a sketch down, and said you'd look glorious with your colouring in burgundy velvet.'

'You what?' said Lucinda, then she burst out laughing. 'Of all the effrontery! The bride decides the colour and the style ... in fact, everything. All right, Giles, I'll go along with this. It looks as if I have to. The sooner they're married, the sooner this farce can end. And Giles, don't, I implore you, argue about that again. I'll bring this to a full stop as soon as possible. Oh dear!' she looked down at what she had been holding in her hand. 'Now look what you've made me do! That's not a dandelion, it's a day-lily! I really think you ought to sack me!'

Lucinda wasn't surprised when Stella and Robert asked her to go to church with them, but had to hastily reassemble her expression, wiping off her surprise when Stella said, 'You'd better come in our car. Giles has to be there early.'

'Why?'

'Because he's on duty at the door this month, handing out the hymnbooks, welcoming visitors and so on. Giles is on the Kirk Session.'

Gracious, one somehow didn't expect the philanderers to attend church even, much less be office-bearers. On the heels of that thought came a more charitable one ... it was just as if Kenneth Darling had spoken directly to his stepdaughter, chiding her for a Pharisaical judgement, asking her who the church was for if not the sinners.

Giles had overheard Stella's last remark as he came in. 'Oh, she can come with me just the same, I want to show her the church before anyone is there. I thought yesterday when I took our stuff in that it's our most beautiful Harvest Festival yet.' He turned to Lucinda. 'You'll particularly appreciate it, I think. The women who decorate are not only artists, but they've got an appreciation of the world scene. In contrast to our own bounty, they've got small tables dotted here and there with displays of the meagre meals of other lands.'

... Even without a single flower this church would still have been breathtakingly beautiful, though the glorious display of ears of wheat, oat sheaves, rowan berries brilliantly scarlet and orange, red geraniums, maple leaves, poplar leaves, dahlias and roses, and the huge orange globes of pumpkins, rosy apples, purple and green grapes, the crusty monster loaf, the glass of water, the open Bible on the snowy cloths, all added to the beauty of holiness.

It was a new church, yet its interior was as hallowed as if it had been there for centuries. Perhaps because the entire back wall was built of enduring stones from the lake and river sides, a grand symbol of enduring things, with a plain empty wooden cross hung against it. A soft gold carpet the colour of autumn birch leaves spread over the floor, and some of the furniture had been brought from the old church to enhance this. It was light oak, carved traditionally and also with native flora and fauna, fitting in a land that had brought its religion from the Old World, to flourish in the New. Giles said, 'Our other

123

church, in this parish, at the Frankton Arm, has a landscape window behind the communion table, looking right up-lake. I must take you to see it. There are two schools of opinion on that. Some think it can be distracting. I don't think so, myself. I even wonder if some day we ought to replace the frosted glass in our side windows here and bring a little of the beauty of lake and mountains into St. Andrew's. But come on down to the Sunday school and see our view from there.'

They descended the stairs and Lucinda caught her breath. There was Walter Peak and the dreaming, bright-roofed town, but silhouetted against the vivid blue of the lake was a cross of Iona, set in a solid green base of polished marble, the gift of a tourist from Los Angeles, a minister who had dearly loved this church.

Suddenly Lucinda's eyes blurred. 'Oh, how Dad and Mum would have loved this. I do wish they could have seen it!'

At that moment the Minister and his session clerk came in and were introduced to Lucinda. She managed to control the tears.

She found it moving the way the more formally attired residents blended in with the casually dressed tourists. A bus drove up and disgorged about thirty people in the older group, but another spilled out a crowd of happy, laughing youngsters in an organized tour from a church three hundred miles away.

She was enchanted to find in the congregation the two doctors who had attended the sick of this area in rugged days, facing great perils of blinding snowstorms, landslips, flooded rivers, on their errands of mercy. Lucinda had read both their biographies, in Kenneth Darling's collection. Giles came and took a seat beside her when the congregation was all gathered in, and gave the preacher his complete attention. He seemed completely unaware of Lucinda at that moment, which was right and proper. The sermon deserved it, too, it was as rugged and compelling as the heights and depths about them.

How complex was this Giles Logie? One moment he was a high country farmer, as rough-hewn as they came, imbuing one with a sense of trust, of dependency . . . and the next as subtly flattering to women as an eighteenth-century trifler—and which was real, she did not know.

It was the week before the wedding when Lucinda overheard a

family conclave beginning. They had no idea she was in the little servery when they came in. At first she took no notice, then she heard Chris say, 'I don't think for a moment she's got a show of getting hold of any of it, but she'll have a darned good try. What do you think, Dad?'

Robert's voice sounded grim. 'Just as you do, son. She'll stir up any amount of mud if it comes to a court case. She'll say how devoted she was to him in spite of it all, the only one to stick to him—on the strength of two visits at the last ... that he'd promised her she wouldn't lose by it. She's so predictable. I have a feeling she won't win, but it would be unpleasant, to say the least. Oh well, we'll try to negotiate, and meantime don't let it get under your skin.'

Chris said, 'I just wish I'd never heard of it, that's all.'

Lucinda decided it was no place for her, got the far door open and slipped away. It sounded like a family turn-up and they'd be horribly embarrassed if they found her there. She'd go over to Leith Lodge.

She found Kirsty backing her Mini out. 'Oh, Lucinda, be a darling and take the children down to the school bus, would you? An absolutely huge lot of tomatoes have come in, and I'd like to start bagging them for the deep-freeze. They're marvellous to have, for later, but my heart always fails at the thought of it. I always wait with the children till the bus comes.'

'Right. Let the others know where I am, will you, Kirsty?'

What a marvellous life this was. Office work couldn't begin to compare with it. Here you were part of a family, appreciated, loved, and the air was like wine, with a sweet breeze blowing off the mountain tops, untainted and free.

There was the faintest hint of dewiness in the mornings now, and little blue hazes clung lovingly to the valleys and the folds of the lavender hills. Perhaps a sign of rain to come. Well, the thirsty land would welcome it.

They waited a few moments. Just as they looked to see the first signs of dust rising that heralded the school bus, a rider turned the bend of the road ahead. Mhairi screwed up her small, adorably pert nose. 'The saints pweserve us! I thought she wouldn't be long descending on us. It's a pity she didn't stay in Austwalia!'

Fergus was derisive. 'You didn't think anything of the kind. You heard Mummy say it to Daddy. See!'

Mhairi was offended and stuck her chin up. 'There's no weason at all why I couldn't have thought of it myself, before Mummy did.'

Lucinda said hurriedly, 'Who is she? She's a magnificent rider, I'd say.'

Mhair said grudgingly, 'She can wide all wight. She's a show-jumper. Another of Giles's girl-fwiends. Here's the bus.'

Fergus said, 'Her name's Sheena Arkwright. *We* don't like her. 'Bye, Lucinda. See you tonight.'

By the time the bus had left, Lucinda had decided not to start up the Mini. It might startle the horse. At least that was what she told herself. In reality she wanted to see what Giles's taste ran to.

Horse and rider looked one. Sheena rode a chestnut, had chestnut hair that caught every glint of sunlight and was carelessly, yet stylishly tied back. She wore a loose marigold shirt over tan trews, and her profile, as she reined in and looked down on Lucinda, was bewitching. She also looked as if she were well aware of all these things.

There was no diffidence in her approach. There was even a slight drawl in her tone which made it faintly patronizing. 'You're driving Kirsty's car, so I have to presume you're working at Drumlogie.'

It was out before Lucinda could stop it. 'Or else I've stolen it,' she agreed.

Sheena looked at her. 'Was that meant to be funny?'

Lucinda's voice was gentle. 'Well, if it was, it just didn't come off, did it?' She pressed the self-starter and the engine sprang to life.

Sheena Arkwright said, 'You've not answered my question.'

Lucinda might be a missionary's daughter, but she could give as good as she got. 'Question? I hadn't realized you asked me one. If you mean your presumption that I worked at Drumlogie—well, yes and no. I'm a friend of Giles's and I give a hand where I'm most needed.'

'Good lord! Still another. Attached or unattached? He never seems to mind which.'

Lucinda knew she was supposed to flinch, but she laughed instead.

One beautifully arched eyebrow rose. 'More humour ... perhaps I'm dull this morning, but I see nothing to——'

126

'I'm sorry. I couldn't help it. It just seems so strange to me to have comments like this from someone I've so recently met.'

Sheena's eyes narrowed. 'I think you can't know who I am. I'm a member of the family. We're cousins.'

'I hadn't realized. Then possibly it *is* all right to gossip about Giles. But anyway, the *affaire* Arlene is as dead as mutton. She and Mark have been here quite recently, just as ordinary guests. I hadn't realized there was more family to come. The only cousins Giles has introduced me to so far are Chris and Kirsty.'

'I'm no relation to *Giles*, I'm Chris's cousin. Through his father.'

Lucinda was instantly aware of disquiet within her. Why? What did a relationship, or lack of, matter to her? Oh, only that she thought this beautiful girl spelled trouble.

She said, 'Is it all right with you if I turn now? It won't startle your horse?'

'My mare,' corrected the girl. She smiled thinly. 'You won't unseat *me*. Go ahead, I'll follow you up.'

Lucinda was surprised to find how ruffled she felt.

As she swung over the bridge to Leith Lodge, she saw Giles emerge with Kirsty, saw his eyes flicker downhill, say something to Kirsty, then they came to the car as Lucinda brought it to a halt.

As she got out, Lucinda was surprised to hear Giles raise his voice. 'Lucinda, my love, I've been looking everywhere for you. Mrs. Swindon wants you for the first fitting of your bridesmaid's frock this morning. Before eleven, if possible.' He leaned forward and kissed Lucinda lightly, full on the lips. He whispered, 'Play up, trouble approaches.'

Another of Giles's girl-friends, Mhairi had said. But this time she'd certainly play up. Even a philanderer like Giles deserved something better than this exquisite creature with the bad manners and waspish tongue. So she turned her face and kissed him back, just a little to one side of his mouth.

She saw the creases deepen at the corners of his mouth. 'Full of surprises, aren't you? But slightly off target. Still practice might put that right. Had a change of heart, love?' His voice was just a whisper.

Lucinda was candid as she whispered back, 'Well, I like this one even less than Arlene.'

Kirsty gave a snort of subdued laughter. 'Oh, Lucinda, you're the one for here all right! I love folk who are frank. So many people these days water things down.'

But they all behaved beautifully when Sheena Arkwright came up with them. In fact they were too, too polite.

They knew she couldn't have failed to notice Giles's affectionate greeting or his words. But she still tried.

'I'd have thought, Giles, that you'd have been letting staff go at this time of year, not engaging more.'

'Why, what do you mean, Sheena? All the temporaries have gone.'

'Oh, I thought——' She gave a wave in Lucinda's direction.

Kirsty and Giles laughed as if it were the greatest joke. Giles said smoothly, 'Now I realize how long you've been away. Though of course it goes back much further than that. I met her in Wanganui, long ago. So she came down here to get acquainted with the Lake County. She's fallen in love with it, fortunately. Are you coming in, Sheena, or do you want to see the others, because——'

'I've a message for you from Rod. He wondered if you'd give him a hand. He's got a bit of fly-strike.'

Giles shook his head. 'Not today, sorry. But I'll see if Neill can. Lucinda and I are going into town. She's got a fitting at Mrs. Swindon's, for a bridesmaid's frock—friends of ours in Wanganui. We're flying up on the thirteenth. Wedding's on the fifteenth.'

The tawny eyes narrowed. 'Some of your Aunt Caroline's brood?'

He shook his head. 'Lucinda's best friend. I'm to be best man. After the wedding he's coming down here to manage a travel agency—a transfer from the Wanganui branch. That'll keep Lucinda happy here.'

Sheena said, 'Things have certainly been moving since I went away.'

Giles agreed with that, suavely. 'Chris didn't tell you anything about it when he met you over there? Oh well, I daresay you and your mother were very, very busy there, Sheena.'

Lucinda wondered at the inflection in Giles's voice. She'd heard him irate and she'd heard him cutting, but never quite that tone. What was it? Despising?

There was a flake of colour in Sheena's cheeks that hadn't been there before. 'We certainly were. After all, *we* got there beforehand, when there *was* something to be done.'

Giles's voice was purring again, 'But not quite enough, it seems.'

To Lucinda's surprise Kirsty walked straight into the house at that.

Giles said, '*They* weren't sent for till afterwards. Your mother could have mentioned it to Chris had she really wanted him there. But it suited her much better to be there alone. Must have been quite a surprise when he *was* sent for. Now, if you happen to want to find out what's going on, I suggest you go up to the guest-house and ask Chris himself. He's with Star and Rob. Lucinda, we've got to help Kirsty with those tomatoes till we leave for town. Goodbye for now, Sheena.'

'Oh, I just came with the message from Rod. Don't forget to ask Neill. Mother and I are not a bit bothered about that other concern. Mother did it because she's built that way, with a strong sense of family duty. I'm sorry you seem to attribute other motives to her. But if I were you, I wouldn't let Chris proceed too soon with the extensions. There's such a thing as counting chickens prematurely. And I'm so glad you have nothing more to fear from Arlene. It was the only thing to do, wasn't it, Giles?—to flaunt another girl in front of Mark. Nice you found a willing one. So long.'

In grim silence they watched the mare disappear over the curve of the hill. Lucinda and Giles were left looking at each other.

'Now how in the world did she know the Arlene affair had cropped up again—and finished?'

Lucinda said, 'I told her. Down at the gate.'

Giles looked enraged. '*You told her?* What in hell did you want to do that for? Someone you'd just met? Spilling it all out! Why, you must be——'

Lucinda held a hand up. 'If I get as angry as you, and I've every right to, we'll find ourselves in a real mess, I warn you. I did *not* spill any beans. That girl was spoiling for a fight. She presumed I was working at Drumlogie. No preliminaries, just that. In accordance with what I thought your wishes would be, Giles Logie, I said no, I was a friend of yours. She wanted to know which kind, attached or unattached. She was trying to set me back, to poison my mind against you. I thought she was a little jealous. You know ... the woman scorned, the green-eyed monster and all that. I was supposed to ask what she meant, whereupon she would have given me a really beauti-fully embroidered version of the Arlene story, which in any case I'm a bit tired of.

'So I gave as good as I got and said the *affaire* Arlene was as dead as mutton. I did not discuss it *at all*. It was to *prevent* gossip that I let her know I knew. It killed it dead. And that's why I played up to you when you kissed me. Now *grovel*, Giles Logie!'

He burst out laughing. 'You win! Sorry, I grovel!' Then he grew serious. 'I'd better put you in the picture about Sheena and her mother. Yes, there would be a bit of jealousy. We did, years ago, go round together in a crowd to dances and picnics, but there was nothing in it. I thought of her as a sort of cousin too. With those sort of looks she's had plenty of chances, but the chaps can't take her tongue for long. But that's not it, really. It so happens that her mother is a cousin of Chris's father. Of course that was how he came here in the first place and——'

Lucinda flung out a protesting hand. 'Giles, do you mind if I stop you? I'd rather not know. Truly. The less I know, the less can I be accused of spreading gossip. See what happened a few minutes ago? You thought I'd been chatting freely about your affairs with a girl I'd just met. I'd feel much safer to know nothing. All families have differences, skeletons in the closet and so on. We—we have a few in ours! You and I will be involved such a short time and I've always understood that after confidences are thrust upon one, a certain resentment follows, because the one who has done the confiding, longs to recall it. No—please! I just don't want to hear. It seems more Chris's business than yours, and he might not like your telling me. I just love Chris, he's got the loveliest, most uncompli-cated nature of anyone I've ever known. He's as nice as—as a teddy-bear. Let's leave it as it is. And there's no need what-ever to accompany me to Queenstown. Kirsty can do with your help. It served you as an excuse not to go to Arkwrights', let's leave it at that.'

The grey eyes were cold. 'What you really mean, don't you,

is that you don't want to be involved in anything unsavoury.'

'I don't, you know. It didn't sound like that to me. Only some family squabbling. It sounded like money troubles.'

She had never seen Giles so white, so intense. 'You have the most horrible knack of putting people in the wrong. It's not money alone, it's a matter of justice, of fair play, and however we hate it, we're involved in it ourselves. Oh, how I detest a holier-than-thou attitude. You won't listen to what I wanted to tell you, yet you'll get all high-and-mighty about something you know nothing about.

'We're just ordinary people here, but at least we aren't smug! I know what it is. You had a father who was so other-worldly he gave you a superiority complex ... something I've no patience with. I can just imagine you thinking to yourself: I've lived a high-principled life ... the temptations and falls of other people don't mean a thing to me. I don't gossip, oh no. I don't want to become embroiled in anything less than perfection.' Giles snorted. 'So you draw your skirts away from more earthy, human folk. All *right*, Lucinda! Stay here till you've satisfied Harvey that you're not still carrying a torch for him. I expect you've lulled your conscience about this pretence we've put up, the white lies we've told, with the sop that you did it for their sakes. Maybe it would have been more honest to admit you were just saving your own face! It's an honour to have people favour you with a confidence. But you don't care about that. It might soil you a little. And it's not a family squabble. It has its roots in a most damnable situation. I think you'd better clear off to the garden and get some weeding done before you go to Queenstown. I'll tell Kirsty—who might also get rebuffed if she doesn't know—that you would prefer to know nothing about the situation, that you hate being involved in such things.' And he flung away.

Lucinda stood for a moment, battered by his anger, then flew after him. She clutched him. 'Giles, I'm sorry. It—it was only that I was so mad because you accused me of spreading gossip. Of course I'd like to know. I—I'm not like what you said I was. I'm human. I'd like to know. Please?'

But there was no friendliness in the face he turned to her.

'You dammed up that confidence for good. And I'm very doubtful about your motives now, for asking to hear it. You just don't like the picture of yourself I presented to you. *Or* you're afraid I'll not want to carry on our masquerade. I will ... because a bargain is a bargain. You tidied up the Arlene *affaire* for me. I'll do the same for you with Harvey. And when you depart from the Lake County, he may not be too surprised at that. He probably knows only too well what a strange, cold girl you are.'

He went into the Lodge, closing the door with a restrained gentleness that was somehow more insulting than a slam and Lucinda clenched her fingers into fists and fled down the hill towards the bridge and into the trees as if a thousand devils were hot on her trail.

CHAPTER EIGHT

PERHAPS it was as well there was so much to do before leaving for the wedding, and that they had an influx of guests, including a conference. To Lucinda's great relief Giles (probably to save his own countenance) must have said to Kirsty simply that Lucinda thought it best not to know. Because Kirsty said to her the next day, 'You must be the most uncurious girl I've ever met. How sweet of you to say that to Giles. I'll tell you all about it, anyway, when it's over. Take no notice of Sheena if you run into her. She's always had an envious eye on Drum-logie and really exaggerated the gossip about him to keep other nicer girls away from him.'

Lucinda had said nothing much in return, terrified lest Giles appear and think she was, after all, prying. She just said, 'Well, these things happen. Kirsty, how much sugar and salt do you want put in these pans of peas?'

Giles was most attentive to her still in front of the guests and in front of the others. She said one day, when he came into the glasshouse where she was watering plants, 'Giles, when we're alone with Stella and Rob I think you could drop the pose. It's pointless.'

His eyes were steel-cold. 'Nothing I do is pointless. You appear to be able to turn your play-acting—and your moods—on and off like a tap. I can't. It's too risky only playing it up when others are there. One could forget.'

She sighed. 'It doesn't seem difficult to me. There are times when, knowing how hard and cool you think I am, I don't find

132

it easy to play up to you and return your show of affection.'

His voice was very controlled, so the insult implied must be deliberate. 'I believe you think that, being a man, I get a kick out of it. Well, you can get that idea right out of your head, Lucinda. I'm merely being thorough.'

Her own voice went icy. 'Then all I can say is that by the time we're through, we'll both be qualified to go on the stage. How glad I'll be when this wretched wedding is over. Thank goodness they're having only a short honeymoon. The sooner they're settled down the sooner we can stage a quarrel.'

'You'll make a big mistake if it's too soon after. You'll wreck all you've built up. They'll smell a rat.'

She lost the iciness, said hotly, 'Well, I can't help it. This is an intolerable situation. At first it was fun. We even liked each other. And if I terminate it sooner than you think wise, then that's *my* funeral. If Harvey and Janice get suspicious, I just don't care! That won't surprise you—you said I was doing it for my own ends, not theirs. And don't argue with me. It doesn't affect *you* now, only me and Harvey and Janice. Arlene and Mark have gone long since. They're out of the picture. So I'll do it when I like!'

There was a longish silence, then he said, rather jerkily, 'I should have told you. They aren't. I believe they're trying to buy a holiday home here. Queenstown is like that. People come for a holiday and can't bear to relinquish all links with it.'

Dismay settled on Lucinda. Then she rallied. 'But in any case it can't go on indefinitely. I want to get on with life, not waste it in this Lotos-land. There has to be some time-limit.'

He didn't answer, which enraged her, so impelled by some emotion of which she was later to feel ashamed, she said, 'I imagine it's Arlene who's under the spell, not Mark. Did you dally with her too through the moongate?'

Had she ever said Giles wouldn't be on speaking terms with a blush? As she glared at him she saw a dark painful red rise up from his collar to mantle his whole face. He turned, strode off.

Lucinda flew after him, clutched him. He stood stock-still, not turning to her, but not wresting away from her either.

She said to his unrelenting back, 'Giles, I'm sorry. That was one below the belt. I didn't mean it. It should never have been

133

said.'

She felt the rigidity go out of him and thought she was forgiven—oh, perhaps now they could get back on to the old, easy footing of the first few days.

But all he said, tonelessly, was, 'Words are the expression of our inmost thoughts, Lucinda. Therefore you thought those things. Well, I've got to take it. When you earn an unenviable reputation you're fair game for such remarks.' He went off to the stables with never a backward look, and in a few moments was heading into the hills on Rufus.

Lucinda didn't like herself much. She kept a guard on her tongue for the rest of the time till they must leave for the wedding. Giles was away from the guest-house a good deal of the time, feeding out to the calves, drafting sheep, fencing, attending to the hundred and one things of the station life, with Neill.

But at nights he was always there, entertaining the guests, doing his fair share. Stella had mentioned the wedding to this batch of guests and they were taking a great interest in it.

One evening they begged Lucinda to put her dress on and parade in it. She felt diffident, but it would be churlish to refuse. Stella helped her dress, then said in raptures, 'That frock suits this house, even if in style it goes centuries back—far past any European settlement of New Zealand. You'll look wonderful coming down our spindle-staircase. Just a moment, I'll run down and tell them to watch you coming down the stairs.'

So Lucinda emerged to see a score of faces upraised and began to descend slowly as the dress demanded she should. The ruby velvet flowed out from a shaped waistline that curved upwards to a high bodice inset with a white tucked vestee and a high choker neck, stiffened and edged with a tiny frill of exquisite lace Stella had produced. Long cowled cuffs fell from the elbow-line and were lined with the same white taffeta. Stella had coaxed a curl in front of each ear in a Jane Austen style and had piled her hair on top, so she could set upon it the cone of the mediaeval headdress from the peak of which cascaded a long slender white veil.

Lucinda felt the flush of self-consciousness rising in her cheeks instinctively as the guests clapped. Her eyes went over the heads to Giles, towering at the back, but his expression

134

was unreadable. She stepped off the lowest step and was surrounded. One very avuncular man in his seventies said, 'Well, we won't be there to kiss the bride, but——' and he bent down to kiss Lucinda's cheek. Laughingly they all followed suit. Except Giles.

He summoned up a laugh, said, 'Well, I prefer mine in private.'

Stella said, as Lucinda turned to the stairs again, 'I'll be with you in a moment, Lucinda, to help you out of it.'

When she came into the bedroom she had a box in her hands. 'Lucinda, what's the bridegroom giving the bridesmaid? Is it a necklace or a pendant?'

'Neither. Earrings, pearl ones to match Janice's.'

Stella snapped open the box and there, on a deep blue velvet bed, lay an exquisite choker of large, perfectly matched pearls.

Lucinda gave a cry of delight at their beauty.

Stella said, 'Not real, of course, just cultured ones, but I want you to wear them with that frock. They'll fit round that high neck beautifully. It's the sort of thing that was worn with that style, three tiers deep.'

Lucinda touched them gently. 'Oh, Star, I'll take the greatest care of them. Have they a safety catch? Oh, yes. Good. I'll carry them in my bag, and give them back to you as soon as we return. How perfectly lovely—it makes me feel really one of the family to have the loan of them.'

She surprised a really strange look in Stella's eyes. The next moment it had gone, and Lucinda thought ruefully it was obvious they all wished she and Giles would make a match of it. No doubt they considered her much safer than some of his fancies!

Stella said softly, 'I don't want them returned. They're for you to keep. Only would you think it odd if I asked you not to mention it to the family?'

Lucinda looked at her sharply, then said slowly, 'Star, a loan would be marvellous. You don't have to give them to me. You're thinking that your own daughter in Christchurch might feel they ought to have been handed down to her. And she would be right.'

Stella walked across to the window, looked out, unseeingly Lucinda thought, at the winking lights far down the lake where the Remarkables brooded. Then she turned round, came back, said to Lucinda, 'My daughter doesn't even know I possess them. In fact not even Rob does. Someone I loved very much when I was just a girl gave them to me. I lost him in the end. But these belonged to our happier days. If *you* have them, no questions will ever be asked, and I would so love you to have them.'

Unwelcome tears that she brushed at impatiently sprang into Lucinda's eyes. 'Oh, do forgive me, Star. You said they belonged to happy days, so I shouldn't feel like this—it's just that I—that I hate to think you had any sadness. That you lost someone dear to you.'

Stella smiled. 'I appreciate those tears on my behalf, and the sting has gone out of the sadness long ago because of Robin. I've been a very fortunate woman. Life is like that. At the time some things are too poignant to bear, to dwell on. But the later years give you something not dreamed of in youth: The faculty of being able to retain the sweet and forget the bitter.' She put out her hands and took Lucinda's. 'I want you to remember that, dear. I don't think this business of Harvey marrying Janice has gone very deeply with you. Or else you've put up a very convincing front, but if there *is* any sting in it for you, don't foster it, don't brood on it. Things have a habit of coming out right in God's good time. It's a good idea to take what else life offers you and not to dwell on the-might-have-been.'

The tears spilled over. Lucinda had to use her handkerchief this time. She smiled through the tears. 'They're happy ones, Star. Oh, how lucky I was to meet up with someone like you at this time. I miss Mother so. We were such pals. And right from the start you've reminded me of her. Not just your colouring, but your way of looking at life, your gaiety of heart. I do wish Mother had known you.'

Stella's voice was shaky with emotion too. 'I wish I had.' She put her arms about Lucinda, kissed her. 'She must have been a wonderful mother to produce a daughter like you. And, Lucinda, we could do with you here. Don't move on.'

She didn't ask for a promise, which was just as well.

Wanganui seemed a great distance away—perhaps because they had three different planes: the small one to Dunedin, the jet to Wellington, the medium one to Wanganui.

This was a welcome interlude. The wedding had no poignancy for Lucinda now. She detected a great relief on the part of Janice's parents when she arrived with Giles. Mr. and Mrs. Gilman were staying in Lucinda's home. Lucinda had told Mr. Ames to take it off the market till after the wedding.

To make the attachment between herself and Giles seem *bona fide* she refused to stay with them there, saying they'd have other relations to put up, in any case, and Giles wanted her to stay with him at his Aunt Caroline's on St. John's Hill.

As they flew over the Wanganui River in their descent, Giles said, 'Lucinda, let's call a truce. I mean apart from our play-acting. We've both said things we shouldn't. Perhaps it was inevitable in our situation, being forced together like this. Maybe our tempers got ragged. We'd both had—well, tempestuous times behind us, emotionally. Let's relax a bit. This won't be easy for you. I'd like to see you carry it through with a high heart.'

Her voice was low but intense. 'Even if you think my motives are not high-minded? If you think I'm only saving my own face?'

To her amazement he didn't come back with a sharp answer or a huffed one. He put his hand across the arm seat between them and took her hand. 'You can forget that. I don't profess to understand you in all things, Lucinda, but then I suppose I'm an extrovert, and not afraid of showing my emotions. In fact I daresay I let them run away with me at times. I'm not very understanding about a certain reserve and coolness in you, but what I said about your motives that day was in temper. I didn't really believe it. I believe you entered in on this deception solely with the view of sparing Harvey and Janice's feelings.'

Reserve and coolness! If only he knew! Why, her every pulse was throbbing because he was holding her hand. Everything within her clamoured to respond to him, to turn to him, encourage him. But she wouldn't. This was exactly what her mother, wise in her own generation, had warned her about. Not to fall for the philandering males. Not to succumb to the undoubted and potent charm of such men, who knew so well how to disarm ... even as now Giles was disarming her, with the caress in the voice, the well-timed apology, the seemingly frank look, seeking an answering look from her and ... yes, she had to admit it ... getting it! But though she would appear to accept his gesture, she would not permit herself to fall completely under his spell. No doubt he was only intrigued because she was resisting him. Once she responded to him, he'd lose interest. This kind always did.

The pressure on her hand increased. He said ruefully, 'How cold-blooded can you get? You're even taking time to consider *this* overture. I'd like to see the chap who could stir *you* up!'

Her eyes flashed. 'Yet once you called me a volcano.'

'So I did. But only in the way of losing your temper, Lucinda. Not in love.'

Her hand moved restlessly under his. '*Were* we talking about love?'

'Blest if I know. This conversation is losing me. If you shrink from the word love, then let's term it the extraordinary relationship that exists in our society between a man and a woman!'

Lucinda burst out laughing and looked up into his eyes. 'Sorry, Giles, I'm getting too intense. Thanks for saying you didn't doubt my motives any more. I admit that *did* sting. Right ... we're down, and taxiing to a stop. Let's get all the fun we can out of this.'

That night, lying awake in the big feather bed Giles's delighted Aunt Caroline had put her into, Lucinda was wondering what her reactions to Giles might have been had she not been made aware so recently of her true paternity, if the wicked irresponsibility of an unfaithful father had not robbed her of her birthright, giving her the knowledge of her mother's betrayal; if her mother had not begged her to use discrimination when it came to choosing a mate. Because if all that had not impinged so recently and devastatingly on her own life, she might blindly, or wilfully, have believed that the episodes of Giles's past life no longer mattered.

Women were like that. Always thought they could reform the flirts. Not all heeded the warning signs....

> '*Your clear eyes glow so steadfast and so true*
> *It seems sheer sacrilege to harbour fears;*
> *And yet, and yet, each time I think of you*
> *Some dark bell peals dire warning in my ears.*'

As Lucinda turned over once again in an effort to find sleep, she wished, not for the first time, that she had never heard of that dark bell.

But after all, they enjoyed themselves hugely. Perhaps because the mutual friends of Janice and Lucinda so wholeheartedly fell for Giles. They found him irresistibly charming and said so. Lucinda laughed over the uninhibited remarks of the young fry, Janice's teenage cousins, who outspokenly envied Lucinda.

'My, but you've got yourself a marvellous guy this time, Lucinda! Fair go! He really puts Harvey in the shade! That mouth, for instance!'

Lucinda, her long brown eyes gleaming fun, said wickedly, 'What do you mean, that mouth? Define it for me?'

'It's the contrast. You must know it yourself. All that craggy sort of build-up, you know ... Jutting eyebrows, like cliffs, tussocky kind of hair, prominent bones, those stern lines down his cheeks, that piercing glance, like an east wind sometimes, then you look at his mouth and ... oh, it would melt mountains!'

Lucinda gave a peal of laughter and fell back on some cushions trying to hush up. Giles came in, demanded, as he looked down at her, 'What on earth's got her? You might share the joke.'

Lucinda got up, sat cross-legged, rocked herself to and fro, said, 'I'll just tell you, Giles, it would make a cat laugh. Nicky said that——' She got no further. Nicky launched at her with one of the cushions and stifled the words on Lucinda's lips. Paula joined in, pinning Lucinda down and keeping the cushion over her mouth.

Giles looked interested. 'What's all this about? It's a real rough-house. Lucinda, my love, you're showing me a new facet of your character. She's been so stately, girls, it's something to see her acting like a hoyden.'

Nicky said threateningly, 'Lucinda ... at the moment I'm letting you breathe ... just ... but if you don't promise to say nothing to him, I'll shove this over your nose too! Just nod your head if you promise!'

Lucinda, winded with Nicky on top of her, nodded vigorously and they took the cushion away. She sat up, tousled, laughing.

Giles said, 'They have a touching faith in your word, darling, more than I have. What was it? Some girlish confidence? Some rhapsodizing over someone Nicky has a crush on?'

Lucinda's dimple flashed out, her eyes danced. 'I shall never betray their confidence. After all, it's marvellous to have anyone trust me as they do, especially after a dirty crack like that from you.'

The four young girls crowded round Giles. 'Tell us, Giles, has she at some time grossly deceived you? It's out of character if she has. Must be the effect love's had upon her.'

He said solemnly, 'That's it. She had all the cunning of Eve *and* the serpent! You might not believe this, but with the sole object of trapping me into marriage she embarked on the most outrageous deception!'

Lucinda gave a startled yelp. 'Giles, for heaven's sake, you utter idiot!'

The girls turned to look at her, eyes widening. 'She—she means it. She's scared,' said Amanda. 'Oh, Giles, *do* tell us. It sounds so romantic. Come on, open up!'

Lucinda said quickly, 'I only meant he was idiotic to make up such a thing. Take no notice of him, any of you. Melanie, don't look at him like that. You'll inspire him into telling you the most far-fetched of yarns. He can't help himself once he starts.'

Giles laughed. 'Look, girls. When we're both old and grey I'll tell you all. When we celebrate our golden wedding. I'm inviting you to that now. You can all come down to Drumlogie and I'll tell of our first dramatic meeting and the greater drama of our second.'

They fell upon him, linking arms around him to make him prisoner. 'Tell us *now*. Well, tell us something if not all. I bet it was romantic. Was it by that dreamy lake? ... be a sport!'

Giles said, 'Well, the second was all that could be desired ... away up in the Chalet, low lights, soft music, wine, dishes served with the gourmet touch, the moon rising over the Trough-of-the-Goblin ... and Lucinda in a filmy burgundy blouse with a vivid green over-dress ...'

Lucinda snorted. 'And the first one, girls, the one he has ignored, was compounded of a wounded hare, stampeding Herefords, a most irate stranger ... one Giles Logie ... and me, *covered with blood and cow-manure!*'

The teenagers gave a howl of frustration and turned indignant faces towards her. 'Now you've spoiled it. And we don't believe it, anyway!'

Giles mourned, 'It's only too true. I shudder to think that some day our grandchildren will ask how we met and I'll have to say I checked their grandmother's headlong flight and shouted at her: "What the hell d'you think you're doing, stampeding my cattle!"'

The girls looked at him and began to believe. They started to giggle. 'But you fell in love with her there and then, in spite of it all?'

Lucinda sent him an alarmed and pleading look. He winked at her. 'It's all right, Lucinda darling, I shan't tell *all*!'

Paula said avidly, 'Go on, go on, Giles. What happened then? You——'

He laughed. 'We went on hurling insults at each other, but she'd grabbed the hare she'd run over, after she'd shoved me out of her way. When I'd quite convinced her I wasn't going to kill it, she permitted me to take it back to Drumlogie and shelter it till it was well enough to fend for itself again. But after an encounter like that, imagine how I felt when I went up to the Chalet that very night, to see the manager and found a beautiful damsel who looked vaguely familiar, sitting all alone at one of the window tables. It was like in a fairy-tale. As if someone had changed a virago into a princess—a decidedly dirty and odorous virago at that! By next day she was staying at Drumlogie. I'm not the sort to let the grass grow under my feet, believe you me! And so it ended, happy-ever-after. Now, brats, I'm taking Lucinda out. It's a glorious evening and the twilight doesn't last as long as ours down South. I want to show her a particular view. Lucinda, my love, retire upstairs and put on thy beautiful garments. That white frock I like.'

As they went out of the room a happy sigh followed them, a collective one, and somebody's voice, 'Isn't he just fabulous!'

Giles cocked an eye at Lucinda. 'Somebody appreciates me, even if not you.'

He headed north from St. John's Hill and towards the coast for a few miles till they came to a cliff-top in the spectacular splendour of a sunset over the Tasman Sea. 'Ah!' he said, in tones of deepest satisfaction as they gained the top of the path, 'there she is ... I was just afraid she might let me down.

Sometimes there's too much cloud.'

There, across far headlands and vast tracts of land, rose up the perfect cone of Mount Egmont, a hundred miles away, silhouetted in royal purple by some alchemy of distance and the evening light, against a sky of smoky bronze, flame, and pure lemon.

The utter peace and beauty of it caught them up. They stood looking into that sunset in a shared silence. There would have been a banality about words that would have robbed this hour of something indefinable.

Finally, Giles slipped his arm about her shoulders and said, 'I scared hell out of you tonight, didn't I?'

She laughed, even leaned against him a little. 'You certainly did! I didn't know what you might let out. Girls of that age are very astute. And there's no holding you in a mood like that. I thought: here we go, of all the irres——'

'You thought: "Of all the irresistible fellows, he's one. Even if I positively hated him a fortnight ago, I've got to admit I'm mellowing towards him." Now, didn't you?'

She looked up at him sideways, the dimple showing. 'Irresistible wasn't the word I was going to use. It was irresponsible. Of all the irresponsible things to do! I thought you'd forgotten the Olivers had been told we'd met in Wanganui long before. Coincidence is a horrible thing. One of these girls might know them, or meet them some day.'

'Oh, what an imagination, Lucinda! Besides, they won't now. They——' He came to an abrupt halt.

She looked up at him curiously. 'What were you going to say?'

He recovered himself. 'Never you mind: I've had second thoughts. It was no more wise than if you'd spilt the beans earlier tonight. I mean whatever it was the girls didn't want you to tell me. Anyway, to heck with that. I don't give a darn now about Arlene and Mark. They just don't matter any more. Lucinda, doesn't a sunset like that do *anything* to you at all? Two people, alone on a cliff-top over a sea like a jewel ... nothing nearer than Australia ... isn't there even a *touch* of magic about it?'

She felt a little breathless ... this wasn't sensible, she knew, but who wanted to be sensible all one's life? Their eyes met, the grey eyes that were sometimes blue, as now, and the brown

142

ones. He drew her round against him, smiling, then shook his head, almost in reproof. 'It wasn't a bit of use your pretending to be cool and indifferent, Lucinda ... not with eyes like that, warm brown eyes!'

His mouth found hers, stayed there. In that kiss Lucinda knew full well why she'd drawn back, instinctively, from the thought of marriage with Harvey. This was *sheer* magic, not just a touch. This was the physical reality of the enchantment that had caught her in its toils when Giles had first led her through the moongate.

For the first time Lucinda wondered if she was right to try to measure her own experience of life beside her mother's. Perhaps Giles had sown all his wild oats. Perhaps now he was ready to settle down. She turned her face into his shoulder, because on the heels of that glad thought had come another, an unwelcome one. She was shaken by a doubt, by a cruel surmise. And she was going to be frank about it.

She lifted her head, looked at him fearlessly. 'Giles, I'd like to ask you something, and please don't get mad with me. I want to know. And please, please tell me the truth, I can take it. In fact, if you say yes to what I ask, I'll just think it was nice and perceptive of you, your good deed for the day. Was that kiss meant to boost my morale for the wedding tomorrow?'

She felt a very slight stiffening within him, then a relaxing. He laughed. 'Oh, Lucinda, you goose! If you can't tell, then you've not had much experience of such things ... which I find rather nice. There are kisses *and* kisses. And though I've got myself the reputation of being a bit of a dope where women are concerned, I've never yet kissed one because I was sorry for her. And I'm *not* sorry for *you*. Harvey's a good fellow for Janice, but you deserve someone more exciting than that.'

She felt a soaring of the spirit immediately. Tomorrow she might regret this softening, but for tonight she was glad, glad.

He said, 'Let's have another, without any doubts.' She had no time to assent. It was something Lucinda would remember all her life and even when she was quite old, she would grow young again, remembering.

She turned round, loosening his clasp a little, to look into the heart of that incredible sunset again. Only a rim showed over the horizon now and the ocean was violet with shadows and advancing night. The last rays made a track of light right to the water's edge and on the black ironsands footprints gleamed silverly. Below, on the Kai Iwi beach, other lovers were walking, the soft murmur of their voices drifting up.

The sun went down and in the far, far west a star gleamed out.

Lucinda was surprised into saying: 'Two places beloved over all ... Kai Iwi in the sunset and Walter Peak seen through the moongate across the Trough-of-the-Goblin!'

'Thank you, Miss Darling,' said Farmer Giles.

CHAPTER NINE

So the wedding was all that a wedding should be and there was no shadow on Lucinda's heart, because, owing to Giles's presence, Janice was as radiant as every bride should be, and positively brimming over with joy in Lucinda's apparent happiness.

As Lucinda finished dressing her she put her arms about her, said, 'Lucinda, the way things have worked out has really done something for me. I feel I'll never be impatient again when things seemingly go wrong. I cried myself to sleep the night you overheard Harvey saying that to me. I couldn't bear that I took my happiness at the expense of yours, especially when I still had Mother and Dad, and you had just lost Uncle Kenneth and Aunt Anne. I couldn't see any way out. It was like being in a tunnel with no exits.

'At first, when I found myself falling in love with Harvey, I thought I'd just clear out, go off to Australia. But once you'd heard us talking about it, there was no rescinding it. Talk about life and death in the power of the tongue! And all the time Giles was waiting for you. And—I'm sure this isn't just wishful thinking—he's so much more the right one for you.'

She caught Lucinda's face between her two small hands. 'He is, isn't he, Lucinda?'

There was no need to prevaricate, to turn it laughingly aside. It was so easy to speak that truth. Lucinda's eyes glowed. 'He is, Janice. I just drifted with Harvey, but Giles is *my* man. So what I overheard you and Harvey discussing wasn't a death-blow. It was life-giving. It gave me Giles.'

A slight sound in the doorway made them turn. Giles was there with Janice's father! Lucinda felt the colour rush up into her cheeks. She said, 'What on earth are you doing here? This is no place for a best man at this time.'

'He's on rescue operations, as a best man ought to be,' said Mr. Gilman. 'I'm afraid this wedding has robbed Harvey of his senses. He's lost the ring. But he's sure it's here. Remember how he brought it over to practise putting it on your finger and you wouldn't, Jan, said it would spoil things? Well, he must have put it down. But don't panic, we'll use your mother's if we can't find it.'

Lucinda said, 'I'm sure I know where it will be. Janice, don't you dare move ... you'll trail your train through some dust if you do. Harvey was slipping it on and off that funny little vase after you said no—the one that's shaped like the trunk of a tree and has a sawn-off branch on it. He was sliding it up and down that bit. Then Mrs. Cummings arrived with that wedding-present. Just a moment.'

She darted off, Giles following her, and Mr. Gilman stayed to admire his daughter.

There it was. Giles's relief was great. Then as she went to rush back to Janice, he said, 'Just a moment.' He went to the door and called out to the others, 'It's okay, that's where it was. We'll be with you in a moment.'

He came back to Lucinda, took her two hands, said, looking her up and down, 'Turquoise ... it suits you.' She was wearing a flared-out quilted brunch coat with ruffles of lace at the neck and short sleeves. Her colour was still high. How much had he heard?

A certain awareness crept into his expression. She looked away hastily. He reached out, turned her chin round, looked at her very quizzically. 'I hand it to you, Lucinda, you're a most convincing actress. We must get you into the drama group.'

She breathed again. 'Yes, I'm discovering hitherto unknown talents in myself. Giles, you must go, I've to get dressed yet. Incidentally, how well you suit formal clothes.' In fact he made her heart turn over.

'Thank you, Miss Darling. I've something for you. I don't see why the best man shouldn't give the bridesmaid a gift as

145

well as the bridegroom. It's a thank-you for your superb reaction that night at the Chalet—a dress ring to match your frock today.'

He brought out a box, sprang it open, and Lucinda gave a cry of delight. A glowing red stone, ringed round with what she supposed were brilliants.

He was pleased at her delight. 'I was terrified you wouldn't accept. You're so unpredictable. And it was a big thing you did for me and for Mark Oliver, seeing Arlene was minded to play the fool again.'

He picked up her hand. She drew it back, laughing. 'Not the left hand, you chump, the right.'

'Oh yes. Well, I'm not in the habit of giving girls rings.' He slipped it on. It fitted perfectly. 'I had a bit of assistance from Janice,' he admitted. 'She pinched that cameo ring of yours for size and met me in town. I don't think you ever missed it.'

Lucinda held out her hand to admire it, looked at the clock, said 'But now you must go. Thank you, Giles, I love it.'

He bent his head, kissed her cheek just as Mrs. Gilman came in saying, 'Lucinda! You *must* start to get dressed. I'm ready. Oh——'

Giles went off laughing.

Janice was starry-eyed over the ring. 'What a beautiful setting ... those tiny diamonds round that ruby.'

'Diamonds? Aren't they——' She took a closer look, started to exclaim in dismay, but had the sense to check it. Janice wouldn't expect Giles to give her just costume jewellery. She had no time to dwell upon it, and anyway, she loved it. She put up a hand to the three-strand choker of pearls when she was dressed. Perhaps, just as Stella had kept this as a souvenir of all-too-fleeting happiness, when it was all over, she would keep this ring when she was gone from sight and sound of the enchantment that was Wakatipu. . . .

She moved as in a dream, said and did all the right things, enjoying with a sort of poignant sweetness, the wonder of being linked with Giles in this way. She even managed to control her tears when Janice's father said to her just before the reception that during the toast to absent friends he would be specially thinking of Anne and Kenneth, and wishing they could see their beautiful daughter.

She felt that the toast Harvey would have to make to her as bridesmaid would be painful for him, knowing that he had once asked her to be the bride, but when he came to it at the end of his thank-you speech for their own toast, he was wearing a huge grin. 'Most toasts of this nature are simply to the bridesmaid, not to the best man, but this is a wedding with a difference. I learned something from my very new father-in-law, after the ceremony, that I felt I must share with you all. I take it it was kept secret only because Lucinda and Giles didn't want to steal any of our thunder, but it's too good to keep to ourselves, and besides, we're departing on a honeymoon and wouldn't like to miss the celebration. The news is that Lucinda and Giles have just become engaged ... would you charge your glasses and drink to their happiness?'

Lucinda only just managed to control her dismayed gasp ... she took a quick look past the bride and groom to Giles, her eyes beseeching him for a lead on how to take it.

Well, she had to hand it to him ... he must have recovered instantly from the shock of it, his eyes were just brimming with laughter. The drinking of the toast gave Lucinda a chance to get her breath. The murmurings and congratulations subsided and it was Giles's turn to rise. He leaned forward a little, looked directly at Lucinda, said, 'Well, the secret's out, my love ... you can now transfer that ring to your left hand....'

In a daze, Lucinda, laughing out of sheer nervousness, and apparently in delightful confusion, did so, spread her hand out and gazed at it, almost as if she could not take it in. She closed her eyes against the room for a moment. Oh dear! Her reassurance to Janice that morning, plus Giles enlisting Janice's aid in getting the ring, must have triggered this off. Well, Giles might have admired the speed of her reaction to his plea at the Chalet, but he certainly deserved admiration for the way he played up to this ... and how much harder it was, in the limelight with the interested gaze of a hundred and forty guests riveted upon him.

'This,' said Janice, as Giles finished his speech and sat down, 'has made my day,' and she kissed her bridesmaid.

At that moment the wine waiter filled Lucinda's glass again. Well, champagne was never meant to be gulped like that, but if ever she needed a reviver, it was now.

Giles and she didn't have a single moment together till after the couple had departed, farewelled with all the trappings by the four teenagers. But at last some of the shouting and tumult died.

Giles was being outrageously affectionate to the girls, paying them compliments, teasing them. With great determination Lucinda detached him from them, which rather thrilled the girls. Amanda said, 'I don't blame you, Lucinda. It's your engagement day and you've hardly had a moment to yourselves.'

Lucinda laughed. 'True, and there's only one place not invaded by guests and that's Dad's study. Giles, come along.'

She turned the key. 'I want no interruptions to what I have to say. Oh, Giles, how sorry I am. Whatever got into Harvey? How could he! I feel so responsible—they're *my* friends and they've positively bulldozed you into this. I—I suppose it's just a combination of circumstances and a bit of wishful thinking on their parts. I mean, they had a guilt complex and we—we played our parts just too convincingly.' She dropped down on to the desk chair, put her elbows on the desk and her head in her hands and moaned.

'If only, only Janice hadn't asked me that question straight out this morning! If only I'd been more evasive. But I got carried away wanting her to have no vestige of guilt left. And of course she tied it in with this darling ring you bought me.' She looked up at him. 'Oh, Giles, if only you'd made it a dress ring, with brilliants, she wouldn't have done this. But a *ruby* and *diamonds*! And all *you're* doing is stand there grinning!'

He burst out laughing. 'Oh, Lucinda, don't be so tragic about it! It was just a confirmation about what we've been trying to put over, after all. Every time I think of the look on your face I just double up! Fortunately everyone put it down to the surprise of the public announcement. It's all right, you goose. Nobody's going to marry you off to me against your will. Engagements have been broken off before now. It doesn't matter a scrap.'

She continued to look aghast. He crossed to her, sat on the corner of the desk, took her hands. 'Come on, come on ... it's done. Let's just take it as a joke. A joke we've put across the lot of them, from the Olivers down to our whole circle of friends. And Star and Rob will be tickled pink.'

Lucinda said, almost piteously, 'Yes, but think how upset they'll be when we break it up.'

He slid off the desk and pulled her up. 'Lucinda, I thought you had more spirit, more sense of fun. Look, I refuse to take you out of here looking like a tragedy queen. Those kids will expect you to come out of here looking radiant ... all dewy-eyed and'—a spark of mischief lit his eyes—'with your make-up smudged! Well, I can certainly fix that!'

His grip was unbreakable and he stopped laughing only to kiss her. Then he lifted his head and looked at her, one eyebrow lifted quizzically. Lucinda recovered her breath. 'Don't you take *anything* seriously, Giles Logie?'

'Life's too short for that. Now I'm going to get that mob out of the hall and we're going to phone Drumlogie with the news.'

Lucinda clutched him. 'Don't be ridiculous! We can't. We'll just tell them when we get there. We can say how it came about then. We can't do that here in case we're overheard.'

Giles said slowly, 'It would be horrid for them if they read it in the papers first.'

Lucinda put a hand to her mouth. 'Oh no, Giles, you couldn't! You wouldn't. Not put an announcement in the papers. That's going too——'

He cried, 'Pax! Pax! There was that woman reporter there. It was nothing to do with me. Didn't you know? She said it was lovely copy for her.'

'But the Wanganui papers don't reach Queenstown—oh, do just let's tell them when we get home.'

'I can see you haven't caught up with things. That reporter wasn't from the dailies. She was from the Sunday papers. It will be all over the Lake County by the time we get home, Lucinda darling—so we've got to ring Drumlogie and Roxburgh. Come on!'

So it was announced to Giles's relations as a *bona fide* engagement. They could do nothing else with guests milling about. Lucinda found herself acting on the telephone as if it were for real. How much those calls would cost Giles she did not know, for Kirsty and Chris were across at Drumlogie and they all had a turn, even Mhairi and Fergus.

Mhairi said, 'Now I can call you Aunt Lucinda, can't I? It's what I'd call a weally wonderful bit of news. And this'll squash Wendy Hillis. I said you'd be marrying Giles for sure and do you know what she said? She said: "Well, he didn't marry any of the others!" and I said, "No, of course he didn't, none of them were nice enough!" Mummy, what are you doing, I've not finished—oh, bye-bye—they're just mean, I——'

They heard Kirsty say, 'You've said more than enough, my darling daughter. Lucinda, take no notice. Though she's right. None of them *were* nice enough for Giles. You're just right for him. Bye-bye.'

'Phew!' said Giles, and they both burst out laughing, but the very tender good wishes and loving joy expressed by the others cut Lucinda to the heart. Marguerite Darroch had cried into the phone—for joy, she had said, excusing herself.

By the time they set off for home Lucinda had schooled herself to accept it till such time as they could break it off. The trouble was, the more delighted the family were, the harder it was going to be to find a convincing basis for the split.

'I never knew such a girl for crossing bridges in advance,' said Giles as the jet soared up over Cook Strait. They were to finish the air trip at Dunedin this time, pick up a new car for Chris, and take it through to Queenstown for him. 'In any case,' said Giles, 'Mother would have expected us to go through by bus so we can see them, after news like this.'

By the time Angus and Marguerite had greeted and congratulated them, Lucinda felt she was being bewitched into a true situation. Marguerite brought out a box tied up in silver paper and blue ribbons. 'Your engagement present,' she said, handing it to Lucinda. Giles's hand found Lucinda's arm, squeezing it. It gave her the strength to be natural. As a box obviously not new came into view, Giles said, 'Oh, I know what this is. Mother always said it would be mine when I married. She's got other things for the rest of the family.'

Lucinda, trembling a little, pushed aside the swathings of tissue and drew out a candelabrum in silver, exquisitely chased. It was George the Third and was by William Fountain and Daniel Pontifex, obviously extremely valuable. Marguerite said happily, 'I'll be glad to have this back at Drumlogie. It's where it belongs. The first New Zealand Giles Logie had

150

it sent out to him by his mother as a wedding-gift. There's a tablecloth to go with it. It was always used on special occasions. It will grace your bridal table, Giles. We'll have the reception at the house, of course. All the weddings at Drumlogie have used it, our silver wedding anniversary, and for the children's coming-of-age dinners. Angus wrote the card himself.'

Lucinda could hardly read it for tears. That inarticulate man had written, 'To the sort of daughter-in-law we've always longed to have.'

Yes, this situation was sticky. How these things recoiled! At first it had been hilarious, something agreed to on the spur of the moment, when a once-met stranger had accosted her and appealed for help. Now they were involving all sorts of dear people.

The Logies had news for them about the road. 'You'll have to go back to Rae's Junction, son,' advised Angus. 'You canna go through the gorges today. There's some more work going on at the Nevis Bluffs. They aren't even opening it for half an hour today. It impedes progress too much, after the blasting. Besides, even if they had been letting them through you wouldn't have dared drive a new car through. Small debris falls and the surface is simply uncrushed rock.'

It didn't matter much to them, Lucinda felt the longer it took them the better. It would give her time to summon up enough courage for facing Drumlogie and the guests.

The winding miles were lovely, but loveliest of all when they came to Kingston at the foot of the great dog-leg lake. The view literally stopped them in their tracks. Giles drew the car to a halt as Lucinda cried out with joyous delight at the sight of it.

He got out, so did she. He put out a hand to her. It was a beauty that had to be shared by the sense of touch, something quite instinctive.

He said, 'Doctor Burns Watson always says everyone should have their first glimpse of the lake from here. But how wonderful ... we've had an early fall of snow ... look at it!' His tone was exultant.

The lake was a long streak of shimmering diamond and sapphire where the sun struck blinding glints from the reflections of a score of peaks and Coronet Peak was dead centre above it. Below the symmetrical perfection of the Peak, the snow-line was as straight as if God had ruled a line and blown away every crystal below it. The Crown Range on the right held a deeper intensity of snow, sheets of virgin whiteness.

They looked up at the immense heights on their right. 'The Remarkables, of course, are too steep for the snow ever to be virgin there ... it falls off,' said Giles. 'It always looks as if the tops get impatient and shake it off, and the sou'westers whip it off too. But look at them, aren't they grand?'

They were, rising sheerly almost from the very road that had been there little more than thirty years. Till then this end of the lake had been inviolate from motor traffic. The railway had come up to the foot from Invercargill, and the steamers had served to bring goods and people to Queenstown.

'That was the way Anthony Trollope had to do it,' said Giles.

Lucinda was enchanted. 'Do you mean Trollope actually came here? My father loved Trollope.'

Giles nodded. 'So does Uncle Rob. His books are in the library. It's a century ago that Trollope and his wife came up here—in winter too, believe it or not! They went back overland to Dunedin by—at first—a buggy drawn by two horses. It was a journey that usually took three days and took them six! No bridges, of course, though some rivers could be crossed with the vehicles loaded on to punts. And from Tuapeka, though he said they had as good a coachman as ever sat upon a box, the horses got buried in deep snow in a cutting and everyone had to help dig them out. The passengers themselves had to drag the coach for the descent and were most thankful when after six hours they reached Tokomairiro below the snow-line and, as he recorded, received great hospitality.'

They came to Drumlogie in the twilight with thrushes whistling softly in the maple grove and blackbirds chit-chatting in a last excited clamour before darkness would silence them.

There were no awkward moments. The instant the car stopped the family came swarming out, eager, excited, unfeignedly glad.

Late that night when they were alone Stella said to Lucinda, 'If only you knew how happy this has made me. You're so right for Giles. You belong here. You did, right from the start. Whatever impulse led you to explore the turn-off to Red Spur Gully, I thank God for it.' She paused, almost as if she thought Lucinda might say something, then went on, 'Drumlogie is a much happier place since you came to it, much happier than at this time last year.'

Lucinda knew she meant that at that time they had thought Giles was going to figure in a divorce case. Stella added, 'And you even have my favourite name for your second name, Rosamond.' Again she looked as if she thought Lucinda might say something.

It was beyond Lucinda to even begin to understand Giles. He seemed so kindred, so understanding, so sensitive and responsive to every mood, to know exactly what to say, to sense a woman's needs, to satisfy them. It added up to experience, of course not constancy—the very thing she must not trust. She must not allow herself to be lulled into an acceptance of this mad engagement. She had been warned. Her mother and that other young wife, long ago, had had no such warning. No dark bell had rung for them, and Sylvester Mordred had ruined their lives. It was all very well to talk of wild oats in the past tense. How could one be sure? And anyway, sometimes the past rose up and hit one in the face.

There was a lull in the bookings. Easter had been early this year and the Anzac Day weekend bookings were never heavy. Everyone relaxed. The trees were at their most golden, the red oaks were beginning to drop their leaves. The green cases of the walnuts were splitting.

Lucinda, standing on the terrace, her hand-fork in her hand, tall and slim in blue jeans and a red checked shirt, said, 'I feel as if I'd like to hold time still, as if I want autumn to stay like this for ever, not to suddenly dim. To beg the winds to leave the leaves alone, not to frolic with them.'

Giles looked at her curiously. 'Autumn will linger a while yet. Most of that snow is gone. As soon as the poplars fade, the larches begin to glow, till the hillsides look as if they're thick with the flames of candles. Especially that hill near Arthur's Point where the larches are baby ones. Besides, there'll be other autumns.'

Lucinda didn't reply. Yes, there'd be other autumns, but not

153

for her ... here. She might see the winter sports beginning. She would like to carry that memory away with her ... guests returning to stack their skis in the big concrete-floored porch, hanging their parkas and ski-caps on the hooks there; when icicles would hang in silver rays from the moongate and Walter Peak would lie beneath the frosty glitter of the Milky Way.

Giles said, 'Star says we're to take advantage of this lull. The Gordons want us to go across to Thurlby Domain and I'm to show you the ruins of one of the most magnificent homes of the area. There are some beautiful trees, planted long before the turn of the century, there. Some are old specimens almost lost to the world. For instance the Cretagus Mollis. It was a native of North America, but was banned from there because of it spreading wheat blight. It's a type of hawthorn. By the time the blight was controlled, it appeared to be extinct, but a visitor from there saw this one at Thurlby, so arrangements were made for seeds to be despatched from there to Canada, for a few years.

'But before we go, I'm going to take you right up the Red Spur. I want you to see the ghost-town there. It has an enchantment all its own. We must go before the frosts get severe.'

'Why, Giles? Is it very steep? Are there rocky faces that ice up?'

'Yes. It's an incredible track. It's amazing the stuff they took up there, packing up miles of pipeline and timber and iron, on horses. It was cruelly hard on the pack-horses, though the men saved the poor beasts all they could—they needed to, the horses were so valuable to them. Some took lighter loads than was desirable because they loved their animals. Every inch of that track is drenched in history, some of it tragic, but a lot of it lighthearted enough. Because when they had reason to be gay, they certainly made merry—picnics, balls, soirées, and concerts galore.'

'Did they dance to fiddles? Or bagpipes? Because of course they'd have no big instruments, over a track like that.'

'Don't you believe it. They had no fewer than two pianos up there, and an organ for the church services. And one of the best-stocked libraries you could imagine. We won't set a day, but we'll leave ourselves free for the first ideal one that comes.

You'll want your sturdiest and easiest brogues, Lucinda. We must get you some tramping boots later on, but they'd need breaking in or they'd raise blisters. Shorts, of course, because we have to ford the river so often. And haversacks. We cross the Ros Scuir at least twenty times, though at present the fords will be low. The early snow has thawed and the freshes are over.'

They picked a dew-fresh morning with a crispness that made them eager to set out. Giles was up early and had the haversacks packed and breakfast ready by the time Lucinda appeared. 'Stock up well,' he advised her, 'you'll be starving again by ten on this sort of track.'

Stella and Rob came out to farewell them. Chris was taking them in the Land-Rover to the far gate where Lucinda had injured the hare.

Stella said, 'You'll take no undue risks, Giles?'

'Not with Lucinda along.'

'And if you were delayed at all. I mean a turned ankle, or a too-deep ford, you wouldn't try Breakneck Crag in the dark, would you? You'd be sensible and stay overnight at the Seven-Mile? We wouldn't be anxious till tomorrow night.'

'I'd do that, Star. Any more Cassandra-like croakings?'

'Yes. If you're showing Lucinda any mines, watch for rotten planking.'

'I'll test every step first. Star, if you don't stop, Lucinda will get so scared she'll turn this trip down! Don't worry, I'm too much of an old campaigner to underestimate this territory. I'll take great care of her—and of myself. Right, Chris, let's go.'

The day really seemed to begin when they were on their own. Lucinda was fascinated with every step of the way. It was as if the wilderness had resented the way men had hacked and hewed into here, changing the faces of the steep river-terraces and even diverting torrents that, after rain, still forced great quantities of water through the narrow channels.

These gullies imprisoned the heat within their narrow rock walls, bouncing it back at one's face. The Ros Scuir—the River of the Red Spur, foamed through these miniature gorges, though at present there was no great depth, except where certain pools had scoured out. If they had followed the

155

tracks of the goldminers it would have been miles longer. The first ones, certainly, had come this way, plunging through, but when they had packed their equipment in, to the strikes, they had had to blaze a bridle-path, and later, when the little town of Red Spur had sprung up, the track had been widened into a hazardous, precipitous road, narrow and rocky in parts, in others a porridge-pot of churning mud where swearing men and sweating horses had dragged incredible burdens.

At times the gorges widened out into sun-filled river-flats, with sweet tussock blowing, each with a hut, each with English trees crowding round it, grown from saplings long ago to provide shade and beauty for future generations. They ate their sandwiches beside one, thick ones filled with bacon and liverwurst, and munched a Cox's Orange apple, freshly picked from the Drumlogie trees that morning.

'It's all right to throw your cores away here,' said Giles. 'In a city street it would be litter-bugging. Here, they'll rot away and the pips will send out rootlets and some day another generation, perhaps our grandchildren, exploring here, will rise up and call us blessed as they pick juicy apples.'

Our grandchildren? Just a phrase ... a general term? Or was he linking them together?

He went on, drawing up his knees and clasping his hands about them. 'I must take you up Tobin's Track across the Arrow some time. There are planks, with netting sides, that bridge it and finish in a many-trunked willow. The children of long ago, from the Crown Terrace farms of pioneer days, used to come right down there and cross to get to the Arrowtown school. Sometimes they were knee-deep in snow, but in autumn they too would come along with apples. I've no doubt they were meant for lunchtime, but from the amount of apple-blossom each side in spring, near the river, I can wager those apples were always eaten before they got to school.'

Lucinda had a sudden vision of those far-off days, with little boys in home-made blue drill tunic coats and girls in white frilled and embroidered pinnies and copper-toed boots, shuffling along in the dust and biting into crisp apples. She said so.

They packed their mugs back into the haversacks, donned them again. Their brogues dangled from the straps, for they were crossing frequently here. Then they left the river bank and climbed high. Suddenly the track vanished in a tangle of native bush, with a small gully cutting it, laced and matted with blackberry. Giles took a small tomahawk from his pack, hacked it away. There, ahead of them, was a huge black pipeline, slippery in places with moss.

'The track's gone here, we'll cross on the pipe. Don't be afraid, Lucinda, it's not far. The irrigation scheme crosses this slip. It's an old scheme, this one, but still used.'

Without Giles she would have been terrified, but she soon got used to balancing for a few yards each time, on the tarry pipes, laughing when she met fine spray forcing up from leaky joins. The cool mist was heaven-sent on a burningly hot day like this. They came over the last pipe, down to a huge river-bed, intersected by three streams, all shallow. Now a steep track rose up, and vanished through a deep cleft on the hilltop.

'They used to bring horses and traps along here when the women and children followed the men. The horses had to be led and coaxed round this bit, though. They had to manoeuvre the carts, first on, then back, on again and again till they got round. One day a woman was coming along here. She was a lass. There are endless tales about her. Just thirty-two and as fearless as they come, Susannah Jetterley. She'd been to Queenstown for stores. She had her little girl and two small boys with her. Just as they got here a wild goat broke cover and leapt from the upper bank across the road and the horse reared. How they didn't go over the bank, trap and all, was a miracle, Susannah must have had superhuman strength that day. But in the first toss, the little girl had got flung right over the side of the cliff. Susannah brought the horse under control, fighting it every inch of the way to the next bend, then she got the boys to hold the horse and flew back, uphill, and peered over, with the most dreadful fear in her heart. Her darling would be lying in the water, on the cruel rocks, far below. She wasn't. Small Genevieve was caught in a tangle of native clematis, as securely as if she'd been in a hammock.

'She was laughing when her mother reached her. "I'm like the baby in the tree-tops," she said. "Rock-a-bye, baby!"'

'Somehow Susannah got down to her and, with the little girl crawling before her, they reached the top The boys couldn't believe their eyes when they saw both mother and sister coming towards them. Just as they reached the trap my forebear,

157

the first Giles, came round the bend, leading his pack-horse. He'd been up to the settlement with stores, and was taking stuff out. He reached them, and Susannah fainted clean away in his arms. He took them back, of course.'

After skirting some steep precipices, the track widened and kept widening. Lucinda stopped and said, 'Look, graveyard ivy, or should I say periwinkle?' Blue stars blossomed everywhere among the green, shiny enamelled leaves.

Giles looked a little sober, stooped, cleared away the tendrils to expose a stone. 'Graveyard ivy is more apt, here.'

He pulled till she could see it all, then took a stick and scraped at the lichens. A flat stone, that must, for all its size, have been levered into position by hand, to mark a tiny grave. 'Mike Jettering carved the inscription himself,' said Giles, and read out:

> ' "Eliza May, beloved daughter of Susannah
> and Michael Jettering, aged two years,
> two months."

'Small Eliza died of diphtheria the year before Genevieve was born. Susannah managed to nurse the boys through it. That was why it was such a wonderful thing that the clematis vine caught and held her other daughter, till her mother could bring her to safety.'

Presently, on a great stretch of green sward, above the river, they came to the township, marked by great splashes of autumn colour and running wild with old, pale roses. Above the derelict houses reared Red Spur itself, a gigantic upthrust of rust-red rock.

'They always called the footpaths sidewalks here, because so many of the miners had been on the Californian gold-fields. See, Lucinda, you can still find them, under the clover.' He took his stick and scratched away. The sidewalks were of flat, schist-like rocks, used as paving-stones. They found small huts, whose sturdy chimneys had outlived the walls, held together as they were with mats of ivy. There were the remnants of one or two more pretentious houses, the caved-in sections of the public hall, with a walnut piano, with great brass candlesconces on it, leaning drunkenly against the far wall, because one leg was rotted right through.

Lucinda took from the top of it a fragment of music, 'Now

is the month of maying.' Had someone from a far, northern clime longed for the may blossoms to bloom in May, instead of November, as they did, here in the South Pacific? But young hearts were the same the world over, and perhaps here, far up the gorges, among these wild mountains, they had sung right merrily: 'Fa la la, each with his bonny lass, a-dancing on the grass.' She was glad it hadn't been all grimness and fear and hardship. She said so.

Giles said, his eyes on hers, 'I'm glad you didn't keep that fancy to yourself, Lucinda. Things like that ought to be shared. Could it be you're losing a little of your reserve?' He reached out for her hand. She freed it quickly, but was amazed at the words that leapt to her lips. 'Giles, you go too fast for me.'

It ought never to have been said. It was only encouraging him. She felt dismayed. But he just laughed. 'I never learn, do I? I charge at my goals like a bull at a gate. I get it from my mother. Dad said to me some time ago, "I think this time you'd better make haste slowly, son." '

A crease appeared between Lucinda's brows. 'About what?'

'About you, of course. The first time you met him.' He laughed. 'I've never taken his advice before, Lucinda. Well, let's leave it at that just now. Maybe it was good advice. Come and see the little chapel. The bell still rings. Stella always gets us to ring it when we come up here. She says it wakens the spirit of worship and the echoes of the past for all the people who lived and died here.'

The chapel wasn't safe to enter, but the bell-tower was of stone, separate, and built for all time. Was there ever such a place as this, so richly endowed with mineral? The rocks had been split by a master craftsman, loving his work, and revealed all the vivid greens, slate-blues, lavenders, roses, of the Waka-tipu stone. And what a bell it was, silver-toned and true, ringing out peal after peal, radiating sound round that charmed circle of the eternal hills, striking back in faery echoes from rock face and canyon wall.

Long after Giles had ceased ringing it, the echoes came back to them. 'Some day,' he said, 'I shall write a poem that satisfies me, to those echoes. I couldn't say how many attempts I've discarded.'

'Oh, do you write poetry?' Lucinda was sparkly-eyed at the

thought.

Giles said, 'I wrote quite a bit in my teens. I've got a bit rusty, but lately——' and suddenly he turned brick red.

Lucinda actually felt sorry for him. She pulled a spray from an old derelict picket fence, 'Oh, look, Giles, honeysuckle.'

It was creamy, with a burnt-orange heart, and its sweetness seemed distilled from the hearts of all the women who had followed their men here and laboured to make a garden out of a wilderness.

As they turned to leave the gardens of yesterday, she was suddenly glad Giles wasn't always master of the situation, that he had his reserves too, that he could redden with self-consciousness. Perhaps—she clamped down on the thought.

Not all bells woke echoes of sweetness. Some were warning bells, dark bells.

CHAPTER TEN

THEY made less pace on the return journey. Their energy was naturally depleted. But suddenly Giles began to increase pace.

Lucinda protested, 'We've plenty of time, haven't we?'

He pulled a face. 'I think there's a thunderstorm coming, despite that good forecast yesterday.'

Lucinda looked upwards, but ahead of them. 'But the sky's so clear. Isn't it just darker because we're down in the gorge?'

He turned her round, to see an inky, heavy cloud over the far peaks, menacing, dropping down. 'It's away back in, Lucinda. That's the trouble. It's right in the headwaters area. A flash-flood can reach here in three-quarters of an hour. We'll be out of this gorge in no time. But there are three more to be negotiated and all those other cuttings, all with straight, precipitous sides. I wouldn't dare risk one of them if that storm breaks where and when I think it's going to break.'

Lucinda said stoutly, 'But didn't you say that once the miners got the track done, they only used the river-bed when it was very low, as a short cut?'

'That's true, we won't be cut off, but I'd never get you through before dark—it's much longer—and believe me, though it's been done in dark in times of great urgency, it's no track for night-time. There's Pluto's Staircase to be negotiated, that's a bit where the old road has given way altogether. You have to climb a face with natural steps in it now, but you need daylight, of course. Never mind, let's get out of here first. It may pass over. If not, we'll bivouac. Stella would never forgive me if I took any unnecessary risks with you. There's Irishman's Hazard and Ryan's Slip too. However, it may pass.'

It didn't. They were only ten minutes out of that gorge when the heavens back in the hills were rent asunder, it seemed. The echoes that lived in the gorges flung back the sound of the thunder till Lucinda, who thought she loved the grandeur of storms, turned and clung to Giles. He patted her shoulder. 'Sounds worse than it is . . . as if all the devils of hell are let loose. Not to worry.'

She shuddered. 'You'd think the rocks would split asunder.'

'They never have. We get slips with heavy rain, but not with the actual roar of the thunder But the catchment area has copped it all right. See . . . that storm-tail . . . it's slowly but surely coming this way. We don't want to get drenched as well as bushed, we'll have to run for Thaddeus O'Brien's hut. Come on, lass!'

They raced across the tussock to where, sheltered by an immense sycamore, was an old stone cottage, in better repair than most. It even had a door that was sturdy yet. They gained it only seconds before the intensity and fury of the storm rolled over them. It was glorious to watch, sheltered by Thaddeus's roof-tree, built to resist elements like this. It even had two rooms, one just a closet of a room, with two cobwebbed bunks in it. The living-room had the usual immense stone fireplace with an old rusty iron kettle hanging from a swee and plenty of dry brushwood piled up in the hearth, and a great stack of it in the alcove.

An old French clock, of marble, stood on the mantelpiece, stopped dead, never to go again. There were some ancient magazines and some books, a few crocks, some home-made chairs and a table, a rough colonial couch, with a mattress on it, and a big chest.

'The chest contains the blankets,' said Giles, 'they get fly-blown otherwise. This hut is always kept supplied. Trampers use it, and so do we, when mustering. It's on Drumlogie property, we reach away in here. Besides, Star put us in some extra food, in case of something like this, and that last flask has soup in it. I reckon the temperature will plummet and we'll be glad of it. Plenty of tinned stuff always here. Chris and I can come up and replenish soon. It'll be a long night, I'm afraid, but I can tell you stories of the old days that will make you feel you're in the lap of luxury, Lucinda. After all, there's a lamp, and plenty of kerosene.'

Suddenly he came across to her, took her hands. 'Lucinda, look up at me. I want to tell you something, whether you want to hear it or not. Something any girl would want to know in this position. There was never anything in that affair with Arlene of which I was ashamed. It's not gallant to give a woman away, but now it's important to me—and, I hope, to you.

'Arlene came up here, as a single woman, got a job with us. I daresay I was still really a greenhorn. Mum was always warning me that some day I'd get into a pickle with one of the girls I partnered round, that some time on of them would take me seriously. But with Arlene, it was just that I was so darned sorry for her. She was years older than me. She put on a great act about having fallen for a guy who didn't want her, and said she'd come up to the mountains to try to heal a broken heart!' He looked at Lucinda sharply. 'I'm telling you the truth. You'd better believe me. I simply didn't know she was a married woman. Mark was so immersed in business, she'd left him, and was ripe for any mischief.

'But one night, apart from that, I realized that she wasn't the broken-hearted woman I'd thought. In fact she was cheap. Oh, Lucinda, a chap feels no end of a heel telling a woman this about another woman, but I'll damned well not let you go on thinking these things about me any more. She was just a bit too sexy. Oh, gosh, I wish there were more words in the English language to explain this sort of thing. It makes you sound such a self-righteous prig! She went too far one night. Thought I was too—well, strait-laced. I got mad and she got mad and called me an inexperienced and callow boy. *Boy!* I was thirty-two. But she was dead right about the inexperience. Talk about the woman scorned! She said she had a husband and had written to him to tell him that there was someone here who wanted to marry her, and hinted that she could give him cause for divorce. Me! Did I go up in the air?

'To do her justice, I think she genuinely loved Mark, only he was all for making money, and his veritable passion for the power and excitement of business made him put less into his marriage than he ought to have done. He's learned his lesson now, though. Mother and Dad and Star and Rob were horrified. Arlene spread all sorts of stories. I couldn't do a darned thing about them, but one thing I wouldn't do was knuckle down to her. It almost amounted to blackmail. She'd told such outrageous lies to Mark; she thought he was going to divorce her anyway, and she'd be left without anyone. So she put the screws on me. I wouldn't take it. Neither could I—quite—expose her to Mark. I flew up to see him—unknown to her—and told him I thought she had deliberately used me to try to make him jealous, that she thought he did not love her. But evidently, about the time you came into it, he'd slipped back into taking her too much for granted again. So, to try to stir him up, she ran away up here again. I hadn't seen her, but it was a sticky moment when Mark got put into the same gondola with me. But you were there alone ... waiting for me, had I but known it.'

Lucinda didn't say anything for a moment, and he said roughly, 'Well, believe me?'

Lucinda's heart was singing, but she didn't want to give too much away ... yet. But she raised her eyes, carefully subduing any outward hint of how she felt, and said simply and truthfully, 'I do believe you, Giles, and I think it was very sweet of you to tell me now when'—she looked away for a moment, then steadfastly back—'when I might have felt very strange, here in this remote hut with you, remembering you'd been almost cited as co-respondent in a divorce suit.'

He gave her hands a tremendous squeeze, then dropped them. 'Thank you, Lucinda. Well, that's one stile taken. This, staying here tonight, is a matter of common sense. It often happens in the mountains, for safety's sake. I give you my promise I won't as much as kiss you. Now, if you would do something about getting the dust off that table, I think we could have that soup. There are still some rolls left—though we'll leave two for breakfast—and we'll open a can of beans. There's a cake of chocolate here and some ginger snaps. Sheer luxury! And you can have the bedroom later, I'll have the couch.'

Before the light faded, when the downpour had been ceased for some time, they put on their wind-cheaters and fared forth to look at the river from the top of the cliff they had climbed. It was a brown, frothing torrent where logs and smaller debris were being hurtled about as if they had been kindling wood. Lucinda looked back at the hut where firelight showed, leaping and dancing, through windows and door. 'That's the most glorious sight in the world,' she declared.

It was a morning straight out of Eden. Giles was busy outside when she woke. She came out to find he had washed in a little stream, but was fingering his chin ruefully. 'Being benighted is much easier on girls,' he vowed. 'Look at you . . . almost band-box smart.'

Last night she had taken her Black Watch trews out of the haversack and had placed them over a chairback. No need for shorts this morning. They wouldn't be crossing any rivers. Her shirt was nylon and hadn't creased. Her dark hair was beautifully layered, so it fell into natural curves about her face and caught the sun in little gold glints. She washed her face in the stream, and applied make-up, Giles watching her with an amused gleam in his eye. They had left-over hard-boiled eggs, a little battered now, and toasted the rolls for breakfast. The mugs of coffee were fragrant and steaming hot.

Giles said, adjusting her haversack straps, 'Well, it's a tough morning ahead of us—Irishman's Hazard, Ryan's Slip, Pluto's Staircase, the lot. Some will be sheer clay after that rain, and we'll be sliding down on our seats half the time, but I think we'll make it by lunch-time. They won't get anxious till night-fall anyway.'

It was all magnificent fun to Lucinda. After what Giles had told her last night, she could face anything. It was a lovely world, and one she need not leave now. The dark bell had rung its last, unnecessary warning. He had never loved Arlene, the womanizing had been local gossip, he'd merely partnered a lot of girls round . . . so, from now on, Lucinda would let things take their natural course.

One thing remained. She would have to tell him she was Sylvester Mordred's daughter by his bigamous marriage. But, for all his pride of ancestry, she was quite sure Giles would

164

just brush that aside. It would not matter. He would be able to tell her where young Sylvester was now, or know enough of his or his mother's whereabouts and subsequent history for them to find them, and then decide how to act. Stella would know. She had lived at Drumlogie most of her life, in fact till her brother Angus had married, Lucinda thought.

They got horribly scratched because the blackberry was rampant and vicious here, and they were stained and bedraggled in no time. But presently, with all the obstacles behind them, they came to the clean sweet tussock-land and were on gentle slopes, dropping down to Drumlogie's lower acres.

There was something Lucinda wanted to say to Giles before they reached civilization again. 'Giles, thank you for telling me what you did, last night. I'd completely misunderstood. That first night—round the lake-shore, after we dropped Harvey, you said you'd taken a pretty hard knock over Arlene. That she'd become reconciled to her husband. I thought you'd known she was married and had taken it badly when she went back to Mark. I thought—with that gossip reaching me via Marny between our first and second meetings—that you were a—oh, Giles, don't get mad with me—that you were a womanizer! I'd been told you were. And our second meeting sort of confirmed it.'

He started to laugh. 'Oh, Lucinda, I can see how it all added up—and Mhairi's clangers added fuel to it, I suppose. Womanizing ... my innocent partnering of the local girls to dances and what-have-you!'

He sobered up, said, looking down on her as they strode along, 'Thank you for saying sorry, Lucinda. We'll be able to make a fresh start now. It's all right ... I won't rush you. I'll give you time to get rid of that old image of me and start again. I'll go along with that cautiousness of yours. I know I rush in where angels fear to tread.'

All of a sudden Lucinda didn't want gentle tactics. Her whole outlook, her whole world had changed. She said, 'Giles, I'd reason for that cautiousness. You know how it is with parents. They want their children to avoid the sort of mistakes they made themselves. My mother was married twice. Her first husband was a ne'er-do-well. She thought he'd sown his wild oats—but hadn't. She had a very unhappy life till she met Kenneth Darling. I'll tell you all about it some time. So she warned me against the womanizers. It's too long a tale to embark upon just now.'

He burst out laughing. 'Careful, Lucinda, or all my good resolutions will go up in smoke. But——' His eyes met hers, then glanced away. 'But—all right, I'd better leave it just now. We'll be in the bosom of the family very soon. And in view of all that's happened, it wouldn't hurt either of us to mark time for a bit.'

They came round a bend in the track to see briar roses festooning a fence. Giles said, 'Lucinda, I'm going to take a slight detour. It won't take long. We've got a private burial-place here. There's a grave I'd like to put some of these roses on. It's through here.'

A track no wider than a sheep-track led to it. He told her it went back to the early days. 'All the Logies were buried here and some of the old-timers who had wished it, including Blue Duck Jake and old Once-upon-a-Time.'

They had made the Little Acre, as they called it, in the V of the small valley; the graves lay there in the sunlight, the epitome of peace. Since sheep moved freely about, the turf was as short as if mown, but the graves were well tended too, and all of them had flowers growing on them. Giles nodded when Lucinda said so. 'Stella comes up here a lot. She always has.'

They walked among the rows, Giles pointing out the graves of his forebears. Then he stopped at a tiny grave, with a scalloped stone kerbing round it, and an open book as a headstone. He dropped down on his knees. There was a hollowed-out circle in among the purple alyssum that covered the grave. It held a vase with some rosemary in it and some wilted sweetheart roses.

Giles said, lifting them out, 'I'll get some water from the creek. Stella can't bear this one to have no flowers.'

It was just as well that he hadn't looked at Lucinda and that it took him a few moments, because she was staring, frozen, at the inscription. It said:

'Jocelyn Rosamond Mordred,
Beloved daughter
of
Stella and Sylvester Mordred,
aged one year and ten months.'

It took Lucinda right between the eyes. *Stella*. Stella *Mordred*. And the child's second name was Rosamond, even as her own second name! They must both have been named for someone belonging to Sylvester. Perhaps his mother. But Stella ... oh, if only Giles would hurry now. There must be some explanation. It couldn't be his Aunt Stella, surely. Oh no, God. Please don't let it be. Don't let it be Star.

He came back, knelt down, picked up the briar roses. Lucinda managed to get her vocal chords into working order, even sounded normal.

'Giles, you said Stella. Do you mean Star? That she was married before to this—this man with the unusual name?'

'Yes. Did she never tell you? I thought she would have done, you've been so close.' His voice harshened. 'He was an utter rat, a complete scoundrel. He not only deserted her, but later made a bigamous marriage. There was a dreadful scandal when it all came out.'

She managed to react as he would expect her to, even though her brain was reeling, and, fortunately, the moment Giles had the roses placed, he got up, held out his hand to her, and they continued on their way.

His voice still held the savage note. 'It was all so public. Even now Stella sometimes feels she's being pointed out as the innocent party in that old scandal. She must have suffered horribly at the time.'

Lucinda said, 'And so must the other woman too. How terrible to find out your husband was married to someone else.'

'I believe Star, being what she is, was as sorry for her as for herself, said that at least her son had a name, one that was legally his—the other woman had a child too. But I've always had my doubts.'

'Doubts ... about what?'

'About whether or not the other woman knew he was already married.'

Lucinda lost her neutral tone. 'What a horrible thing to even think! And anyway, surely no woman would go through a form of marriage she knew to be bigamous. That would make her a bigamist, too!'

He laughed and patted her arm as they went striding on. 'Oh, Lucinda, you're just like Star, always flying to someone else's defence. Dad was the first to voice that doubt, I believe, and Star really went for him, said she was ashamed of her brother. Of course this is all hearsay, it happened long before I was old enough to know.'

Lucinda persisted, 'Why would a woman do such a thing?'

'Oh, Dad had worked that one out. Because her parents were in a good social position in Singapore, and they hadn't been pleased when he started courting her. They thought he was a no-good. If she was madly in love with him—I think he *was* a charmer, you know—then she might have taken this way out.'

'I couldn't believe that,' said Lucinda hotly. 'I just hate to think you could even entertain such thoughts!'

He chuckled. 'Oh, Lucinda! We shall never know, shall we? Those people are never likely to cross our paths again. But all right, it was a mean thought, I apologize. I can see I shall have to watch my step. You've just realized I'm not a philanderer. If I'm not careful, you'll be labelling me hard-hearted next!'

Lucinda said, 'But I hate to think Star was treated like that. It seems incredible that it happened to her—though you did say, the day you read me that poem in the library, she had known sadness.'

'He was a gay, irresponsible sort of chap that people couldn't help falling for, at first, I believe. Dad said his parents were far from happy, though they liked him too, to start with. But he was so fond of the women. Star thought he had sown his wild oats, that he would settle down. He was a spendthrift. They lived in Queenstown at first, but Sylvester fell behind with the rent, piled up debts. My grandparents let them have the little cottage with the garden, in Red Spur. I told you long ago of a girl who'd made that garden. I didn't tell you who then, because I hardly knew you. Stella was great at makeshifts. She sold their furniture to pay the debts, and borrowed old stuff from Drumlogie. Times were bad, the world was just recovering from the Depression. As fast as she got them debt-free he ran more up.

'Little Jocelyn fell ill. Sylvester spent most of his time in town with his wild, irresponsible friends, gambling, drinking. I don't suppose any of us can guess all that Star endured. He wasn't even home when Jocelyn died ... and Aunt Stella was expecting again. Mother and Dad were with her that night. It certainly sobered Sylvester up when he got home and for three months or so, till after her son was born, Star had the highest hopes he might really have reformed for good.

'But he couldn't take the duties that come with fatherhood, broken nights, the fact that Star was tied to the house. Her family used to baby-sit sometimes, but she didn't care for the company he took her into, and was terrified at the state he was in sometimes when they drove home in his rattletrap of a car. She often thought he'd never take the bend at Arthur's Point. She thought he might kill them both and her baby would be left fatherless. So she stopped going out with him. And one night he just simply didn't come home. Stella had the publicity of a search ... but he was never traced. The war broke out shortly after.

'It wasn't till someone from Queenstown, years after, visiting Singapore, found out he was there, apparently married, sponging off fairly wealthy in-laws, that it all came out.'

There was a question Lucinda was dying to ask, but she must phrase it very carefully. Where then was Stella's first son? Where was Sylvester Mordred Junior, her half-brother?

Mercifully, Giles, all unknowing, supplied her need. 'After Sylvester disappeared, Stella couldn't bear to call her son by his father's name. It reminded her too bitterly of him. The baby was only a few months old, so she had his name changed to Christopher, the name she herself had wanted to call him from the start. Then later, when she met and married Uncle Rob, they changed his name to Adair. Uncle Rob legally adopted him.

'Stella never heard from Sylvester again after the trial and his imprisonment. She was tempted to go to him, to try to help him, but my father persuaded her not to, that if she did, Chris could come under a very undesirable influence. She was granted a divorce, and years later, she married Robert.

'Then, out of the blue lately, we had word that Chris's real father was dying in Brisbane. He'd written to Chris, calling him Sylvester Mordred, of course, and it reached him, as he'd sent it care of Drumlogie. It gave Stella an awful turn when she collected the mail at the gate. It was only a line or two, saying he was far gone, and had come into money, and had made it all right for his son, and would like to see him. Chris and Kirsty went across right away—they were there when you

169

arrived, remember—and Robert followed them a day or two later.

'They got there too late. Chris hadn't wanted to go, had wanted nothing to do with him, but Stella thought Chris deserved something from his father, and if it was left to him he'd have to accept it, anyway. But no will was found—so I expect when everything is sorted out, it will come to Chris. This is what I wanted to tell you, ages ago, Lucinda, but then'—he smiled—'you didn't want to know. Now you must.'

Now you must know. She knew what he meant. He thought that soon this pseudo-engagement would become a reality. Last night, and earlier this morning, she had thought so, too. Was it only last night she had been so happy? Was it possible? Because now an immense gulf, not of days and hours, but of cruel circumstance, separated them.

Because Star had already suffered more than enough. She couldn't marry into any family without telling them the truth about her parentage, much less this one. It was the one thing she couldn't and wouldn't do to Star. Lucinda would remind her in every way of the manner in which she had been betrayed. No wonder Robert had seen a likeness to Mhairi in her. A hot resentment boiled up in Lucinda. She didn't want to resemble her scoundrel of a father. She didn't, she didn't!

Giles said, 'Oh, here's Chris now. We won't let on that we've been talking out this. It's weighing on his mind as it is, with all the legal business.'

Chris was in the Land-Rover, heading their way. He drove up, hopped out, laughing at their muddied appearance. 'We thought that storm had made the crossings impossible and that you'd get out, by the old track, about lunch-time or just after. So I did a bit of work up here, fixing that fence over the creek, in case you'd like a lift for the last mile and a half. Lucinda looks a bit bushed. She's quite white on it.'

He put an arm round Lucinda, hugged her. 'Don't let that hefty cousin of mine wear you out, girl. He's a tough hombre, that one!' Lucinda wanted to hug him back. He was her half-brother, and he was so gorgeous, so uncomplicated. Stella had made a grand job of bringing him up, solo, with help later from Robert Adair. But Chris would never know she was kin to him.

As they drove, Chris said, 'We reckoned you might have

made Thaddeus's hut. Stella hoped it was some hut, anyway, because that was one mighty downpour!'

Lucinda hardly knew how she met Stella, knowing what she did. Later tonight she would have to decide what to do. It must be well thought out. Whatever happened, Stella must not be hurt again. Imagine if what Lucinda had dreamed of last night had happened . . . that she had married Giles, then found out. Stella would have had to live the rest of her life with someone who would constantly remind her of the man who had almost ruined her life.

It was the early hours of the morning before Lucinda slept. As Kenneth had instilled into his children, she had prayed for guidance and then set herself to use her mind to work it out. That, Kenneth had said, was what God expected of you.

She couldn't stay. Even though it would tear the heart out of her to leave Giles—now. And to leave Stella, in whom she had found so much of her own mother. Oh well, she'd read somewhere that men tended to run to a pattern in the women they married.

At least Sylvester Mordred had been a good picker. And Harvey and Janice were married and well settled in. They would be disappointed when she went away, breaking this engagement. Only the last time they'd been out here, they had asked when were they setting a date. But they'd get over it. They'd just have to. Because Stella was the one who mattered. And Giles . . .

It wasn't just a case of how it was going to tear her own heart out, but of what it was going to do to him. She must do it soon before Giles declared his feelings too plainly. But he'd said he wasn't going to rush her. Oh, what irony, when all she wanted now was to capitulate! But anyway, he loved Star so much that if he knew the truth, he would turn from Lucinda.

She wasn't quite sure how she would do it, but she would try to make it appear to Giles as if, after all, her feelings had not become involved.

One thing she had still not resolved. If Chris were going to inherit the money, with no bother about it, she could burn that will. Then nothing would ever come out about her being Sylvester's daughter—but she mustn't act rashly about that. What if other claimants happened along, and Chris lost his inheritance, or a great part of it? Lucinda knew very little about the law.

In the morning she got the document out and even the sight of that legal form scared her. Must she stay here till she was sure Chris was going to get his father's money? A longing to have it over and done with rose up and nearly choked Lucinda.

One thing she settled in her mind. When it was all over, she would join the twins in England, taking some position not too far from them.

She told the family she had letters to write, shut herself in her room and wrote to Mr. Ames, saying she wished to put a hypothetical case to him. In the event of a girl who suddenly found she was another man's child, falling joint heir to his estate, with his legitimate son, by a will that had been sent to her, not her co-legatee, if the girl did not wish any part of the estate because it meant stirring up the mud of long ago scandal, seeing it appeared the whole estate would go to her half-brother as the father had seemingly died intestate, was the girl justified in burning the will? It would save many people untold anguish if she did.

Mr. Ames's answer was prompt and decisive. Among other things he said he was horrified (though he admired the motives that had prompted it) to think of any will being destroyed. It was not ethical, apart from the legal aspect. The wishes of the dead must be respected. And possibly it could be done with a minimum of publicity or embarrassment. But at this distance, and without any further discussion on the matter, he didn't feel competent to advise her. She had said a hypothetical case, but he thought it was more likely to be concerned with the letter he had sent her, at her mother's request, on her twenty-fifth birthday. He would like her to fly up to consult him as it was a matter of great importance, but if that were impossible, he could supply her with the names of some reputable solicitors in either Dunedin or Invercargill.

Lucinda felt worse than ever. Her mind was in a turmoil. Was one ever wise to act against expert legal advice? Yet she could not bring herself to reveal to Star that she was Sylvester's daughter.

She kept the letters and the will in her old deed-box, locked. Though no one here would pry.

Stella complained that Lucinda had lost weight, that she

172

was looking pale and drawn, which was odd now the heat of autumn was over and the bracing frosts beginning. Giles was waxing skis and doing up the toboggans which delighted the children who came to stay in the winter and spent most of their time on the toboggan run on Ben Logie. Everyone expected an early snow-sports season and they certainly hoped for it. Once the ski-instructors arrived from Europe they were impatient for the season to get underway. Lucinda had thought the Trough-of-the-Goblin sheer scenic perfection in the sapphire stillness of autumn, but nothing could compare with the remote splendour of the reflections of early winter as seen through the moongate, with the triangular outline of Walter Peak, with snow down to the halfway mark, admiring itself in the iridescent waters below, and with sunsets that were living miracles of rose and amethyst and mother-of-pearl on the jagged peaks of the Remarkables.

Then, just as winter seemed to be closing them in, they had day after day of Indian summer weather. An enchanting, lovely world, but one she must soon leave.

Chris had flown over to Brisbane again. Giles told her he thought the estate would soon be settled. If it was, then Lucinda was going to burn that will and quietly slip away, leaving a note for Giles to say she had decided, now Trudy was starting a baby, that her future lay in England with her own folk, that it had, after all, been a bogus engagement, and she was afraid if she discussed it with them first, they would all try to persuade her to stay.

She had sorted out many of her things, ready for a quick flit when Chris was back and she was sure he had come into his own.

CHAPTER ELEVEN

CHRIS came back, but they didn't tell her much. Lucinda had to pluck up courage to ask Giles. She made it simple.

'How did Chris get on this time? I mean if there had been other claimants, they would have popped up long since, wouldn't they?'

'I expect so. They advertised well. But there's been some

173

hitch. Hope it doesn't take long. Not that it matters much, but any reminder of those days does something to Star, I think. She's seemed a little distraught lately, I thought. Of course it has entailed a number of discussions with Chris, and I expect it's brought it all back. I've not asked much because it just gets Stella brooding on the past, which is unlike her. Robert spoke to me about it the other day. As soon as it's over and done with he's going to take her for a good holiday. Perhaps even a cruise round the Islands. He said that with you here, they could take a month.'

Lucinda knew alarm, but before she could say anything, Giles said, taking her secateurs from her, 'I know what would take her mind off it, of course ...'

Lucinda fell into the trap. 'Oh, what? What are you planning?'

'A wedding. All women love a wedding. She was asking me the other day what our plans are.'

Lucinda said quickly, 'I suppose that's natural enough. I expected something like this long ago. In fact your mother did ask, last time she was up, when we were on our own. She pointed out that a spring wedding—September—before the busy tourist season is upon Drumlogie, would be ideal. I just laughed and said we'd have to wait till Trudy has the baby and can travel out to be my matron of honour. I felt I'd turned that one off very neatly.'

Giles plucked the yellow jessamine twigs she had picked for the vases out of her arms and threw them on the flagstones. 'And you've turned *me* off very neatly too. I've been a very patient man, Lucinda, ever since that night in the hut. I've been giving you time. But I was seriously suggesting that a wedding would take Star's mind off "old, unhappy far-off things," as Wordsworth puts it. And I'd like an answer, Miss Darling!'

Lucinda decided she could make this the thin edge of the wedge. 'Giles, you make me cross! You know perfectly well this was only make-believe.'

'Heavens, Lucinda, you don't have to be coy with me. I pretty well declared myself on the Red Spur Track. It started that way, yes, but you know as well as I do that we've grown together day after day ... that we suit ... so none of this nonsense. I'm not letting things drift much longer without crossing my t's and dotting my i's. You——'

'Well ...' Lucinda sounded quite cross. 'What a time to pick! Star is waiting for these flowers to fill the last urn for the big hall. Now scram!'

How hard it was to be off-putting with Giles. He put his head back and roared. 'What a time to pick for a proposal ... and how prosaic of me! Never mind, love, there'll be a new moon in two nights. I'll take you through the moongate then and do it properly. This must be the oddest proposal since time began ... asking a girl to marry you, *after* she's wearing your engagement ring!' and he scooped up the flowers and thrust them at her just as Star appeared on the top step to find out what was keeping Lucinda.

Lucinda said, in a sort of low hiss, 'And it's cold-blooded too, let me tell you ... it's not exactly the sort of thing you make an appointment for.'

'Well, it is, if you want the time, the right setting, and the loved one all together. Chris wants me to go over some accounts for him tonight, and tomorrow night I'm speaking at the Young Farmers' Club.'

'And the night of the new moon, let me tell you *I'm* going to Thurlby Domain for a demonstration of floral decoration by the Garden Club!' She pulled a face at him and ran up the steps. She mustn't appear to take him seriously till she knew Chris's legacy was in the bag.

Every moment was precious now, enhanced by the knowledge that soon it would be just a memory. Soon she would never again be able to look forward to seeing the sunrise over Ben Lomond, lighting up the snow crystals with rainbow tints; never again to see dusk enfolding the tiny streets of Queenstown in purple wings; never again to see Giles, tawny and tanned, striding up to the house from the stables, or erupting into rooms where she sat, with all the masculine vigour and enthusiasm he brought to everything.

They had a spell without guests. Two days of it had refreshed them. The next morning at breakfast Robert said, 'Well, Neill can manage on the farm today. Rena and Meg can attend to the phone and have a bit of a loaf. Chris and Kirsty are off to Wanaka. I'm taking Stella down to see Angus and Marguerite. Why don't you and Lucinda go off for a winter picnic in this glorious sunshine, Giles? It can't last much

175

longer.'

Lucinda said quickly, 'I'm sorry, I've got a hairset at eleven-thirty in town, and I've some shopping to do too. Trudy has a birthday coming up soon, and one of the guests showed me a gorgeous *paua* brooch and earrings set round with marcasite and brilliants. I want to see if Wilkinson's has another. I want clothes too. I've got the whole day planned.'

Her eyes met Giles's. His were cold and grey. 'Well,' he said shortly, 'it's your way of spending a day like this, I suppose.'

Stella protested, 'Giles, don't be so grumpy. Lucinda's too considerate to break an appointment.'

Lucinda dodged Giles and left for Queenstown when the others did. She didn't want to be alone with him. She'd have to try to get a hair appointment. It would never do to come home as she had gone. Chris and Kirsty were going to be home by the time the school bus brought the children, and she'd go across to the Lodge with them. Giles had the air of a man who is tired of shilly-shallying. If only Chris could get word that his legacy was safe!

She drove up to the carports, saw Chris's car was there, and began to stroll across to Leith Lodge. She saw an unfamiliar car parked right in front of Drumlogie. Some guests must have arrived. Oh, well, Meg and Rena were there.

The side door of the annexe flew open and Giles appeared, looking, she thought nervously, like an avenging doom. She'd never seen him look just like that before.

His shout halted her in her stride. 'Lucinda, I want you up here. Right away!'

Her heart raced madly. Oh, she knew all right. Here was her unmasking! But how——?

She tried to appear nonchalant as she mounted the steps, saying, 'Hasn't it been a glorious day? What a waste it was to spend it under the dryer.'

He didn't answer her. It was almost as if he didn't hear her. Anger, bewilderment, and all kinds of emotions seemed written on his face. He was gazing at her face as if he had never seen it before. Her heart thumped even more, her breath quickened, she felt queasy.

He gestured her into the room and to her great shock, she found Sheena Arkwright and Mrs. Arkwright there. Why in the world should *they* be here? Stella, for instance, couldn't stand them. Lucinda said inanely, 'Oh, hullo, isn't it a lovely day?'

No answer. She bit her lip and stood there, feeling as if she must be on the mat, especially as Giles had taken up a stance on the hearthrug and looked about as forbidding as a Victorian papa at his worst. Lucinda swallowed.

Mrs. Arkwright said, waving towards Lucinda, and using a most contemptuous tone, 'See what I mean!'

Lucinda looked blank. Giles looked savage and said, 'Don't be so ridiculous. It's preposterous!'

He turned to Lucinda and said, 'Lucinda, I want you to tell this mischief-making woman and her daughter that you are *not* Sylvester Mordred's daughter. She has some crazy notion that you are!'

His eyes met hers, blazing, confident ... and with a hint of triumph.

Lucinda's eyes almost went blank with the horror of what she had to do to him, to destroy that lovely confidence. She felt the blood leave her cheeks.

Then she looked him straight in the eye. 'But I *am* Sylvester Mordred's daughter. I wish I could tell you different, but only the truth will serve now. My mother was the one Sylvester married bigamously in Singapore.'

She'd never seen such a change come over anyone's face. She could hardly bear to look at him. His colour ebbed to such an alarming degree she took a step towards him, putting out a hand as he swayed. He stopped her with such a gesture of repugnance that she did not reach him.

She tried to speak, to explain, but that hateful Mrs. Arkwright got in first. '*Now* perhaps, Giles Logie, you'll apologize to me and to Sheena for all you said before this—this girl arrived!'

'Like hell I will!' He ground the words out. 'You may have been speaking the truth, but you got a horrible enjoyment out of it. Damn it, I'm engaged to the girl, or *was*!'

He turned to Lucinda, but was overridden again. Mrs. Arkwright said to her, 'I'm sure I don't know what your game is, but one thing I do know ... a neighbour of my cousin's—my cousin Sylvester—has told me you are in possession of a will that ought to have been in the hands of the Brisbane solicitors long ago.'

Lucinda was staring at her. 'But what's it got to do with you? Why come raging over here saying who I am? It's entirely a matter between my half-brother and myself and Stella. It's nothing to——'

'It's everything to do with me. I was the only one to show Sylvester any kindness. I mean to see I don't lose by it, so——'

But she lost out to the fury that was spilling out of Giles.

'Be quiet, woman! None of that matters—yet!' He turned on Lucinda, who visibly shrank. 'What *does* matter is that *you* came here, tarred with the same brush as this woman, wormed your way into our lives ... even into our affections, trying to snoop and find out how much Sylvester left and if you could cash in on it. To think I loved you more than I thought I could ever love any woman ... and all the time you were pretending you didn't know Stella's pathetic story ... oh, you hypocrite!' His face twisted for a moment. 'But none of that matters, really. What does matter, matters most damnably, is that you made *Stella* love you! How dare you do such a thing? Have you no pity in you? No regard for other people's feelings? Her life was devastated by that skunk years ago and now it's all going to be stirred up again. But I'll get you out of here before she and Robert get home tonight, believe me. I never want to set eyes upon you again!'

Lucinda set her mind against all those latter words and for the sake of justice and truth, concentrated on something else.

She waved him down with such an imperative gesture, he stopped.

She said to Mrs. Arkwright, outwardly as cool as a cucumber, entirely in control of the situation:

'What makes you think *you* were left a legacy? Facts, please, not torrents of abuse, or reproaches. Because I *must* try to make sense out of this.'

'Because he thanked me for all I did, nursing him, and said he'd see I didn't lose by it.'

Lucinda said clearly, 'From all I've heard of my father, he was extremely good at pie-crust promises.'

Mrs. Arkwright snorted. 'He was fond of me. I was the only one he had left. I nursed him.'

Lucinda's lip curled. 'Did you know he'd come into this

178

money before you went across to him?' and though she got no reply she had the satisfaction of seeing Mrs. Arkwright redden. Lucinda continued, 'But he didn't keep that promise. Or if he did make a will in your favour then, or left you something in one, he made a later one, when he knew he couldn't recover. He wanted to make it up to Chris and me. If he didn't tell you about it, I imagine it was because he thought you wouldn't send it on, so he got his neighbour to do it. *I* didn't want a penny of his money. But Chris is his legitimate son. I thought if I concealed the existence of that will, Chris would get the lot as next of kin.'

Giles uttered an incredible sound. She swung round on him. 'Yes, perhaps you think that's quick-wittedness on my part. You might as well say: "Tell that to the marines!" as snort like that. But it's true. Well, there's one thing I can do—and that is, prove for my brother's sake that there's no other will likely to turn up. I'll just get it.'

She turned and went flying up the stairs to her room, grabbed the deed-box. Then she had a second thought. She yanked her case out from under her bed, thanked heaven it was almost packed, thrust in an armful of clothes, still on their hangers, from her wardrobe, scooped up a few things from her dressing-table, but not the box with the choker of pearls, slammed it shut.

She put the case in the hall, very quietly, went into the room where Sheena, Mrs. Arkwright, and Giles were standing as stiffly as if they were tableau figures.

She crossed to Giles, that unnatural calm still upon her, and put the papers into his hands. She said, 'You'd better take great care of these. Read the will to this woman by all means, but don't let her get her hands on it. I wouldn't put it past her to destroy it. My solicitor's address is on that letter. I'll get him to set the necessary machinery in order to deed Chris the lot. It ought to be his.'

Giles gazed blankly at the papers, took a step towards her. 'Lucinda——'

She grimaced. She did not want him to know she was leaving, that he would never see her again. She said, 'See me later ... I'd get this woman off your plate first, if I were you,' and she closed the door, picked up her suitcase, and went out of the far door, praying the girls were not about, or Chris and Kirsty.

She wanted no one to see that case.

She flung it into the boot of the car, thinking that possibly no flight had ever been accomplished so speedily and suddenly. Giles would probably be occupied for some time to come, with two hysterical women.

She was along the Skippers Road and almost into Queenstown when in her rear vision mirror she saw what she was certain was Giles's car coming after her. She got a terrible fright. She wanted nothing more to do with him. Anything that must be done, she would accomplish from the safe distance of Wanganui and under the aegis of Mr. Ames.

She couldn't stay here, a poignant reminder to Stella of Sylvester Mordred. A clean cut and a fresh start must be made. But Giles was a crack driver. If she made for the Kawarau Gorge to go to Dunedin, or the longer way round by the foot of the lake, there would be no escaping him. He would edge her into the cliffs either way, and force her to stop.

What he wanted her for, she knew not, but she would never return. Probably it was only because he felt she had had the last dramatic word and there was a terrific lot more he wanted to heap upon her.

But where could she go to escape him? She turned down a street that would lead her to the Frankton Road which she'd have to take whichever way she left the lake, and inspiration came to her. If she turned right instead of left, before he got round the corner, she could go a little way along the Glenorchy Road, and tonight, when he had given up, she would sneak out of the Lake District and out of their lives.

In a flash she was round and before she reached the next bend, had the satisfaction of seeing him head out of town in the wrong direction. She hoped no one would see her. It was hardly likely, though, that the Drumlogie folk would broadcast this day's doings. She went into the narrow green tunnel-like road that led to Glenorchy past the One-Mile.

She was too numbed to be nervous, though she sounded her horn at the blind corners and, thankful she was driving a Mini, kept well to the left in case some huge truck came round.

She didn't pass a single car and drove on till she came to White's Point where a viewpoint was situated and where the road was widened out over the lake. Here she and Giles had sat for a while and had a cup of coffee that happy, happy day they had gone to Glenorchy.

She got out of the car in the tingling air and spread a rug out to sit on. There would be a longish time to wait. But what did that matter? What did anything matter?

It must have been an hour later, an hour of unremitting misery, when she heard a car pull in, hoped desperately that no tourists would come across to speak to her. Then a voice said, 'Why, Lucinda, what on earth are you doing here, all alone?'

She looked up. It was Annabel Darroch.

She sought for words but couldn't find them. Her powers of invention had failed. Annabel saw the distress in her face and said gently, 'Lucinda, there is something wrong. Why are you looking like that? Oh, you *must* tell me. I'll understand, whatever it is.'

All of a sudden the fog in Lucinda's mind cleared. Yes, of all people, Annabel would understand.

She put her hands out to Annabel. Annabel took them in hers. They were ice-cold. She said, 'Come and sit in the car with me. You're frozen.'

She tucked a rug round her, pulled off her own gloves, warm with her own heat, made Lucinda put them on.

'Now, everything! I'll understand. I take it you've quarrelled with Giles. Only that could make you look like that.'

Lucinda said, 'You *will* understand, though few people would, because you came to this lake seeking *your* father—and found him. Well, I didn't, in fact; even if he had been still living he wasn't the sort of father anyone would want to find. I'm not Kenneth Darling's daughter. I—I suppose you know the old story and the subsequent scandal about Stella's first husband?'

Annabel just nodded, didn't look surprised, which made it easier.

'Well, I'm Sylvester Mordred's daughter by that bigamous marriage, though I didn't know it till I was already on my way to Queenstown. It's a long story, Annabel, and very involved. You see, you don't even know that our engagement was only a mock one. But I'll tell you now . . .'

Annabel did not interrupt. Only the pressure now and then of her hand over Lucinda's showed sympathy and love. Lucinda finished, and for the first time her lip trembled. She looked up at Annabel.

'Oh, Annabel, the things Giles said ... that I'd insinuated myself into the household in order to see if there was any chance of cashing in on my father's estate. Oh, I don't blame him, his concern was all for Star. He'll never believe I didn't know who Stella was. He'll realize now that I went up the Red Spur road to see the cottage. He'll think I knew all along.'

Annabel said thoughtfully, 'Well, there's one thing, once he saw that letter you wrote to Mr. Ames, he's going to know that you weren't after money. That would be it, Lucinda, if he was chasing you along the road, it would be to apologize. You must give him the chance of taking back what he said.'

Lucinda's voice had no yielding in it. 'That's not the point. Yes, no doubt he could apologize for that. The thing that can't be changed is that I *am* Sylvester's daughter. Giles would never forgive me for that, for intruding into their lives. He would never bring so permanent and agonizing a reminder of her past into Stella's life.'

Annabel's eyes filled with tears. She put her arms about Lucinda and they cried together. That meant she knew the situation *was* hopeless. Presently they both mopped up. Annabel knew that those tears would have done Lucinda a power of good.

Then she said briskly, 'You're coming up to Canaan with me. I won't take no for an answer. It's completely beyond me to leave you here, and if I don't arrive on time, Gideon will have the whole of Glenorchy out looking for me. He hates me going to Queenstown on this road as it is, and if I'm not in by tea-time he'll be fit to tie.'

Lucinda gave in. Annabel said the folk at Olivet, her father and stepmother, were away in Norfolk Island for a holiday and the house was shut up. No one save herself and Gideon would know Lucinda was there and it would give her time to recover. Lucinda said, 'I'll come on one condition, and that is that you promise me you won't ring Giles and tell him where I am. I don't care what he thinks or doesn't think, nothing can be done about the situation. I'll contact them through my solicitor in Wanganui later. I will do nothing to hurt Stella.'

Annabel promised.

It was most peaceful at Mount Carmel. Annabel had taken Gideon aside and explained it. He came to Lucinda, put an arm about her shoulders, said, 'It's a damnable situation. I've

182

got to admit that, but I'm glad you came to us. I can't see my way through it at the moment, Lucinda, but from my experience of life, things have a habit of resolving themselves, if we don't burst any bonds asunder in the first overwhelming misery of such things. Stay here a week or two, just letting things take their own course.'

But what course could they take, except severance from everything she wanted most in life? Almost a week passed. Lucinda was refreshed physically, but the pain was no less. She had a dread of what she must do to get away from the Lake County. Oh, if only there was more than one road. If only the one to Fiordland was through! But it would take years. Then she wouldn't have the fear of being seen by any of the Drumlogie people when she passed through Queenstown. She thought she would go in a day or two.

She packed her things in her case and put it under her bed. She would tell Annabel and Gideon at breakfast tomorrow morning that they had seen her over the worst, but now she must go. She would book a passage for England as soon as she had instructed Mr. Ames on what she wanted him to do. Annabel had promised not to tell Giles, so she was safe.

Meanwhile, she would saddle up one of the donkeys and go for a ride. She couldn't find Annabel, so she left a note on the kitchen table to say what she was doing and went off to catch Adoniram. Just as she neared the stables she heard Gideon say, 'It's just nonsense, Annabel. *I'm* not breaking a promise, I didn't make one—you did. Giles is a grand chap and a close friend. He came through that business last winter in a very good light. And he must be desperate if he's advertising for her in the Dunedin and Invercargill papers. I mean it's bound to cause a bit of talk, even if he's worded it very cleverly to make it look as if they've just lost her forwarding address. If I thought she'd respond to that advert, I'd show her, but I'm sure she won't. That's why I hid the papers yesterday. I'm simply going to ring him and tell him she's here and then it's over to him.'

Lucinda didn't wait to hear more. She sped away, never pausing till she reached the house. She looked at the note on the table, added: 'Five minutes later—I heard Gideon talking to you in the stables, Annabel. I'm not cross with Gideon, don't think that. It's out of friendship for us both, I know. But

183

I must act as I think best, and go out of the lives of the dear Drumlogie people. I may never see you again, but God bless you both for the shelter and comfort of the last few days, and I love you dearly for all you tried to do.—Lucinda.'

It was the work of a moment to get the case, get her car out, drive as fast as the road allowed, down the Canaan Road alongside Mount Judah.

It couldn't have been a lovelier day ... every exquisite mile mocked her. All she wanted to do was get safely to Queenstown and from there she would take the Kingston Road in case the Nevis was closed.

Of all things, a grader was on the road, sweeping it and levelling the shingle. Even when she got past it there were long ridges of shingle he'd turned up from the edges, to negotiate, not an easy thing for a Mini. The boulders bounced up and smashed against the under-carriage. She hoped no serious damage would result. How ghastly to be stranded here, with only two stations on the way. Not only that, but they knew her, those station-owners, and she wanted no word of this to be spread. Those people would have seen the advertisements. Oh, how could Giles do such a thing?

But as the miles fell behind her a little of the dread lifted from her spirits. She would get through safely and away through Queenstown unseen. Nevertheless, she did wish that that greasy bend in the bush hollow was behind her. It was quite ridiculous, because a culvert would have taken care of all that drainage long ago. Even in the autumn it had been a patch of black ooze and Giles had said an agitation was going on for a culvert. The trees grew so tall there, and the tree-ferns and mosses crowded so closely, the sun never reached the road.

She came down the incline, turned the bend, then stopped, dismayed. They were putting the wretched culvert in and the road was blocked! Oh, well, the afternoon was getting on and she thought the day's work ended at four-thirty, so she would just have to content herself to wait. Nothing else for it.

There were only three men. They had the ditch for the drains dug, but oh, horrors, none were in yet. How long did it take to lay them? The men had stopped for smoke-oh, and were enjoying a cup of tea. One of them leapt across to her and said, 'It's okay, lady, less than an hour will see it finished. Steve, what about filling up the cup of the flask for the lady?

It's mighty cold down here.'

They handed him a box across. Oh, how short a distance it was. Any pedestrian could step over. And here she was, stuck with the car! Oh well, don't panic. This is the day of the big sale at Wanaka. Gideon wouldn't get Giles on the telephone today. And you've made good speed despite everything, till now.

The man on this side, Les, they called him, handed her a box of home-made cookies. 'My wife's. Try the caramel tarts.'

Lucinda found she was hungry. The men enjoyed her tucking in like this. They weren't to know how grateful she was. If she had food now, she need not stop till well past Kingston for a meal. The only thing was that her friendliness encouraged the men to talk instead of getting on. She thought they'd never start laying those drains! They said, 'You needn't fear you'll sink when we finish. We'll run the dozer back and forwards till it's packed solidly. Why don't you walk back up the hill till we've done? You look cold. It's sunny up there out on the bluff. The sun's gone right round to the west and it's shining straight down the lake.'

It was good advice. Lucinda turned to go up the wet and steep road. She heard a car approaching from the opposite side. It came round the bend and stopped. Lucinda's heart gave a great bound. It was the Holden. That was Giles ... *and Stella*! She was half behind her own car. Was it possible they were not on this road with the express intention of stopping her? There was just the slenderest chance that something was taking them to Mount Creighton Station. In her heart of hearts she knew that Gideon Darroch must have contacted them.

Nevertheless, she slipped into the trees, and into dank, wet undergrowth. She clambered madly uphill as quickly as was possible on that grade. She turned the bend, stopped because of a stitch in her side, then, out of sight, scrambled down the bank, across the road, up through the trees on the other side and out on to the sunlit bluff overhanging the lake. She stood there, panting, with a hand to her heart. She'd wait till the culvert was in. Then, if they were not in search of her, and drove past, she'd slip down and drive on.

She heard someone shout behind her. Shout her name. Slowly, unwillingly, she turned. Two people. Giles and

Stella!

Giles helped Stella over the last rock, got her on to the soft leaf-mould. Stella flew over it to Lucinda, half laughing, half crying, holding out her hands. Lucinda couldn't believe it. There was *gladness* in those blue eyes, *love* in that smile, those outstretched hands. But ...?

Stella caught Lucinda to her. 'Oh, Lucinda, Lucinda Rosamond ... you goose, you goose! I've known for so long, but I couldn't make out if you did. I didn't dare say a word in case you didn't know, in case it was just a coincidence that brought you here. In case it would make you feel sad for your mother, or shamed for yourself ... you see, you and Giles met so much by accident, over that hare. I thought it could be one of those sheer coincidences that you're always reading of in the papers ... you know, two people from Piccadilly meeting in the middle of Timbuktu and saying: "Isn't it a small world?"

'Oh, I just didn't know how to go about finding out if you knew or not. And I made up my mind to wait till after you and Giles were married, then you wouldn't feel so embarrassed. I thought it was meant to be when you and Giles got engaged. That you could stay at Drumlogie, that every day I could thank God for the miracle of having my little Jocelyn Rosamond reincarnated for me. It's been so wonderful. I'm always thinking "That's how Jocelyn would have laughed at this age," and watching your one dimple flash out. She had only one too. I always used to tickle her gently under the chin just before she went to sleep, to see it peep out. Oh, I thought it was wonderful when Mhairi was born, that there was a resemblance, but it was nothing to the way you—well, you *are* Jocelyn!

'I hoped that living at Drumlogie with Giles in my girlhood home might somehow make up to you for all your mother suffered at the hands of my first husband. I longed to do something for her, and I did write to her, answering a very nice letter she wrote me, brave girl, and in it I said if there was anything at all we could do for her or her child, just to ask. But she didn't write back. I suppose she just wanted to forget, to close that chapter in her life and——'

At that Lucinda found her tongue. 'But, Star, she never got that letter. She said so in that one she wrote me for my birthday, that explained things. She said you had never replied to her letter. Though the trouble was, she only referred to you as Mrs. Sylvester Mordred. That letter must have been a casualty of the postal service either here or in Singapore. It was wonderful getting her letter, because I'd felt very bitter that they hadn't told me of my paternity, that I'd had to find it out in a letter written by my real father, when he was dying . . . the letter that only reached me when I was on my way down here, purely to visit a renowned beauty-spot. So that part *was* coincidence.'

Stella shook her head, and for the first time tears starred her eyes. 'Not coincidence, darling. Fate . . . or, as I prefer it, the Hand of God.'

Lucinda said bitterly, very aware of the man standing silently waiting, 'But whether or not Giles will ever believe that, I neither know nor care.'

The next moment she took a step back as he suddenly leapt in front of her and took her by both arms. He shook her. 'Stop it, Lucinda, of course I believe you. It was only that the shock of it got me off balance. Damn it, I was so confident in you, believed in you, loved you so much, I thought that flaming woman had gone out of her mind and I was waiting so proudly to hear you denounce it as utter rubbish.

'When you said it was true, I felt as if someone had knocked the props from under me. Then I was appalled to think what this would mean to Star. The thought that she might already have guessed never for one instant occurred to me.' He gave her another shake. 'Lucinda, look up at me . . . looking's believing . . . you *must* know I love you. Look, I don't give a damn whether you're going to forgive me or not, I'll absolutely pester you till you marry me. The minute I read that letter you wrote to the solicitor I realized what agony of mind you must have gone through, even though then I didn't know the whole story. Poor Mrs Arkwright, I don't think even she deserved what she got then. I just unleashed my full fury on her. Though serve her right. She was responsible for half the trouble between Sylvester and Star long ago. Anyway, after I tore strips off her, and bustled her and her poisonous daughter out of the door, I tore up to find you—in your room, I thought.

'Rena and Meg thought I'd gone clean demented. I sprang round the whole house yelling for you, then saw your car was gone. Talk about burning up the dust! I shot off at such a rate

187

from the yard, Chris and Kirsty rushed to their windows to see what was happening. I nearly went mad when I got right along Frankton Road and knew I'd missed you. I dashed into a shop and rang Kingston, in case you were hooling along there, and got a friend who has a farm near the main road. I said he was to stop, at all costs, a green Mini that was probably coming along, and to hold you till I got there. How you would react to him, I neither knew nor cared.

'Then I set off for the Kawarau Gorge. I was terrified lest, in the state you were in, you'd lose control and finish up in the river. I got to the Nevis to find it closed and you not there. Back and down to Kingston, where this friend was faithfully parked. Imagine how long he'd sat there! I'll never forget his face when I just told him I'd tell him some day what it was all about, and charged back to Queenstown, searching madly everywhere for you. Knowing you were fleeing me, I never thought about Glenorchy!

'Then when Stella and Rob got back, she knocked the pins from under me again by calmly stating she'd known most of the time. And Chris is tickled pink to have you for a sister. And I——' He stopped. Then he couldn't get started again.

Stella broke in. 'I can't stand it a moment longer, and if you keep on shaking that girl, she won't have enough breath left to tell you that of course she loves you and will marry you ... look at her, Giles! Can't you see it in her eyes? Go on, kiss her ... I'll turn my back!' And she did.

Giles stopped shaking Lucinda, put his head on one side, looked deeply into those warm brown eyes, liked what he saw there, and bent his head.

Just as he slowly lifted his mouth from hers and said, 'Okay, Star, you can turn round now,' a stentorian bellow reached them from the trees and a stocky figure emerged from them, then stopped dead from sheer surprise and embarrassment.

Giles laughed the most carefree laugh, his eyes dancing. 'Those men must think we're the most unconcerned motorists they've ever held up ... and what they're going to say when we decide *not* to take the Holden over their beautiful culvert, I don't dare to think.'

He waved a hand at the man. 'Coming, mate! Didn't think you'd be done so soon. I was just filling in time.'

'And a more pleasant way of doing it, I can't imagine,' said

188

Les, and guffawed. They all joined in. It was a terrific anti-climax.

Giles knew the other men. One of them said, as they reached the dip, 'You'd better bring the Mini over first, lady, then Giles can bring the Holden through.'

Giles grinned. 'We aren't going to Glenorchy now. Your culvert saved us a long trip, mates. We were going to Glenorchy to get Lucinda. I take it you've met? By the way, she's my future wife.'

Giles was making sure this time. And not asking her. He handed the men a five-dollar note. 'Have one on me when you knock off. Stella, you'll drive the Mini, won't you? I think Lucinda is safer with me.'

As they drove towards Queenstown, he said, 'I'm simply terrified to let you out of my sight. When I found your ruby ring on your dressing-table I nearly went out of my mind. Oh, yes, *I* put Harvey up to that ... said you hadn't wanted to steal their thunder, but how about making the announcement at the toast and to save you scolding me, say Mr. Gilman had let it out. Lucinda, I had to. I was trying to make sure of you.

'But you aren't getting it back yet, you mad, crazy girl. You've kept *me* waiting long enough. You can wait a bit longer to wear your ring again. Till about eight tonight, in the moongate garden, under a not-quite-so-new-moon!'

Stella, eyes ashine, managed a late but ceremonial dinner. The lace cloth was on the big oval mahogany table, the candelabrum had new candles in it and their leaping flames lit a very contented family scene. As Mhairi and Fergus were being looked after at the Lodge, with Rena and Meg in attendance on them, they could all talk as freely as they wished. To-morrow Giles and Lucinda would go down to Roxburgh to tell Marguerite and Angus.

Stella said Lucinda was so like Sylvester and Jocelyn, she had wondered from the start, but seeing she'd thought her married sister would be older than her, had put it down to sheer coincidence. But the night they had brought Fergus and Mhairi home, she had known for sure.

Lucinda, sparkling, as she sat beside Giles, her jasper pendant swinging against the green of her woollen frock, said,

189

'But how? Even the fact that I was born in Singapore and was the eldest of the family couldn't have made you as sure as that. I mean, it was such a wild surmise.'

Stella said, 'Put your hands out, Lucinda.'

Wide-eyed, she did just that, then said, 'Oh . . . I see.'

Stella said, 'Sylvester told me, when Jocelyn was born and I saw that her little fingers had only one joint, that his mother had them, Rosamond Mordred. It ran in her family—one in almost every generation. Chris missed them. But I loved Lucinda too much to tell her something she might be happier not to know.'

Robert broke the tension up. 'And then they say women can't keep secrets! Well, Giles, you and I have got ourselves two that can. Folks, I didn't put this Sauternes out for nothing. Let's drink a toast . . . to Giles's bride-to-be, to Chris's sister, to our new daughter!'

Giles made his explanations later, under that not-so-new moon that shone down on the garden beyond the moongate. The honeysuckle no longer scented the air because where its blossoms had been were now little puffs of seed-bearing down, starring the vines, but the wild thyme under their feet still sent up its bruised and pungent perfume. It was cold, but Giles had pulled up the hood of Lucinda's wind-cheater over her hair. It was red, and lined with white fur, framing her face, and anyway, she couldn't feel cold with Giles's arms about her.

A single and very curious star had slid right down the blue vault of the heavens till it had got stuck fast in the snow on the very tip of Walter Peak, as Giles said, laughing.

Then, not laughing, he said: 'Oh, Lucinda, I loved you long before you loved me. I can pinpoint it, in fact.'

'Oh, yes?' she asked breathlessly.

'It was that night when—to set the stage for our further deceiving the Olivers—I sang you that song of Burns. And I experienced a most remarkable thing. When I sang,

> "Till a' the seas gang dry, my dear,
>   And the rocks melt wi' the sun;
> I will luve thee still, my dear,
>   While the sands o' life shall run."

190

'It hit me between the eyes. I felt as if I were taking marriage vows. But I had to go carefully with you. You had this reserve. Later I thought it was because I'd gained myself a bit of notoriety over Arlene. I realize now it was this knowledge about your parentage. You felt you'd better not fall for anyone the slightest bit that way, didn't you?'

'I did.'

'You didn't dare let yourself care too much?'

'Well, I tried not to, but I didn't succeed, did I?'

She was kissed for that.

'I was always terrified that once you felt Harvey and Janice had settled, you might decide to move on. That's why I told that thumping lie about Arlene and Mark.'

'What thumping lie?'

'About them looking for a holiday home here. They've gone to Australia—permanently.'

'Oh, Farmer Giles!' She started to laugh. 'What time we both wasted!'

'Exactly. So let's stop talking now. Or is there anything else you want to clear up, my love?'

'Just one thing, darling.' She lifted up her pendant. 'Kirsty let out long ago that the gold links in this chain were real, made from the dust and small nuggets you washed out of the Ros Scuir from the time you were a little boy, so I knew that it wasn't the souvenir trifle you made it out to be on my birthday, but you promised you would tell me, some day, the meaning of that Maori proverb you quoted then. Giles, please?'

She knew that if she could have seen them in a stronger light, his eyes would have been burningly blue. He said it in Maori first. Surely there could be no more beautiful language in the world in which to murmur endearments. The vowel sounds were liquid, like creek water purling over a rocky bed.

'E iti noa ana na te aroha.'

His voice deepened. 'A small, ordinary thing, but begotten by love.'

The moon looked down and saw that inquisitive star on the top of Walter Peak. She sailed discreetly behind a cloud immediately, blocking out its view, and left the world to darkness and to two people halfway up a mountain above the Trough-of-the-Goblin.

FREE!!!

Did you know......?

that just by mailing in the coupon below you can receive a brand new, up-to-date "Harlequin Romance Catalogue" listing literally hundreds of Harlequin Romances you probably thought were out of print.

Now you can shop in your own home for novels by your favorite Harlequin authors — the Essie Summers you wanted to read, the Violet Winspear you missed, the Mary Burchell you thought wasn't available anymore!

They're all listed in the "Harlequin Romance Catalogue". And something else too — the books are listed in numerical sequence, — so you can fill in the missing numbers in your library.

Don't delay — mail the coupon below to us today. We'll promptly send you the "Harlequin Romance Catalogue"

FREE!